We ~~~~~~ ... the universe.
The existence of extraterrestrials has been
well-documented.
We have learned about them and
their way of life.
Loving extraterrestrial beings are a lot like us.
They have been with us for a very long time.
They interact daily with families as ordinary
as your next-door neighbors.
They marry Earthlings and create
children with us.

This is the true story of
Denise and Bert Twiggs.
In 1989 they began an exciting journey.
They awakened to what had been happening
all their lives: Extraterrestrials had been visiting them for years. They opened themselves
up to the truth and befriended the extraterrestrials, who offered Denise and Bert a glimpse
of a better life: a life without materialism, a life
of peace and loving and communal harmony.
Eventually they intermarried.
They still live happily together today.
This is their story.

SECRET VOWS

Our Lives With Extraterrestrials

Denise Rieb Twiggs and Bert Twiggs

BERKLEY BOOKS, NEW YORK

SECRET VOWS

A Berkley Book / published by arrangement with
Wild Flower Press

PRINTING HISTORY
Wild Flower Press edition published 1992
Berkley edition / April 1995

ISBN: 0-425-14685-5

BERKLEY®
Berkley Books are published by The Berkley Publishing Group,
200 Madison Avenue, New York, New York 10016.
BERKLEY and the "B" design
are trademarks belonging to Berkley Publishing Corporation.

PRINTED IN THE UNITED STATES OF AMERICA

10 9 8 7 6 5 4 3 2 1

**This book
is dedicated
to
our children of
both worlds!**

About the Authors . . .

Bert and Denise Twiggs come from similar middle-class backgrounds. Bert works with electronics, and Denise spends most of her time home-schooling their three children. Nothing in their upbringing prepared them for what they have faced as adults. As parents, all they wanted was to work, have a home, raise their three children and enjoy life—but this was not to be. A few years ago certain events triggered past memories, and a new world opened up to them—one they had been living subconsciously for years. Not only were they living a concealed life, but their children were doing so as well. Learning that one has made *"secret vows"* with extraterrestrials is not easily assimilated into one's everyday reality. Luckily for them, they are a strong family, and as a family they have had to cope with reactions from relatives, their church, the children's friends, their own friends, etc. This has not always been easy. The Twiggs are reserved, kind people, and they do not seek notoriety. However, they feel strongly that their story must be told, because they believe and "have been told by their unseen friends" that they are not as unique as they first believed. The process described in this book is happening to many other people!

Acknowledgments . . .

We would like to express sincere appreciation and thanks to the friends and family who have helped us through our experience . . .

To "God, the One Creator," whose unwavering love for all of his creation has made all of this possible . . .

To Jesus, the man, who created the path . . .

To our parents, whose love, encouragement and faith in us gave us the strength and the confidence to face our experiences . . .

To Christy, Christopher and Stacey, whose innocent understanding and acceptance helped us to see things more clearly . . .

To Madaline Allen, who helped us with the initial shock of our involvement and helped us through hypnosis . . .

To Ron and Lisa, whose love and friendship will always be cherished . . .

To Larry, for his understanding friendship . . .

To Debbie, for her love and unwavering support . . .

To Kelli, for her lone courage, she's not alone anymore . . .

To David Huggins, for his preliminary cover artwork and the sharing of his experiences with us . . .

To Marcella Bateson, for the final cover artwork on the original edition of this book and her patience as she brought the pictures from memory to life . . .

To Beek and Magna, whose patient love has brought us through the awareness of them . . .

To Dets and The Androme peoples that we have come to know, for their courage to join two worlds . . .

To Brian and Pam, whose encouragement and patience has brought about the birth of this book. . . .

Original Publishers' Note

One Sunday afternoon a couple of years ago, we were sitting in the back of an auditorium at Clackamas Community College listening to one of our authors, Dr. James Deardorff, lecture about the extraterrestrial origins of the Christian faith as told in the document *The Talmud of Jmmanuel*. At the break a man whom we had never met came up to us and asked, "Are you the publishers who are supposed to be here?"

"We are publishers, and we are here," one of us replied, "but I'm not sure why we are *supposed* to be here. Who told you that we would be here?"

Bert Twiggs was a bit evasive on this point. He said that he had a manuscript, and we asked to see it. He said that it was very sensitive and he insisted that we come to visit him and his wife, Denise, to talk about it. So we arranged to see them at their home.

At that time, Denise and Bert Twiggs lived in a ranch house near Molalla, Oregon. Their dogs, cats, parakeets and several children running about suggested nothing out of the ordinary. But their story was anything but ordinary. As we got into it, we turned back to our question at the lecture. "Now who told you that we would be at that meeting?" we persisted.

"They did."

"Who are they?"

"The Andromes," [pronounced andrommies], Bert said. "And they said you would publish our book."

"Did they, now?"

"Yes."

"I see."

And we did. You are holding it in your hands.

Such are the times we live in and the kind of books we publish. It is a new world.

—P.M.C. and B.L.G., book publishers, Wild Flower Press

Letter from Madaline Allen—Hypnotherapist

February 20, 1991

Bert and Denise came to me in early summer of 1989, because they wanted me to hypnotize them to "help them remember something." When I asked what it was they wanted to remember, Denise said, "I think we were taken by extraterrestrials."

"This sounds interesting, but I need to meet with you both," I remember telling her.

At the appointed time on a Saturday morning, I met two nice, young, clean-cut people, both appearing to be centered and honest.

I shall not forget the initial interview on that very warm morning when suddenly the room became ice cold, and the energy around us changed. It was very obvious to me that the energy was not that of a spirit. It was very fast and caused our hearts to beat faster. Our breathing quickened, and each of us became dizzy and nauseous. It was much like motion sickness.

"They" knew Bert and Denise were with me, and they wanted us to know that they knew. Then, as suddenly as the energy appeared, it disappeared.

And so our meetings began that opened the doors to Denise and Bert's adventure. Because I am a psychic (a sensitive), I was able to travel with them and "see" what they saw during their sessions with me.

The hypnosis sessions with me opened the doors to the deepest recesses of their minds to when it all began. They left me to continue on their own with "their" guidance and help, and are still experiencing the incredible journey even today.

This is a story that is unbelievable and intriguing. As a professional psychic, I can tell you that I have experienced the lights going on and off, the "light" shows, and the music suddenly playing when the stereo was off, as well as other strange occurrences.

Although I can only speak for myself and for Denise and Bert during the time they came to me as clients, I leave the rest to you. You decide what you wish to believe. "They" are here, there, and everywhere. If they are not with you now, they may be soon, and your life will be changed forever. Don't be afraid!

Sincerely,
Madaline Allen
P.O. Box 467
West Linn, Oregon 97068

Contents

	Foreword	xiii
	Introduction	xix
1.	The Lonely Road	1
2.	The Return of the Sliver	25
3.	The Thing at the Window	47
4.	Fairies and Diamonds	79
5.	Long, Bony Fingers	95
6.	Passenger in My Womb	99
7.	Double Motherhood	109
8.	A Four-Ring Ceremony	117
9.	The Unreborn Soul	123
10.	Building a Blended Family	129
11.	The Evaluation Committee	147
12.	Physical Evidence	155
13.	A City on a Ship	177
14.	Attacked by Humans	203
15.	Companions Along the Way	211
16.	ETs on My Couch	221
17.	Cast Out with the Demons	245
18.	Compassionate ETs	257
19.	Balancing on the Edge	263
	Appendix	269

Foreword . . .

Amazingly, humans can walk through life and totally ignore anything out of the ordinary. If it doesn't jump up and hit us in the face, we step around it and go about our daily business. Or we wonder to ourselves how odd a particular event was, and we store it away in our memories—uninvestigated. We may even conclude that a ghostly, psychic or religious experience occurred and leave it at that. Or we finally conclude that we've been working too hard, and we need a well-deserved vacation.

In order for our "awakening" to begin, we needed to know that there was something to wake up to. Awakening to an experience that does not fit in with anything in your reality is a difficult process, and the first shock can be devastating. Much preparation precedes the initial shock of recognition. This preliminary work is directed by the extraterrestrials and yourself within your subconscious, and the extraterrestrials know what is needed to convince you that something different is happening.

We wondered why they didn't just come up and knock on our door. But we realized it is more complicated than that. Many people have heard stories about extraterrestrials coming down and zapping someone into a submissive state. The person feels powerless, both physically and emotionally. This is a common misconception of the conscious mind. The human consciousness is easily deceived by its own set of rules. The conscious mind sees and hears without really looking or listening.

The conscious mind is earthbound and very much controlled by the rules and ideals with which we are raised in our society. Overriding these rules and ideals can be complicated and shocking. If you are a person who has been involved with extraterrestrials for a long period of time, you know they cannot just come up to you and say hello. A complicated period of memory recall would occur too fast, and it would be too shocking for an individual to control their emotions and retain their sanity. One must awaken over a period of time and learn about the portion of one's life that the conscious mind has not witnessed. The individual must allow the conscious mind to live through past subconscious memories for the first time. This is what my husband Bert and I learned through the different phases of our awakening.

At first it seemed almost experimental. We thought perhaps these "beings" were controlling us and our progress through each of the phases. We could not see through our own conscious emotions at that point to allow our subconsciouses to reveal what we had in our own memories. In this first phase of our awakening our fears were magnified, and we felt nothing but shock and fear.

As we entered into the first phase, we tried to remain open in our minds and hearts. Although we did not understand anything but our own feelings during that first shock, now we also understand the pain and stress that Beek and Magna, our extraterrestrial spouses, went through while they kept many hours of constant, invisible watch over us. We have learned that there were many times when they wanted simply to come up to the door and knock so that we could see them and learn of them. We learned also of many times when they cried, because they could do nothing to relieve the conscious confusion and fear we felt. Sometimes our subconscious selves even met and cried with them, knowing that only so much could be given at one time to the conscious mind's efforts to learn of the existence of our ET spouses.

As we went through the first shock, we tried to expand beyond our own emotional needs, and we found that on the other side of consciousness we had friends giving us all their help. We also began to discover that we were not the only ones going through this. We began to notice that certain people we knew seemed to be going through similar experiences. They had experienced or were currently experiencing the same strange occurrences as we were— occurrences we call "symptoms."

Some of the people, including ourselves, have experienced *missing time*. Some have experienced driving in their car and seeing some odd lights or odd people on or above the road ahead. Then the odd sighting was gone just as suddenly as it had appeared. Yet when they arrived at their destination, they discovered that they somehow had lost time, or that they had arrived much later than was expected.

Some people may never become aware of having missing time. Perhaps they were not aware of the time to begin with and therefore did not notice that a discrepancy existed. Perhaps the missing time occurred while they slept. If you went to bed at your usual time and woke at your normal time, then you would not know if you were missing time. In that case, the only unusual occurrence you may have noticed is that you may have awakened feeling more tired than when you went to bed or you may have felt that you tossed and turned all night.

Some of the other "symptoms" we experienced are as follows:

• Vivid dreams
  We wrote down all of the vivid dreams that could be recalled throughout our lives. We then wrote down all of the stress periods in our lives. We found a correlation between the dreams and periods of stress. The dreams were not always about extraterrestrials. We wrote down any dream that was so vivid to us that had we not

awakened in bed the next morning, we would have thought it was real.

- Stress periods

  After writing down these periods, we analyzed each one and looked for other correlations and other "symptoms."

- Nosebleeds

  We had nosebleeds that were sudden and gushing or just spotty on the tissue. These nosebleeds were not due to a blow to the nose. (We had blamed them on heredity, anemia, weather, pollutants, etc.)

- Restless nights

  We often woke up tired, sometimes having had vivid dreams.

- Paranoia

  We went through periods when we were sure there was someone in our house because we heard odd sounds. At times we felt that a ghost was haunting us.

- Marks

  We found that scars had suddenly appeared on our bodies. We discovered wounds or bruises that we couldn't account for. We checked our heads, finding a red mark or marks. These ranged from a single dot to a large circular pattern of dots. Some even resembled a birthmark. But once the mark was located and monitored it was found to relocate itself overnight.

- Headaches

  We experienced odd pressure headaches. This type of headache would come and go throughout our lives. We found that aspirin didn't do a thing for them. At times we would experience dizziness with them.

- Blinking lights

  We experienced a lot of blinking lights in our home. Light bulbs seemed to be constantly burning out.

- Stereo

  Our stereo would switch stations by itself or adjust its own volume.

- Street lights

  Whenever we walked near them, they seemed to go off.

- Locks
  Our locks suddenly broke. We replaced them with new ones which mysteriously began locking and unlocking themselves.
- Clocks
  We would find our clocks off time. Alarms rang when they shouldn't.
- Pets
  Our pets became jittery. Friends of ours found that their pets were also becoming nervous.
- Sounds
  We often heard high frequency sounds both internally and externally. However, they were more frequent externally.

These were just some of the more common "symptoms" that we and other people we knew were experiencing. Each one on its own could be explained logically. Yet over time these accumulated experiences began to tally up and summarize the extraterrestrial equation.

That is why in this first phase it was so important for us to begin a diary, writing down everything—dreams, odd occurrences, appliances acting up, etc. We recorded every time we woke during the night, and we recorded each memory we could remember and the dates and times of the memories and odd occurrences. It was through the use of this diary that we were able to compare notes with others like us and to begin to understand the phenomena that had been taking place. Reviewing the diary, we were able to realize that there was an actual phase-by-phase advancement taking place. It showed us the growth taking place in our personalities as well as in our understanding of our own world and other worlds. It also proved to be a valuable reference, freeing us from depending on memory alone as we began to write about our experiences over the past several years.

Introduction . . .

It has been over three years now since our journey began. What we have learned defies available scientific information. We have discovered other facets of human existence that cannot be ignored, and we have gained information relevant to questions humans have asked for centuries.

The "we" I refer to is my husband, Bert, myself, and our "extraterrestrial" spouses, Beek and Magna Solunjeno. My husband is an electronics design engineer. I am a housewife. Beek and Magna are extraterrestrials from another planet. Beek works on an extraterrestrial ship in engine control, and Magna works with their computer systems. Between the four of us, there are a total of thirteen surviving children. Three of these are the children Bert and I had together and the only ones we consciously knew about until three years ago. Although we have chosen to use our real names in this book, we have used fictitious names to protect the identities of others who have shared some of our experiences with us.

Throughout time humans have questioned the reality of UFOs, aliens, other inhabited worlds, other dimensions, ghosts, reincarnation and psychic phenomena. Are these subjects related? If so, how? Many religious leaders, psychics, cults, UFO believers and others have claimed to know the answers. Who is right and wrong?

Three years ago Bert and I had no particular interest in extraterrestrials. We were busy with our day-to-day lives and had no idea that our lives were about to change drastically. We have always believed in God, psychic gifts, spirits and aliens, but we didn't know much about UFOs, abductions or how aliens might behave. The rules of society had not interfered with or prejudiced our views concerning other beings. But our beliefs, our very personalities, were put to the test one day when we discovered that those mysterious beings from other planets were actually a part of our lives and that they had been a part of our lives for a very long time!

We have termed this realization as "the awakening." This "awakening" took place in several stages involving vigorous mental and physical changes. These changes have not been easy. This book has been written in an effort to help other individuals who are going through similar experiences and to inform many others who want to know why extraterrestrials are here. Bert and I aren't the first people to have discovered the existence of extraterrestrials in our lives, nor will we be the last.

—Denise Rieb Twiggs

SECRET
VOWS

1

✧

The Lonely Road

It all started Memorial Day weekend in 1989. . . .

The first step seemed innocent enough. We made a quick trip to our neighborhood store to pick up groceries and a prescription for myself, since I had had hand and foot surgery four days earlier. The surgery was for carpal and tarsal tunnel syndrome. I had developed the syndrome in both wrists and ankles. I had had the first surgery the prior September on the right hand and foot, and now had had the left hand and foot corrected. In addition, a sliver discovered in my left hand when I was five years old was removed.

Since it was a sunny Sunday afternoon, the whole family went along. We decided to stop at a bookstore and look at the crystals. We had developed an interest in crystals after reading a book by Edgar Cayce.

We entered the small store and went our separate ways looking over the crystals and other paranormal articles. I am fascinated with rocks and the chiseled crystals, whether paranormal in energy or not, were definitely a geological wonder. I picked one of the crystals, a light amethyst in color, which came with its own carrying pouch. After choosing the rock, Stacey, our four-year-old daughter, and I tracked down Bert and the older two kids. As I walked up to Bert, he showed me a book he had been flipping through.

The book was called "Uninvited Guests" by Richard Hall. I looked up at him and gave him a teasing smile. "We are standing in the middle of all these books on psychic phenomena, and you go and find a book about this?"

He smiled, shrugged his shoulders and put the book back in place. He started browsing through the other books. It had always been a joke between us that if there was anything on space or electronics, he wanted it. This particular book was different because it was not about space flights and NASA, but about UFOs. It wasn't long before he had found his way back to that book.

Finally deciding he couldn't put it back on the shelf, he grudgingly decided to buy it, wondering why, since just a few feet away were several Edgar Cayce books. While Bert paid for our purchases, I was drawn to the shelf full of advertisements. Normally I ignore ads, but I felt compelled to pick a few up along with the bookstore's newsletter.

Once we arrived home Bert sat down and read through parts of the book before putting it down and continuing on a software program he was writing. It was Sunday, May 28, 1989, Memorial Day weekend.

Next our oldest daughter Christy picked up the book, and began reading it. She had been reading for approximately an hour when Bert asked her if she found it interesting. She said it was and continued reading for a while before putting it down and going outside to play with her younger brother and sister. Later that evening she picked up the book again and continued reading.

We didn't have anything planned on Memorial Day and I decided that if Christy was going to be reading this new book, then I should read it myself. She is a very intelligent ten-year-old, but this book is intended for adults, and we have always tried to monitor the reading and viewing material of our children. By doing so we can explain any questions they may have, or in some cases, say it is out of bounds until they are older.

I was partly through the first chapter when Christy came in. I asked her if she understood the book, since I noticed that some of the words and phrases might be a little more advanced for her. Her expression was odd, and she agreed that she had gotten stuck on some of the words. I told her that if she needed any help with the words she should ask for help. She agreed she would. She didn't pick the book up again that day, and by the next day we decided that for the time being we wouldn't let her read any more of it. I continued reading the book after Christy left the room. It was good, and it recounted typical sightings that had started in the 1940s—nothing unusual about that, since everyone has heard about these sightings. Although we had never seriously spent hours talking over the subject, Bert and I had always agreed on one thing—logically, if space is that vast, then it is ridiculous and egotistical for us humans to believe that we are the only beings in the universe. If there is other life out there, it probably wouldn't be at the same techno-logical level that we are. This was basically the extent of our few conversations on the subject.

The book also covered abductions, but stories of this type had been circulating for as long as I could remember. We never discussed that issue or went out of our way to find out more about it. I suppose we believed it could happen. We always felt that if aliens landed we wouldn't be frightened or try to hurt them. We are open-minded people and would just go up to them and say "Hi." As I read on I came upon a particular sentence written by an abducted person who was describing her experience of being in what she called a "cloud." I can't explain how I felt other than it shook me to my very soul. I looked up from the book and said loudly, "My God! That's our cloud!"

Bert looked up from the computer and asked me what I had said. I stared for a moment longer at the book. My body was tingling all over, and a sense of fear and confusion seemed to be settling into my bones. I finally repeated, "Bert, that is our cloud! This book has our cloud in it! It doesn't say the cloud was from God!" We had originally concluded that our encounter with an odd cloud many years before had been a religious experience.

I must have looked the way I felt, because he came right over and I showed him the sentence in the book. He read it

and looked stunned himself. He took the book from me, and
I gave it up willingly. I didn't want the thing in my hands.
He spent the evening reading through the book thoroughly.

We talked it over later that evening and felt it couldn't be!
We were nervous and upset. For 12 years we had retained a
wonderful memory of our cloud. The comfort that we felt
from feeling that God had enveloped us in the cloud for our
protection was suddenly crumbling away, leaving in its
place a terror we could not understand.

The next day we went to the public library to find out
more on the subject. We had to find the answer! We felt
almost embarrassed as we found and chose the books we
needed on UFOs. These were not the usual reference
materials we had gone to the library for in the past. As
we walked through the library we tried to hide the books
under a couple of other books and hoped the librarian
wouldn't read the titles as she checked them out.

Bert spent the evening reading through passages in the
books, stopping now and then to ponder on what he had
read. Later that evening after the kids had gone to bed we sat
down for a long talk. He explained that the books mentioned
memory blocks and how people make illogical explanations
to themselves about odd events, which later under hypnosis
proved otherwise.

We decided that we should review every aspect of that
night, 12 years before, when we were in that "cloud." We
never had a detailed conversation about it before. For all
these years it had just always been our cloud. We had been
in it. It had felt weird, so out of time with the world. Bert
had said that while we were in the car he couldn't
understand how he had maneuvered the car around the last
corner. He remembered trying to steer, or that he had been
thinking he should turn the wheel to get us safely around the
corner. I remembered sitting on the passenger side feeling
very relaxed. Everything seemed to be moving in slow
motion. Then suddenly we were out of the cloud. We sat for
some time wondering what we had experienced. We felt that
time had elapsed and that because of the unearthliness of the

cloud, for some odd reason, God had reached out to us to prevent us from dying. Perhaps the highway we were headed for had a drunk driver on it or something and God delayed us. He slowed down our pace so that we wouldn't be on the road until after the danger had passed. He saved us. We went to Bert's home shaken, even thinking that one of the cars we passed on the highway was the culprit. Bert was seventeen at the time, I was sixteen. After we arrived at his house we didn't relate our experience to anyone. We couldn't tell anyone since we hadn't been where our parents had believed us to be.

We decided we had to start from the beginning. We began recounting the events of that night so long ago. Piece by piece, looking for an answer that might leave our memory of a religious experience intact so that we could laugh over our own imaginations.

It all began sometime during Christmas holidays in 1976–77. We can't remember the exact date, whether it was in December or the first few days in January.

I picked Bert up in my parents' car that evening. We were going to spend some time together while I did the laundry at the laundromat for my mother. We had a washer and dryer at home but my mother didn't want to put the larger blankets and throw rugs in our machines. After getting the laundry done, we headed out to a trailer court where I used to live. It was about five miles from Rapid City, South Dakota. This was the first time that Bert had been in my car since we started dating in October. We planned to drive out to visit a friend of mine, but she wasn't home and so we left.

I was going to take a short cut that would take us over to another highway and ultimately to the other side of town where we both lived. The road between the two highways was a long, deserted gravel road, which was exactly what Bert seemed to be looking for at the time. We still had plenty of time before either of us were due home, and the short cut gave us enough extra time to look for a place to park on this quiet road.

Bert gave me quite a time about being driven on a date by

a girl, which wasn't part of his upbringing—the man drives, not the woman. I thought that was funny, and that driving this old gravel road would not only show him that I could drive, but that I was actually good at it. The topic was dropped as we tried to find a good place to pull over and park. We slowed down at several prospective spots, but we felt uneasy. The road suddenly had not seemed quiet. We felt anxious, and it seemed that we were not alone. Finally, knowing we weren't far from the last corner before the highway, we pulled off into a field. But we still felt nervous. We had parked a couple of times before in other areas and had felt perfectly fine, but this time was different. We still felt anxious and were sure someone was watching us. We were almost to the point of changing our minds and leaving, because the feeling was so real. We thought perhaps a farmer was out there somewhere, since the road was an access road to several pastures, but no one was there. Reluctantly we tried to forget our fears and began to neck.

As we recalled the events of that night, we could remember so clearly how paranoid we had been about being watched. As we continued to talk of that night, we began to experience new fears—fears that were very real and confusing.

Soon after we began kissing, we again began feeling very scared. There had to be someone else there besides us. The feeling was too real, too frightening. As I adjusted myself in the seat to start the car, Bert picked his comb up off the floor where he had dropped it. He then scooted himself next to me, moving the rearview mirror so that he could see out of the front window also.

I started the car, the wheels spun in the mud, and we both looked at something off to the left of the car. There was a cow looking at us! I must have said it out loud, because Bert remembers me saying something like that. Oh, those eyes—I remember those eyes! Those weren't cow eyes! I was afraid . . . so afraid. I was trying to get away from the window—those eyes were at my window. Bert was trying to grab the steering wheel.

Suddenly we were in a cloud, on the gravel road, at the last turn before the highway intersection. The cloud was so calm . . . so quiet—there wasn't a sound. I felt as if we were in a vacuum. No sound could get in or out, even if I had wanted to talk, which I didn't. The cloud was so soothing. I wanted to stay forever. The gravel road couldn't even affect us, there were no bumps or vibrations, just a slow, forward motion. I could see Bert sitting there mesmerized, just staring straight ahead into the cloud. I looked out the front window.

In a moment the cloud was gone. We didn't remember driving out of it, but we must have, since we were on the bridge heading for the stop sign. We had to stop. Normally I sit with one leg under me, next to Bert, but I wasn't this time. I felt like a Barbie doll sitting there perfectly posed. I could feel my arms by my hips, and my feet were flat on the floor. I was over by the passenger door and sitting straight.

The *passenger* door?

Suddenly I felt my heart hit my stomach. "Oh no! Oh no! This couldn't be, I must be remembering wrong! This wasn't happening, Oh no!

"My God, Bert, *I* was driving that night, not *you!*" I almost screamed at him.

His face went ashen as he realized it too. We were in *my* car that night. I was showing him how well I could drive! When we left the field *I* was driving. While we were in the cloud and afterwards, *he* was driving!

Neither of us could say anything for a moment as the impact of what this meant hit us. All these years we never thought about it, never talked over the events leading up to the cloud. But it was true, and now we had to deal with it. We had to go on. We had to try to remember more.

"What was your first impression?" one of us must have asked. Funny, but I can't remember who asked it, and neither can Bert. The question was pertinent though, what did happen? Something happened. What was that cloud?

That was when we rationalized about God and how he had, for some reason, delayed us and protected us. Our reasoning even seemed to be justified, because as we turned onto the highway that night, we watched a car pass a semi-truck at the top of the hill. The driver was using our lane, and as he tried to get back into his own lane, he overshot it, and in trying to realign his car into his lane, swerved back into ours for a moment. After he drove past us, he even turned onto the same gravel road we had just left.

Bert then looked at me questioningly. "We thought God had delayed us? We even thought we saw the car we were being protected from, right?"

I didn't understand what he was getting at, all the realizations up to this point had me going in circles. "Yes, what about it?"

"Don't you see?" Bert explained. "If God delayed us so that we wouldn't be in the path of that car, then we probably would never have even seen the car. As it was, we were right in its path when it swerved coming over the hill."

He was right. Why had our thinking been so illogical? "Now that we remember more, we know God was probably not personally involved. I think we have a problem, a big one! We have to remember everything!" A mixture of fear and decisiveness crossed Bert's face.

We went over it again, but nothing new emerged.

"OK, what happened after we got to my house? What do you remember?"

I said, "I remember everyone was awake because all the lights were on. It was noisy, and the noise just added to the nervousness I felt. We went downstairs to the utility room and someone was in the next room watching TV." I could still clearly remember the way I felt. It was as though all my nerve endings were on fire.

"Yeah," he said, "that's what I remember. Then the phone rang."

"I won't ever forget that phone ringing. We were next to it, and the sound made all of my nerves go off like a bomb and it scared me!" I continued, "It was for me because I was late."

"That's right," Bert remembered, "because you had to leave, and we wanted to stay together. We needed to stay together."

"You know something else?"

"What?"

"Don't you see, when the phone call came that night right after we got to your house, and it was for me because of how late I was."

"Yeah, because . . . because you were late." He answered slowly, cautiously, because he knew what it meant.

I nodded. "To have had anyone looking for me I had to have been at least two hours overdue, probably longer. They would never have called otherwise."

"Do you realize what that means?" he asked. "We weren't just delayed! When we headed onto the gravel road we were relaxed about time, because we were ahead of schedule, and that's why we had time to park!"

"We weren't parked long because we were too nervous. The drive from the field to my house should have taken only a maximum of 15 minutes! They called just as we got into the laundry room downstairs!" Bert finished, his breathing, like mine, was becoming quicker.

"You've got to call and confirm that with your parents! If they remember how late you were, then we will know just how much time we lost. We didn't just have a time delay. We missed a large amount of time." Although his voice didn't reveal his panic, I knew we were both feeling the same thing.

I didn't call my parents that week. I waited. I didn't want to explain to them why I wanted to know about an incident that happened 12 years ago. I was worried they might think we were crazy, but once the memories were stirred, we couldn't seem to stop them.

Each night we sat up late talking, thinking and recounting every odd experience in our lives. We were not only sure that something was terribly wrong about our memory from 1976–77, but we were terrified that this might not have been the only incident. It may have been only the first of several different occurrences.

By now we felt like we were drowning in our memories—things that were odd, that we had explained away and ignored, memories that we had kept hidden from ourselves, forced away into the depths of our minds.

Bert grew up with the philosophy that you should continually improve your mind and constantly strive for knowledge. He has a very logical way of thinking. All knowledge is available either in reference material or by deductive reasoning from source material and logical thought processes. However, even he had to remain open to the fact that perhaps unearthly possibilities existed as we encountered certain oddities in our lives that had no explanation.

I, on the other hand, was raised with an understanding that the scientific world was not the only basis for life, that a sixth sense did exist, and that this was a gift from God. I had grown up knowing that psychic phenomena do exist and that on a limited basis I was even able to tap into that sixth sense on occasion.

Our religious belief, although similar in expression of faith, had developed from separate bases. His was a middle-class upbringing, starting with Sunday school as a young child and continuing with church every Sunday. Although his logical mind had trouble on occasion accepting a belief without proof, his faith seemed to grow slowly within as he matured. It quietly grew until he felt less need to explain it logically.

I was brought up differently. I didn't attend church on a regular basis. This was something my family, to the dismay of relatives, didn't seem to need. I believe this was hard on my mother, who was brought up within the church. But our faith was strong, and from my earliest childhood memories I remember my own faith being strong. God was a part of my life in a quiet way. I stood on my own with my faith in God. I was taught by my parents that God was in the heart and that if you couldn't walk with God within, then no number of Sundays in church would bring you any closer to Him.

So our faith together as a married couple developed into a quiet, strong faith. We didn't join a church because our church was in our hearts and in our home. We used this faith to explain the undefinable events we encountered over the years.

Perhaps Bert thought I was just a bit nutty the first time I told him I had a ghost that followed me. I believed it started when I was about 14 years old. Something odd would happen. A ring would disappear, or an alarm clock would ring at odd hours. Always a presence seemed to find me whenever my family moved. I learned to accept this "ghost." I believe there is a God and an afterlife, and along with my belief in a psychic gift from God, I decided that I was perhaps sensitive to these people who had passed on to the afterlife. I tried not to fear the "presence" when it would again find me, and I calmly tried to wait out its periodic visits.

I'm not sure what Bert thought at first, but when he felt the "presence" he had to accept the fact of an afterlife. These times seemed always to be mai ed with stress. This could be explained logically because the stress seemed to be centered around jobs, budgets problems or health issues. However, everything was under control. We worked through the hard times, and we waited out further visits of this "presence."

Our lives developed and grew together, as our family and responsibilities grew. The unexpected "presence" resulted in temporary upsets that made us pray harder during those times.

But now, our "presence" and these new revelations had catapulted us into a world we couldn't explain, a world that we were unequipped to handle. We felt that we were being thrown into a world we could not deal with logically or psychically, and we felt the structure of our faith being threatened. To add to the confusion, we slowly realized that we were hiding secrets that our minds had refused to acknowledge consciously. It was amazing to us that a part of us could so effectively keep hidden secrets of our very own experiences.

The night I finally called my parents, we had an appointment with a UFO investigator from one of the organizations we had read about. We tracked down the phone number through an address in one of the books.

Bert got the kids ready for bed while I talked with my father. I had about ten minutes to fill Bert in on the results of my conversation before the investigator arrived.

My dad remembered that night. He couldn't remember the exact date any better than we could. He said that I had been late, but he couldn't remember how late. What upset him the most was the condition of the car—it was covered with dirt and weeds. The call seemed to verify what we had feared—I had been late.

The appointment we had that night with the investigator left us feeling cold. He gave us the impression that this was not his field of expertise and that he really didn't want to be involved in abduction cases. He assured us he didn't think of us as the nutty type and he went on to explain that he had run into some people who were. But we had the feeling that he couldn't give us his wholehearted support either, nor could he give us answers to our questions.

He asked a lot of questions, and although we could logically understand the necessity for them, we were also somewhat offended by them. He explained the need to ask these questions, since he didn't know us, but they seemed personal and non-applicable, such as did we drink, or use drugs, then or now. We didn't use drugs then nor do we now. We didn't drink then, and only occasionally do we have a drink now.

What we needed at this point was someone to listen to us and ease our fears. We needed to hear him say, "Yes, you have been abducted, but here is a solution." Or, "No, you haven't been abducted, and you don't have anything to worry about." Instead, all he could do was to give us a noncommittal response, taking down a report that may or may not be reviewed.

We talked it over later that evening and decided that Bert would call him and tell him to tear up the report. We decided we didn't want to endure a lot of red tape and have it end up as just another of the many reports stamped "unknown." We needed answers, and we didn't want our lives to become an impersonal, unexplained report.

So we started the journey on our own. We began to review our lives piece by piece, and we wrote down any and all odd or illogical experiences that we could remember.

Bert and I stayed up late each night, booting up the word processor and typing in all that we could remember. We wanted to recall everything we could think of that related to those particular times, everything that had been out of place and everything that had been explained by our "ghost" or by stress.

The first experience had been on the deserted road when we were teenagers. We had remembered all we could about that event on our own.

The second experience occurred while we were living in Puyallup, Washington in 1980. We rented the upstairs of an old two-story house from a nice, elderly woman who lived downstairs. The second floor, which she had turned into an apartment, supplemented her monthly Social Security income and provided her with immediate assistance. As far as we could remember, things began happening just after Christmas. Our only child at the time was two-year-old Christy. Suddenly she began having nightmares that she was convinced were real. Before that time she had never had nightmares, at least none that woke her up crying and upset, like these did. She kept telling us that something with a "pig" face and red eyes kept coming to her bedroom window and asking her to go with him. This was very upsetting to us since, for one thing, we were on the second floor and for another, we had recently read "Amityville Horror." A pig face? My God, were there bad spirits here? We had noticed other strange things such as peculiar odors and the sense of being watched when no one else was physically present. Separately, both Bert and I, when we had been up alone late at night, heard footsteps and thought that the other was sneaking up in order to give a good late-night scare. In each case we found the other sound asleep.

We honestly felt that we had been invaded by something very evil, that perhaps our "ghost" wasn't going to remain just a "presence" any longer. We began to pray for help. Our lives were very stressful. Bert had gotten fed up with his job, and he complained constantly. His back hurt so much that he went to a chiropractor for treatment. I felt like I was coming down with my first case of housewife blues, and Christy suddenly wanted to be alone all the time. She and I began to have nose bleeds with no apparent cause.

This situation continued until sometime in March when, just as suddenly as they had begun, things went back to normal. We felt that, with God's help, we had cleansed ourselves of the evil that had tried to interfere with our quiet way of life. Shortly thereafter I found out I was pregnant, so everything seemed normal and happy again, as we prepared for our second child.

This second odd time in our lives we couldn't remember much more about except that on the two occasions when we had heard footsteps late at night, neither of us could remember anything that had happened afterwards. On the night that it happened to me, I stayed up late to watch a television show. I heard Bert walk from the bedroom and stop just before entering the living room. I waited, thinking he was going to jump in and try to scare me. When he didn't I got up and went to see where he was. I found him sound asleep in bed. I don't remember returning to watch the show or even turning off the TV.

On the night it happened to Bert, he woke up and went to the bathroom. He thought he heard me walk down the hall and stop outside the bathroom door. The door wasn't locked, and he waited for me to jump in and try to scare him. After I didn't, he got nervous and came out to check, only to find

I was still sound asleep in the bedroom. He can't remember going back to bed that night.

The third odd occurrence came in 1984. We had just moved to Portland, Oregon. The company Bert worked for in Washington had been purchased by a Portland company, and we were relocated. By now Christy was six years old, and our son Christopher was almost three. Our youngest daughter, Stacey, had just been born in October. We moved into our house in November, and things seemed to be going fairly well up until about the middle of December. We were feeling a lot of stress. The new job involved a lot of out-of-town service calls for Bert, which became hectic for all of us, and I felt that I was going through a late spell of post-natal blues. Both Christy and Christopher had periodic bloody noses during the night. Christopher began wanting to be alone, and Bert's back began bothering him to the point that it was necessary to seek out a chiropractor.

We began to feel there was something in the house. We felt that the ghost we had left behind had returned. It felt so evil, and it had the same odd noises, shadows and smells. We began to add a prayer to our regular prayers to rid us of this "haunting" again. We read books from the library on Edgar Cayce, hoping to find an answer. We began feeling some hope that we could again overcome this evil presence. Mr. Cayce was a very religious man, and we felt that our concentrated prayers for help would be the answer.

The worst experience we had during the short three months we lived in that house happened early in January, 1984. This had never felt like a dream to me, it was so very real. As I began recalling it to Bert (he typed as I spoke), the memory became clearer. A late night ghostly appearance and what I thought was a subsequent fight of good and evil suddenly took on new dimensions.

It woke up one night feeling that I had heard something come in the room. It seemed to be at the end of the bed. It was not standing. It was floating. It wasn't very tall, because I could see the major portion of the closet doors behind it. It was black and evil. It had come for me. I never knew how

I knew that, I just did. I sat up, I was so scared. There was a blue light over us, and I thought that it must be our auras. As I turned to wake Bert, the blue light radiating over me seemed to turn to green, and the blue light stayed over Bert. The light was like nothing I had ever seen before. I have always been able to see the energy field that radiates around a person, but never in colors. It was always white. I believed that this light had to be our auras. I felt very scared, but I couldn't move. Bert woke up and began swinging his arms. The blue light on him began to change. The blue darkened, with red mixing in. He wasn't going to let that black thing take me. His good aura was fighting the black evil. I just sat there, unable to move or scream. I was thinking that my aura was not as strong as Bert's, and that was why he was fighting it and I couldn't move. Suddenly it was all over, and I was lying beside Bert, who was already asleep.

Until now I had never questioned that memory. I always felt it wasn't a dream, because it was too real. I simply believed that I had witnessed a fight between good and evil, and that we had won.

Bert recalled a similar event. He had been sleeping in bed when he was awakened. He thought that he saw evil aliens and that they were shooting ray guns of colored light at him. He wanted to fight back, and he needed one of the ray guns they were using on him. He recalled that his dream was so real to him that the next morning he began to conceptualize the ray gun he was going to build in case they came again.

The last week in December, 1988, seems to be the start of the next episode. Our best friends moved to another state, and Bert remembered that it seemed to be bothering him more than it should have. They were our best friends, and we had all been together for four years. But they weren't that far away, and weekend visits were very possible. Besides, Bert was very proud of the fact that he could always hold his emotions at arm's length.

Bert also started having a heavy load of field service trips again. Between his job and mine, (I had been working for two years for an answering service on the graveyard shift), it seemed that we almost never saw each other anymore.

During this same period Bert again started having a lot of back and side pain. He went to a chiropractor for his back and to specialists for his side, fearing he had kidney stones. The pain in his side was eventually traced to his back.

In March, 1989, Christy came down with a mysterious rash. The allergist couldn't find a cause. Stacey had to be taken to the hospital for an asthma attack, a condition that had been under control since December. We were all stressed out, and I gave my notice at work. Budget problems or not, I couldn't handle everything we had going.

In April things got worse. Christy's rash reappeared, and she was getting unusual bloody noses. For the first time in her life, she had a problem with math. She would cry for no reason, and she began sleep walking.

Christopher seemed very ornery with everyone, and this was not normal for him. He was coming in almost every night to sleep with Bert and me. He would wake up crying, and one night, very late, his nose started to gush for no apparent reason. He also acquired a mysterious rash.

Stacey began wanting to be alone. She had another asthma attack that required hospital attention, and her nose was constantly bleeding. She was coming into our room almost every night to sleep with us, and she would also wake up crying.

Bert and I both started having blood each time we blew our noses, and at one point mine suddenly bled heavily. I started giving everyone iron supplements, but they didn't help. I was getting dizzy quite often, and the pressure in the back of my head kept coming and going. Bert and I began to feel that our "ghost" had found us yet again, since we were experiencing nocturnal noises, unexplained sounds, odd smells and increased stress. Even the dogs restlessly roamed the house all night. They started sleeping in the children's rooms instead of their usual place in the living room.

We were convinced we had our "ghost" back again when

one night as we lay in bed I awoke to the sound of something coming down the hall, straight for our room. It came into the room. It was the same male "ghost" as the last time, although not as black. It felt evil but physical at the same time. The next thing I remember was Bert and me standing side by side, our auras blending together in a soft white light. We were standing up against this thing. Then I remember lying down next to Bert and going to sleep. I awoke feeling very anxious. It was approximately 4:00 A.M. I was so impressed with what had happened that I began writing it down. I didn't give much thought to the details, but I concentrated instead on the feeling that I experienced when Bert and I had stood together with our auras merging into one white light. We had stood up to this thing, and we had been very firm.

Bert and I discussed it later. I told him that it was like the last time—it just could not be a dream, since it was so real. I really felt as if we were stronger this time and that we could get rid of this ghost more easily than the last one. Bert commented that we did it before, and we could do it again.

A year later, as I thought over what had happened that night, I remembered more. I heard this thing come down the hall, and it stood just inside our room with his arm raised and pointed at us. Then it seemed as if Bert and I were standing next to each other outside like statues. The light was not from us but on us. The thing that stood in front of us was talking to us. We had been firm, but we had not been standing up to it, we were agreeing with it. We were firmly agreeing with it! The next thing I remember is lying down beside Bert.

All of these memories seemed to be getting out of hand. It could not be happening—we must have been remembering incorrectly.

On June 6, 1989, we decided that we should talk to the kids. While the older children were at school, I decided to talk to Stacey, who was now four. She and her brother had been playing with an invisible playmate they called "ET." This game started during the first part of the year, right after we had rented the movie "ET." It had lapsed for a while, but since April the game of ET had resumed with a difference. Stacey seemed preoccupied with this game and seemed to be confusing reality with the movie. This was something she had never done before. We had always been very conscientious with the children regarding movies and television shows, consistently teaching the separation of fact and fiction.

At one point, Bert, who had just returned from a hectic service call, got upset with the kids. We were in the car, and they were playing ET again in the back seat. He turned and spoke very firmly, telling Stacey that ET was not real, that it was only a movie, and that she couldn't play ET anymore. She had become very quiet.

As I began talking to her this day, I chose the ET game she used to play as a starting point. I asked her what ET played when she played with him. She replied with a question, "Which ET?" I was stunned, so I asked her what she meant. Her answer scared me.

"The movie ET or the alien ET?" She looked so sincere and so serious. It was just a normal question to her, and she wanted to know which one I was asking about.

I desperately tried to hold my fear in check. I couldn't let her see how her question had affected me. So I tried to be as matter of fact as she had been, and I asked her who the alien ET was.

She replied with an explanation, "Daddy was wrong. He didn't know I was playing real alien ET."

My heart should have stopped at this point. What kept it going, I'm not sure—probably fear! I asked her, "There's a real alien ET?"

"Yeah, not the one from TV," she replied.

"It's not the one from the movie?" I asked.

"The movie ET isn't for real," she answered with the innocence of her age.

"Do you mean the other ET is for real?"

She gave me this "Oh, come on Mom" look. "You know the real alien ET doesn't say 'phone home!'"

I can't even begin to express how I felt at this point! I kept my calm and controlled my panic as she went on to tell me how the real alien ET comes at night and wakes her up. She said that there are a lot of these ETs, girl ones and boy ones, that come at night with these "flash lights" that she described as "real white light." They come at night and wake all of us up, and we walk with them out of the house. The ETs are real nice, and she has ice cream with them.

As she told me about her experiences she finally looked up at me and said, "Geez, Mommy, you know, you were there, too!" But she continued on anyway, telling me how these alien ETs bring us back home and tuck us back into bed.

I asked her to draw me a picture of this "real" alien ET, and she did! Oh boy, did she! I grabbed one of Bert's books and opened it to several pictures of aliens drawn by hand from abductees. "No, those aren't right," she told me. I asked her why. She proceeded to point out different pieces of each of the pictures that were correct. These included the head on one, the eyes "sort of" on another, the legs on a third and the arms and tummies of others. These pieces made up the ETs she knew.

The shocks for the day had just begun. When Christopher got home from school, I had Stacey put on the headphones and listen to one of the children's tapes we had gotten from the library so that she wouldn't hear our conversation. I began by asking Christopher, now seven, why he started sleeping with us back in April and part of May. He replied that it was because he had been having scary dreams. I asked him what these dreams were about?

He answered, "Aliens."

So I asked him to tell me about these dreams. He told me how this alien had come into his room while he was dreaming he was asleep and woke him up. He left the house with this alien, and they had a nice time. They played ball, and it was light. He was confused, however, as to why he had dreamed he was asleep at night . . . playing ball with an alien . . . in the daylight . . . in his pajamas! He didn't know why he felt afraid of the dream, because the alien had been so nice to him. The alien had even brought him back home and tucked him in! And that was why he and Stacey liked to play ET, because the alien in his dream was just as nice as the movie ET.

I was still in shock—this was too much! I asked him to draw me a picture of the alien in his dreams. His picture was very similar to the one Stacey had drawn earlier, although he had not yet seen hers. I again grabbed the book and opened it to the pictures, asking him if any of these looked like the one he dreamed about. "No," he said, "they aren't quite right."

I asked him what wasn't right about them. He looked at them and proceeded to piece together a picture that was correct to him. All the pieces he picked were exactly the same as Stacey had chosen! Every one!

I called Bert at work after the kids went outside to play. I was shaken and scared. Even over the phone, Bert sounded just the way I felt, and he told me to question Christy when she got home.

I did, and she told me she also had a dream involving aliens, and that they had mistaken her for an alien herself. They had done this because she thought it was Halloween and she was dressed as an alien. She has never dressed up as an alien for Halloween. Curiously, she said the trees and weather were springtime in her dream. They took her on their ship, where she sat down on a white box and they talked to each other.

I asked her to draw me a picture, without her knowing about the other children's dreams or pictures. She drew the same image! Again I grabbed for the book, opening it to the pictures. She also told me that none of the pictures were the same as the aliens in her dream. I asked her to show me what was different. She also picked not what was different, but what would be right. Picture for picture, limb by limb, she chose what the other two had chosen!

Once Bert got home he had them repeat what they had dreamed except, of course, in Stacey's case. To her, this was not a dream. Bert apologized to her for not realizing she meant her real alien ET instead of the movie ET. This, to our horror, seemed to be a great relief to her, that her daddy was no longer mixed up about her ETs!

So that was how we started this journey. Memories that in the past seemed to have simple answers, as well as odd problems that we rationalized as the result of stress from work and sudden allergies, now began to take on new meaning.

But how could we explain the children's memories? Were they dreams? We just didn't know. We could always try to explain our memories as imagination, too much media coverage or something else—anything! But how could we ignore the memories of our children? Where could we go? We were having a problem that went beyond anything we had ever coped with in our reality!

Nothing seemed to make sense to us any longer, although we felt that we had begun to find the truth. We had to ask ourselves many questions. The thing we believed in before seemed so confusing to us when we thought of what had been happening to us. And what would we do if our memories held secrets that we weren't prepared to handle?

The first realization of aliens in our lives was a great shock to us, and it was a very frightening and confusing time. Further into our awakening we learned that the first shock and the way in which it is handled by the individual is very important. It is at this point that the decision of whether or not further progress can be made is evaluated. If the conscious mind cannot accept that something seemingly unreal is happening, it can close up and refuse to accept anything further. How the conscious mind processes what is happening also becomes a deciding factor as to whether the awakening can continue. If the awakening threatens the person's sanity, the process is stopped.

This all sounds very logical to us now, looking back, yet we haven't forgotten how confused and frightened we felt in the beginning. At that time we had no concept of an awakening or any phases of the procedure. From our attempts to find answers in books and from our muddled attempts toward the truth with the UFO investigator, we turned to a new source. We enlisted the help of a psychic who was also a trained hypnotist.

2

The Return of the Sliver

JUNE 1989

As we approached the office of Madaline Allen, we wondered what we were doing there. Had things really seemed so odd to us that we needed to see someone like this? Always when either of us thought of a psychic, we thought of a gypsy woman reading palms or looking into a crystal ball. But this psychic was a professional and a trained hypnotist.

As we approached the door a woman stepped out. We did not experience anything unusual, except the fact that we felt we had seen her before. It was not déjà vu, but she seemed familiar to us. She was a pretty, middle-aged woman with dark brown hair that was styled short and curly. She was dressed casually in jeans and a sweater. She welcomed us and tried to make us feel comfortable, perhaps knowing that we weren't completely at ease with the situation.

Her office was small but comfortable. The air was cool and smelled lightly of incense. She had soft music gently playing from a cassette stereo. Her desk was in front of the window, and on it was a lamp, the cassette player, a large crystal ball and various papers and office supplies. To the right was a book shelf filled with books on psychic phenomena, meditation and self-help.

Bert sat in an easy chair, while I chose a typical office

25

chair directly in front of her desk. Following us into her office, she asked us if we had expected someone weird. We answered that we hadn't, and we added that we had hoped she would not be.

So there we were, Bert and I sitting in a small office facing a psychic, and our business meeting was about to start. After formally exchanging first names she began, "First, I would like to know what brought you to me? How did you find me?"

"Well, we picked up one of your advertisements in a bookstore," Bert answered. He was recalling the odd circumstances that had led us there in the first place. It still didn't seem to make any sense to us, and an ominous feeling still persisted as Bert and I mentally recounted the events of that day in the bookstore.

"I see, so that is when you called, and the receptionist sent you to me? Why did you call in the first place?" Her curiosity about how we had come to be here seemed extremely important to her. I could see that she had a feeling that the circumstances were strange. Bert and I already knew that, but trying to explain it was difficult.

"The ad said that one of the things you do is past-life regression. So we thought that if it was possible to regress a person into a past life," (at that time we didn't know if such a thing existed) "then it must be easy to regress back twelve years into a person's current life. The clinic also seemed to be the only place that might be open-minded enough to take our problem seriously."

Still looking for something odd she questioned us further, "So the receptionist gave you my number?"

"She had felt you would be interested in us," Bert answered.

We knew what she wanted to hear, but neither Bert nor I would say it aloud. We didn't want to admit that perhaps we had been led here for reasons we couldn't comprehend.

"Yes, I am very interested in this case." Her face was still a mixture of excitement and curiosity.

"I had thrown the ad into our scrap paper recycling bag

and then dug it out later," I said. I had to say it; the urge that made me go dig for that silly piece of paper had been strong. Bert added the rest of the story.

"We went into the store to learn what crystals were all about, and out of all the Edgar Cayce books available, plus all the psychic phenomenon books, it was so strange to me that I felt I had to have a particular one on UFOs. Denise even teased me about it, asking why I had passed up all the others for the one I bought. I can't explain it myself." This had been hard for him to admit, with his logical mind.

Our answers must have been the ones she was looking for.

"You see!" she said, "We are supposed to be together. I don't know why! This is interesting!" Her mind seemed to be thinking fast about this encounter and how it had come to pass. "Well, why don't you tell me what happened all those years ago. Denise discussed a little of it over the phone with me, and I am really interested in hearing all of it."

"Well," Bert began, choosing his words carefully, "We had an unusual experience approximately twelve years ago. You may think we're crazy, but we believe we may have been abducted by a UFO."

"What happened that made you remember this?" she asked.

Bert and I glanced at each other. We knew how strange it must sound to her because it was extremely strange to us. Yet after what we had just gone through in the past two weeks recalling our memories, this memory was only the beginning and the least strange of all.

"Well, it was that book I had bought," Bert replied. "Denise was reading it one day. She stopped and pointed out a sentence to me." He looked over at me, so I continued.

"It was this particular sentence I was reading, and it hit me. My God, that is our cloud!" I can still remember that moment clearly; that sentence had hit me so hard.

"She showed it to me," Bert added. "The story was a typical UFO abduction case, but the lady told about this cloud she had been in. That was our cloud." His own face was showing that he remembered the initial shock of rereading the passage.

"So twelve years ago you saw this cloud, or you were in it?" She questioned.

"We didn't drive into it, we were just suddenly in it, then suddenly out of it." Bert answered.

"You see, all these years we had thought we had had a religious experience," I added, trying to explain.

"Why did you think that?" Madaline asked.

"At the time we felt that God had delayed us, and we had a strong feeling of being delayed," Bert continued, "I guess we rationalized that there was going to be a drunk driver or some other danger on the highway we were headed for, and that God held us back with this cloud.

"At the time when we were out of the cloud, we knew something very strange had just happened to us. There was never any doubt about that. The cloud or whatever it was could not have been anything that came from this Earth. It had to have been God. Only he could have created what had just happened." At the time and only until recently, Bert and I had been positive in that belief.

"So you knew something had happened?" She seemed to think that was odd.

"Yes, we stopped, or anyway we were sitting there at the stop sign. One of us, I can't recall which of us, asked 'What was the first thing that crossed your mind' One of us answered 'a drunk driver . . . we were delayed so that we wouldn't die.' We both seemed to feel that way, that for some unknown reason God had stepped into our lives and prevented something from happening." Bert added, "It doesn't make any sense now—in actuality, the delay could have actually put us in his path."

"Where were you when this happened?" Madaline asked.

"It happened when we were first dating. We lived in South Dakota at the time," I started.

Bert grinned and finished, "We were looking for a place to park."

"So then you were on a quiet road?" she asked, but she already knew that answer from our embarrassed looks.

"A very deserted old farmer's gravel road," I answered.

"That is usually when it happens, you know, a dark deserted road," she commented.

"Yeah, it was the typical deserted road. We handed ourselves right to them," Bert grinned ironically.

Pulling a book from her shelf, she began showing us pictures of possible abduction cases as well as actual photos of possible UFO wreckage. "You see your story fits the pattern—the road, the loss of time, the feeling that something strange had occurred and the illogical explanations to yourselves."

"Yes it fits, but it all seems so strange. Why after twelve years? The things we have been remembering are frightening." I guess I was still reaching for something that might make sense, something to pull me closer to a reality I could understand.

"That's not unusual, in most of the cases I have heard about, the people don't remember for years. It usually seems to take something that triggers the memory, and it can either all come back quickly or bit by bit. Sometimes because of the memory block, it may take hypnosis to uncover it." Madaline continued, "I don't think they always come by spacecraft. There are theories that possibly they are simply coming from another dimension. I think that is how they can get into and out of people's homes in the middle of cities without being seen."

Bert responded, "That's interesting. You see, a few months back a friend of mine bought a book, *The Awesome Life Force* by Joseph H. Cater. I bought my own copy recently. It describes an old scientific theory that is based on ether. Ether is a true usable energy in the air and can also be used as a medium or type of wavelength like radio or TV signals. Today psychic researchers call it PK or Psychokinetic Energy. With this energy it may be possible to move through doors or even power a spacecraft. It is most likely the medium a psychic uses."

"That is very interesting. Some day perhaps it will be proven or disproven." She stopped for a moment and then added slowly, watching each of us for a reaction, "That probably was not the only time they have picked you two up."

Bert let out an uneasy breath before answering, "No, we have begun to realize there may have been several other times."

Her face lit up as she realized we did know. In her excitement she continued, "This may sound weird to you, but it's not. I watched you two pull up. They must have come with you; the energy all around the two of you is amazing!"

It all seemed so unreal, so dramatic! But whatever it was that was almost always with us, it was also here in a stronger than usual sense. It was almost visible; its sparkles of light energy almost formed a thin cloud. It actually was starting into the room we were sitting in. Bert saw it too, as well as felt it. He knew it was with us again.

"That's our ghost. He always finds us," I tried to explain, surprised that someone other than Bert and me had actually noticed it.

"We used to think it was a ghost, but now we aren't so sure," Bert corrected.

I noticed the presence in the room move from behind Bert off to his left side near the desk. It was strong today, it left the top of my head tingling, along with the typical up-the-spine chill. It was not new to me. If anything, I was wondering why it was so bold today. It was unusual for it to make such a spectacle of itself in front of someone other than Bert and me.

Madaline stood up, showing her excitement, and as she tried to explain (perhaps not to scare us), she spoke in a low voice, "There is something in this room. Can you feel it?"

Before we could answer, her hands went to the top of her head, "The energy is amazing! My head is just tingling with it!"

Stunned, I stared at her, "Tingling? The top of your head is tingling?"

"Yes," tracing an invisible path around her head with her hands, she explained, "That is the psychic band. It is where your psychic energy expands."

"But that is what my head is doing! Is that psychic power?" I asked excitedly.

"My head is just tingling with this energy. It is right here with us now. This is amazing, it just came right in here with us!" Answering my question, she said, "Yes, the tingling is from it being used."

"I never knew that. Whenever the ghost is around I tingle."

"It has such energy. It must know why you are here, yet it hasn't stopped you. It wants me to know that they know you are here. For some reason I think you two are supposed to be here with me." She seemed astounded over this concept, "It is not a ghost, I don't know what it is, the energy is very fast."

"It's not a ghost?" Bert and I both echoed.

"But this presence is what follows us, no matter where we move, it always shows up." Now Bert looked astounded. "It is also funny that you would say that we are supposed to be here. Denise said to me the other day that she thinks we made an agreement with them, that some type of decision had happened between us and them."

"After what just happened here, I'm not surprised. I think it may be leaving now. Do you see the air clearing?"

The air was clearing. The energy that had been so strong a moment earlier was easing off, and the tingling in my head had also started to lessen. But it wasn't gone. No, our friend was still here, over by Bert again, quietly watching. Apparently it had just wanted to be acknowledged. We didn't know if Madaline could still sense it or not, and she didn't say.

Looking at me, she announced, "I think they have been around you a lot longer than you think, maybe even since you were very young."

"Yes, I was afraid of that," I replied. I hadn't wanted to hear her say that. I was terrified she was going to, and then she went and said it. While trying to recall memories in the previous weeks, I knew that I probably had been visited since I was an infant. Memories had been slowly coming back, including the resulting panic.

Looking over at Bert I had to say something to break the panic that was slowly threatening to put my stomach into a death grip.

"Sorry I got you into this!"

He laughed and shrugged his shoulders.

"No, maybe not. Bert, it is possible," she speculated, "that they also may have been tracking you since you were younger."

"Well that's just great," Bert tried to answer humorously.

"Why do you think they would want to track us?" I asked. "We are no big deal. We are very quiet people. We don't do anything important." I hoped she wouldn't have the answer.

"I don't know why. No one knows why. But they do track families, generations even. The current thought is that they are scientists studying us just as our scientists would study a new animal or plant."

The thought that we were lab animals wasn't something we wanted to hear.

"Well, I think our next step is to go ahead with the hypnosis. What do you think?" she asked.

"Yes, that may be the only way to try to prove any of this. We have to know what is going on," Bert answered her.

We made an appointment for me on the next Saturday, June 17th at 10:00 A.M. and one for Bert one week later at the same time.

We left her office feeling that possibly we were not totally alone with this problem. Perhaps we had found someone who would be able to walk us through our journey in attempting to discover what was happening to us.

As we drove to the babysitter's house to pick up the kids we used those last few minutes of privacy to talk it over.

What was happening to us? It seemed too unreal, too

impossible to believe that we could have been abducted by people from another planet. How could that have happened to us, and why?

Until recently we believed the chances of the existence of other life forms was high. But now that there was a possibility we were involved with them, we tried to convince ourselves that they did not exist.

However, our own memories and feelings were telling us something different—telling us that we had every reason to worry because our fears were justified.

So where did that leave us? What was going to happen to us? Had we both gone mad at the same time? What could possibly make two adults suddenly begin to wonder whether or not they had been abducted by aliens?

JUNE 12, 1989

Madaline "scanned" us during our initial meeting. She explained that she could see our energy pattern. As she "scanned" my energy with the palm of her hand, she seemed to think there was something on the back of my head that felt different compared to the energy readings she was used to getting. She did not, at any time during the meeting, actually touch my head.

She could not have known there was something different with the back of my head, yet her first impression was "What have they done to you?" She had no way of knowing that was the exact place where I get an odd sort of pressure headache, which, although not very bad, has come and gone for as long as I can remember.

I asked Bert to check my head, and he was stunned! There at the same location was a patch of spots that he described as small, circular, red marks approximately .05″ to .3″ in diameter with a bumpy look but smooth to the touch. As Bert began pressing on the area, the pressure began. That was it, but what was it?

Could this be our evidence? The next day I checked our

children as they returned from school, starting with Stacey. Yes, there was a similar patch of spots in the same location! Christopher's mark was also in the same location, but it was slightly different in that it was one large, circular, red spot. Christy also had one. Hers seemed to be more like scarring than circular spots, but the location was identical. I called Bert at work to tell him what I found, and we were both stupefied. What were the odds that all four of us could have birth marks in the same spot?

Bert also checked the areas as soon as he got home. He pressed on each one, but only Christy complained of a kind of headache in that area. Hers seemed to give her the same type of pressure as mine did.

Then I had Bert sit down, and I looked at his head. Sure enough, he had a spot identical to Christopher's in size and location.

Bert and I agreed there was no way we could all have those marks unless they had been put there for some unknown reason.

This raised more questions. If something had been "planted" in our head, what? And why? And how? This was unreal. This was something we just were not ready to handle!

JUNE 13, 1989

Madaline called this morning and relayed a strange experience that she had had on the evening of the 12th. After she returned home from a meeting and was locking up for the night, her tape deck in the living room suddenly started. She had been in the hallway at the time. She returned to the living room and felt a chill and a presence. She told me that she had never encountered a presence like this before, and she was sure they wanted to let her know that they were there. She also said that she slept restlessly that night and awoke at 3:59 A.M.

I explained our experience of finding the marks on all of us and how odd they seemed.

She relayed that she did an automatic writing on us the previous night and explained exactly what automatic writing was. I didn't know if I was ready to deal with this right then, but I listened as she continued. "The extraterrestrials wrote that they do not want you two to be afraid, that they would not hurt you and that the tape player coming on had been their doing. Also, you should be aware that there will be more physical evidence."

We also discussed a feeling that Bert and I had that perhaps they might want something from us or want us to do something. She thought maybe she was to write about it, or help other people who had been abducted. We could understand those feelings since I felt a strong need to write about this, and Bert felt that we were to help other people who were going through what we were. Had these extraterrestrials been planning our futures?

That same evening before going to bed, we all became irritable at 7:30 P.M. It was strange. One moment we were all in a good mood, and the next we were grumpy with one another. I felt strange most of the evening, and at one point the lamp next to the couch blinked about five times. Bert and I glanced at each other uncomfortably. That light had never blinked before, and it was peculiar. That night we all slept very restlessly. The dogs were jittery all evening, we found Stacey sleeping the wrong way in bed, and finally, Christopher woke up frightened and slept with us the rest of the night.

We wondered what was happening to us?

JUNE 14, 1989

I called Bert at work after talking on the telephone with Madaline, who had called me the first thing this morning. She wanted to tell me how odd her evening had been, and how she had become irritable and had been having a problem with blinking lights (we are serviced by different power companies). Then I described our evening to her.

Bert and I talked about how really bizarre our situation was becoming! The same things that seemed to be happening to us now seemed to be happening to her as well. I mentioned how odd it was that we both had similar experiences with our lights. Bert asked me what I meant, and so I reminded him about the blinking lamp. He couldn't remember it, and that scared me. It was something we had acknowledged at the time, and now he couldn't remember it. Why? We had both glanced at each other when it happened.

Bert and I went to bed at 11:00 P.M. I was tired, and I had just sunk down into the covers when I felt a chill in the room and became conscious of the presence again. I was tired and in no mood for its sparkly thin cloud of light energy, its "light show" or the ultimate adrenalin flow that comes with it.

By now we figured since we couldn't stop them, we'd just try to go to sleep. However, as I was drifting off to sleep, I heard someone in the hall. It frightened me, and I lay very still, listening. I felt that I was still lying with my back up against Bert. I heard the footsteps go up the hall, and I waited for the bathroom light to turn on, thinking it must be Christy going to the bathroom. When it didn't, I turned to get out of bed, fearing she was sleepwalking again. I suddenly froze because Bert wasn't in bed. I quickly grabbed my glasses and came out to the living room, scaring Bert as he turned from where he was looking out the back door. I told him that I was so sure he was still in bed with me until I turned over. He told me he was tired but couldn't sleep, and that I had missed another "light show." I told him that I knew when it had come into the room, but that I purposely missed it. He said he felt nervous and had come out to the kitchen to look around.

We talked for an hour about whether or not we were going crazy. We didn't feel that we were. The things that were happening just couldn't be ignored. We felt uneasy about what the future was going to hold for us and we felt a certain destiny was beginning to unfold. Although in some ways it was scarier than we had ever imagined, we also felt that we had been invited, and this felt "right."

Because of the odd things that happened that night, we asked the kids how they slept. Christy and Christopher said they slept fine, but Christopher couldn't remember why he had awakened or why he had been crying. Stacey said she slept and had "no dreams all night." The way she said it seemed so strange that I thought it couldn't hurt to ask her straight out if she had seen the aliens again.

She said that they had come during the night. We asked her if she had dreamed about them again. No, she had not dreamed any dreams last night, but the alien ETs did come again.

This, of course, was very disconcerting. Stacey knows the difference between reality, pretending, dreaming and teasing. She is not given to "flights of fantasy," and her attitude during this conversation was very matter-of-fact. She was not talking about a game of pretend or relating a dream. She was describing reality.

She told us how five real alien ETs had come into the house that night and awakened all of us and taken us with them. We all lay on giant mattresses and took a nap. Then the ETs brought us back home.

This was shocking to hear, because a four-year-old, if she were pretending, would probably not pretend that. She would pretend to play or do something. It was spooky to compare the conversations we had had with all three children in early June with this one.

JUNE 15, 1989

None of us slept very well again the previous night. About 10:30 P.M. the lights in the kitchen and both bathrooms began blinking off and on in a strobelike effect (from January to May the house blew five light bulbs). Stacey also woke up crying and came into our room to sleep with us.

This morning the lights periodically continued to blink. After seeing Bert off to work and getting the kids off to their last day of school, I went in to take my shower. Stacey usually comes into the bathroom with me, plays with her toys and then takes a bath when I'm done. Suddenly, while I was standing under the water I felt the presence again. This time I had a definite sense of something physical. I might have tried to convince myself I was paranoid or crazy, if it hadn't felt so real. My heart was pounding so hard I could hear it in my ears, and at the same time I heard two separate sounds either in the kitchen or living room area. The parakeets started screeching so loud that I could hear them above the sound of the shower. The light also blinked, and I was glad I had locked the bathroom door (not that it would have made a difference). I quickly left the shower, and as I was wrapping a towel around myself, the phone rang. The birds quieted, and although I had the feeling of being "alone" again, I was reluctant to open the door. I finally got up my courage, and as I went to answer the telephone, I didn't notice anything unusual.

It was Bert and I told him how glad I was to hear his voice. I explained to him what had just happened. There really wasn't anything else to say or do at this point, so all we could do was continue with our daily routine. Bert wanted me to drive him to the airport so he could rent a car to make a service call about an hour and a half drive away. He would be back in time for dinner. (Some of his service calls can last as long as two weeks and be anywhere in the United States.)

On the way to the airport, Stacey told us that she woke up last night because the ET aliens came again, but she said she would only tell Mommy what happened.

On the return trip Stacey was with me while Bert followed us home in the rental car. She told me that the aliens came but they did not awaken her. It was the noise they made in the other room that woke her up. She also told me that she wasn't supposed to tell Daddy or Mommy about them, but she wanted to tell me anyway. At that point I didn't know what to think. This couldn't be happening! I told her the aliens must have gotten mixed up, since she should always tell us when they come. I told her that the next time they came we would tell them they were mixed up. This seemed to relieve her, but not me.

After we got home, I took Bert aside and told him what had happened in the car. Like me, he didn't know what to make of it. We know our little girl. It is not like her to make up something like this, and how could she possibly relay things to us that seemed to be textbook scenarios of UFO abductions without ever having been exposed to them?

Then Bert revealed what he held back from me on the previous night. He had gotten out of bed because he felt nervous after the "light show," and as he started to drift off he heard someone call his name so clearly that he thought it was me. After he thought about it further he realized that the voice had been in his head, not in the room.

After Bert left to make his service call, the remainder of the day seemed fairly normal, except that I noticed that one of the two bathroom light bulbs had blown again.

In Bert's absence, the kids and I took the opportunity to go shopping for a Father's Day gift. Upon returning home about 4:30 P.M., we found Bert was already there. Things seemed to be normal and happy again. He teased the kids, grabbing at the sack, and they ran giggling to hide the present in Christy's room.

After dinner we used the rental car to go for a drive. The car was rented for the entire day and we paid for the gas. We have always enjoyed these drives since the age of our car didn't allow us to do that very often. The rental car was new and, of course, had been routinely maintained. Bert had just driven it more than 200 miles on his trip without a problem.

The drive started out as a fun ride. We pulled over at a rest area to allow the kids to tuck their coats under them so they could be safety belted and still be high enough to look out the windows. Just before we reached the rest area, I started feeling a familiar pressure in the back of my head. A pressure sensation that had come and gone periodically, with fairly long painless periods in between. For the past few months, however, it had been happening much more often, and the pressure had become intense. It had never really bothered me previously until I realized that the pressure occurs whenever I feel that presence.

We continued our drive, having a good time, goofing off, teasing each other while watching the scenery and trying to figure out what kind of cargo the semi-trucks we saw were carrying. Approximately thirty-five miles out of own, we took a road through a little town that would take us to another highway and ultimately to a very scenic drive home. The pressure in my brain at that point became very strong. I couldn't say that it actually hurt, but I felt extreme pressure.

At the first stoplight we came to, the car engine died. Bert thought it was extremely odd, since he had been driving the car all day without a problem, and it was new. At the next light the engine died again, making it obvious there was a problem. Bert could get the car up to about 35 mph, then it would die. He threw it into neutral and restarted it, then it ran about a block and died again. It was obvious we had to get the car back to the rental agency and let them know something was wrong with it. We turned around to make the return trip on the same highway we came in on, since it was the quickest way to get home. Just before we got onto the return highway, the pressure on my head let up, the car stopped stalling, and it didn't stall again during the entire drive back to the house. The kids drove with me in our car, except for Stacey, who asked to ride with her Daddy. We dropped off the rental car at the agency, and it didn't act up during the entire 20-minute drive from our house.

After we returned home and put the kids to bed, Bert and I sat down to talk. We couldn't explain the action of the car, and I couldn't explain why the pressure I felt in my head eased off just when the car quit stalling.

"Do you know what this reminds me of?" I asked Bert.

"What?"

"When Madaline told us about the automatic writing and

that there would be more physical evidence for us to watch for." I paused. "Remember our lights blinking last night and this morning, now our experience with the car?"

We looked at each other and smiled ironically, shaking our heads. No, it couldn't be.

"Well, if that's what they call physical proof, it isn't enough to convince me, and they better try harder." Bert laughed.

"I suppose until one of them comes up to you and shakes your hand, you won't have enough proof," I joked back.

"That's about it!" Bert responded.

"Yeah, but what if they just want to give you some evidence without giving you proof?" I asked.

"They could still show me a photograph or just simply appear," he answered.

"Things are getting stranger," I answered more seriously. "I just don't know what to think anymore."

"I don't know the answer either," Bert said. "It's hard to believe everything that's happening, but something is definitely happening and has been happening for quite a while. There is no other explanation."

He began to tell me about his conversation with Stacey on the drive out to the airport to return the rental car. She had told him what she had told me, that she wasn't supposed to tell us and he had told her that she should. She then told him that the aliens fly in a kind of helicopter that has lots of colored lights. She also told him that she was told that they would be back. She said the aliens told her where they live. She could not remember the name, but it was out in space near the moon.

Bert loaded our Polaroid and placed it on the stand beside the bed before we went to sleep. He answered my questioning look with, "If they are coming tonight, I'm going to get a picture of them!"

"What if they don't come tonight, and what if they don't exist?" I asked.

"I don't know," he said, "but it won't hurt to have it ready!"

We fell asleep that night with many questions running through our minds. What do we do now? What is happening? If they do exist, what could they possibly gain from us? We don't do anything fantastic. We aren't super-scientists or powerful politicians. Are we just lab rats to them? Are they even here? What do they want from us?

And what of these strange bits and pieces of memories we have, the things that seem odd and the dreams that seem too real? Is there more to these memories? Is that why we've never forgotten them? Is that why they seem to keep flashing back to us now? What are we going to find out when we undergo hypnosis?

JUNE 17, 1989

At a little after 3:00 A.M. we were sitting across the table from each other trying to figure out what had just happened.

"I was floating!" Bert told me with astonishment.

"I know. So was I. I felt so breathless!" I was just as amazed.

"I tried to tell them something," Bert said, "but I can't remember it. Whatever it was I think it came out mumbled."

"That was what first woke me up," I told him. "I heard you say something, then when I opened my eyes, I felt breathless but not like I couldn't breathe. I was beside you and I could see the top of the dresser over our feet."

"They were in the room with us, and I think I tried to yell at them to take me with them!" Bert went on.

"Is that what you said? I was just looking around, one was by the closet, and one was by our feet. Then you yelled, and your arms shot out in front of you. You startled me. I tried to grab for you, then everything went black until you talked again." I could still remember how his yell had surprised me out of the relaxed state I had been in.

"Yes!" remembered Bert, "You hit me with your elbow just after I yelled!"

"Sorry, I was trying to grab your arm."

"I tried to get a picture of them. I had the camera in my hand," Bert said. "I had a terrible pain in my finger, and I couldn't hit the button!"

"You tried to get a picture of them? You remembered to grab the camera?" I was surprised because I wouldn't have thought to grab it.

Bert smiled. "Yeah, I want a picture of them. I got the impression they didn't know what I had. I think I surprised them. The clock was floating at that time, like an invisible hand had picked it up and was turning it at angles like it was being examined. Then it felt as though the camera was taken out of my hands, and it was beside the clock, floating and being examined at angles."

"You're kidding," I said. I didn't see any of this.

"No! It looked like someone had been examining the clock, then when the camera was taken from me it was beside the clock in the air. The clock wasn't moving anymore, like someone was just holding it, but the camera was being tilted at angles."

"I didn't see that," I said. "As I told you, after I grabbed for you, everything went black."

"Then," Bert said, "the one by the closet looked like a ghostly image, white with large black eyes, and he waved his arm and his hand in a motion to have me moved. The finger he pointed was long." Bert moved his own arm and hand to try to demonstrate the motion. "I can't move mine the same way. It was like the finger moved more, I guess because it was so long."

"What else do you remember?" I asked.

"I was just lying there, and I believe I said something about them being here, or they just were here."

"I remember you saying 'They were here,'" I said. "When you said that I woke up completely."

"It must have been a dream, but it felt so real!" Bert said.

"We both couldn't have had the same dream!" I commented.

Bert tried to rationalize what had happened. "I guess you

could have heard me yell and then started to dream that I was yelling."

I smiled and said, "Sure, that's why I can tell you exactly what you were doing and what was going on in the room at the time."

He smiled back. "I think they did something to my nose. I can remember before all that happened I couldn't breathe out of my right nostril. I even reached up to check for blood. Something was in my nose." Getting up from the table, he got a pen and paper. "I think I can draw what they put up my nose."

I watched as he drew an odd object.

"I think this is pretty close," he said as he turned the drawing towards me. "My nose is tender here." His finger pressed the cheek area just under the bridge of the nose on the right side.

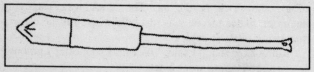

The instrument Bert remembers being inserted into his right nostril. The tip was blue like a gemstone, the center section was red or black and the handle was either chrome or silver.

"Can you remember anything else?" I asked.

"No, I'm not sure. When I felt something in my nose, I don't think we were in our room though."

"I don't know. Everything went black after you yelled," I told him. "Then when you said 'They were here,' I opened my eyes. I was lying on my back, and I was sweating."

"I was lying on my back, too," Bert said. "In fact my arms were crossed over my chest. I don't normally sleep like that."

"My arms were crossed, too, and I not only don't sleep like that but with this splint and my surgery, it hurts to lie with my hands like that," I explained.

"This couldn't have happened. It had to have been a

dream, but yet I know I was awake, and it was real." Bert seemed to be fighting reality with reality.

"It could happen," I continued. "It has happened before. You tell yourself that you were in bed, you had to have been dreaming, but out of even the most vivid colorful dreams I've ever had, none of them felt that real. These dreams really happened. You wake up, and you know they happened! What happened tonight was real. We couldn't have dreamed the same thing!" Since there was nothing else we could do, we went back to bed.

The next day I got up early, since I was going to have my first hypnosis session. I felt as if I was going to take a test, and that no matter what I did, I was going to fail. If I didn't have any memories revealed then I would probably feel like a fool—a happy one, but a fool. If there was something to all of this, would I really want to know? And what was it that really happened the previous night?

So many questions were going through my mind as I got ready for my shower. I began to remove the temporary splint the doctor had placed on my lower left arm and hand the day before. The stitches had been removed, and the incision had been checked. He had said I was healing just fine and another ten days in the temporary splint would, for the most part, complete the post-surgical recovery. I had asked him about the sliver that he had removed from my hand. We had both looked at my hand where the sliver used to be, and he explained the removal procedure.

He had said that it was a very unusual and curious sliver. It was made out of a very thin metal, and it must have been in my hand for a very long time, because he had to scrape it out instead of pulling it out in one piece.

As I removed the splint for my shower, I noticed a spot of blood on it. The spot of blood was on the back of the splint and the incision was on the palm of my hand. The incision was past the point where there had been any bleeding. I looked at it and part of it did look a little different, yet there was nothing open that could have caused any bleeding. There wasn't any blood on the inside palm side of the splint only the one spot on the back. It didn't make any sense. Then I noticed something else near the incision. Just next to where the old sliver had been, was a new, very small incision and a new sliver! I wasn't sure what to do. I decided I wouldn't say anything to anyone for now.

3

✧

The Thing at the Window

Bert and the kids drove me to my hypnosis appointment and dropped me off. It was about 9:45 A.M., a little early, but that would be all right. They were supposed to come back at around 11:30 A.M. to pick me up.

Madaline talked to me until I was relaxed and ready to begin. I closed my eyes and listened to her, allowing her words to relax me. True hypnosis is odd—you feel very relaxed but you are still in control.

During the hypnosis I even prayed to myself, and my brain was still thinking that I liked being where I was—so deeply relaxed. It makes remembering easy, and you don't have to fight to find memories. Events I wasn't ready to remember simply remained closed for the moment, and I didn't fight that feeling. I would find them when the time was right—when I was ready.

This is my recollection of my remembrance of the 1976–77 event as brought out under hypnosis. It is not an actual transcription:

As we were getting ready to leave the field, we were nervous and feeling that we were being watched. I started the car while Bert reached to pick up his comb and adjusted himself in the center of the seat. I started to step on the gas, and the back tires spun twice. I took my foot off the gas. Bert was saying something to me about putting the car in low gear and slowly giving it gas, and that way I would not get stuck.

At about that time there was movement on the driver's side of the car that caught our attention. I looked out my window and there were eyes looking back at me. My initial reaction was that a cow was looking at me. That changed quickly, however, as my eyes adjusted. It was no cow. It wasn't human, and it wasn't the only one. There were two, maybe three more coming up behind the car, and the one that was already at the door just kept staring.

I was so scared. I may have screamed or yelled at this point. My mouth moved, but I don't recall any sound of any kind. I leaned into Bert, trying to get away from the window, and our hands were slapping each other's as I tried to move away and he tried to get to the steering wheel. Suddenly I was up and over his lap. I went right over his lap and couldn't take my eyes off the window. Bert moved into the driver's seat. His head was bent close to the steering wheel. He was looking at the dashboard and trying to turn the key. He was trying to get us out of there, and the thing at the window was stepping backwards away from the car. I could see it over Bert. It was raising an arm and pointing something cone-shaped at the door. The lock popped up. There was light from behind the car, just enough light that I could see what it was doing, but everything else was very black. The headlights and dashboard lights must have been off, and that was why it was so dark.

I was very afraid. The door was unlocked, and Bert couldn't get the car started. That thing was stepping toward the car now. It was going to open the door! I could hear something behind me at the passenger's window now.

As the being began to open the driver's side door, I suddenly felt very calm. I was watching everything now, but I didn't feel afraid. The inside of the car was being lit from somewhere. It was such a soft, white light, and so comforting somehow.

The being that had opened the door was holding it so that it wouldn't shut while two others came up closer. Bert was starting to move out of the car, and he was taking the arm of one of them. It had motioned for Bert to come and he did. He wasn't afraid anymore. He moved very slowly and was very relaxed.

I was still sitting in the same position I had been in when I had crossed over Bert's lap, and I saw the beings step away from the car with Bert. When I could no longer see him I turned my attention to the being who was holding the door open. He seemed to know me, and he wanted me to get out of the car. He was letting me know what he wanted, but I still didn't hear any sounds or anything like a voice. He knew my name. I thought he said my name. Was he transferring his thoughts to mine? I moved towards him and out of the driver's side door.

I stepped out of the car and faced him. He wasn't as tall as I was and he had some sort of pendant around his neck. He was wearing a long white gown. He didn't want me to be afraid, and he wanted me to turn around. As I turned around I could see Bert up ahead. There were two of the beings, one on each side of him, and a third following behind. They were heading towards a square light, possibly a ship. It looked like a spaceship—it was big and round. It was hard to see it clearly, because my eyes were drawn to the light. It was a door into the ship, and they were taking Bert in there.

The being that was with me suddenly put his hand on my shoulder. I still had my back to him, but he must have been speaking to me with his thoughts again: I wasn't supposed to worry; they would not hurt Bert; they had to check something. I thought I knew what he meant, but I just couldn't remember what it was about. The being behind me knew me well. He knew everything about me, but did I know him? I sensed that his emotions toward me were very protective, and I knew he would not hurt me.

Suddenly my memory hit a black wall. The door was shut. I had remembered all I was going to for today. My brain seemed to be protecting me from absorbing too much at one time.

As we got into the car to go home, I was glad Bert and the

Our memory of the 1976–77 incident, where Bert is being led by
"aliens" to the meeting ship. I follow behind with another being.

kids had gone with me. I still felt lethargic, and I didn't
seem to be able to concentrate on anything. I believed from
the way I was feeling that I was in shock, because the
memories didn't seem to bother me much. I felt as though
they had always been there. Perhaps the immediate shock
was removed while I was under hypnosis. My reaction,
though, was that I had just had a terrible shock of some sort.
Part of my brain seemed to be non-functioning, because it
was busy trying to sort out what had just happened. I could
now remember almost everything that took place under the
hypnosis, but could I accept it? Yes, the memory was there;
it was real, but how could it be? That couldn't have
happened to us, to someone else perhaps, but not to us. How
could I handle the changes in my life that acceptance of that
memory would bring about? This particular memory and the
others that are partially there had no place in our lives. I
couldn't allow this memory to tear up and destroy our tidy
world, demanding that I acknowledge it and live with it.

I spent the remainder of the day cleaning the house and pulling weeds in the flower bed. Trying to concentrate on anything else would have been futile. Bert kept asking me if I'm going to be OK? To my self, I scream, "No! No, I'm not! I can't accept this! It changes everything!" But instead of saying it out loud, I just give him a simple "yes." I couldn't tell him I wasn't OK. Not only could I not find the words, but we had agreed not to discuss any memory derived from hypnosis until we both remembered it. It was the only way to establish trust in our own memories. If we both remembered details that were identical, then we would know it had really happened.

I went to bed thinking that this memory had to be wrong, that somehow my mind had fooled me. I would not allow myself to wonder why this memory felt so familiar, why it has been there for twelve years. And what would happen the following week? Bert would have his hypnosis appointment. What if his memory were to recall the same events as mine? If that were to happen I couldn't reject my memory as just my imagination, I'd have to accept it as the truth—but how would I be able to cope with that?

JUNE 18, 1989 Father's Day

Although I knew that they had come the previous night, I seemed to feel much better than I had the day before. The shock seemed to have worn off and I felt normal again. I decided I would refuse to accept my own memory without physical proof.

We spent the day pampering Bert. The kids showered him with presents, some handmade, some store bought, and he gave out tons of hugs and kisses. Father's Day, like Mother's Day, is wonderful, because the kids get so excited and try so hard to make the day happy for us. They watch us open the gifts with the same excitement they display on their own birthdays and at Christmas. The greatest gift of the day is the love they show.

After opening gifts and watching Bert's new movie, we went to the science museum to see the new display. From there we came home and had a special Father's Day dinner and dessert. It was a wonderful day. Our lives appeared to be as normal as anyone's.

JUNE 19, 1989

Monday is major house cleaning day. Everything seemed fairly quiet most of the day dusting, mopping, etc, instead of just the routine straightening up and vacuuming.

Everything seemed quiet until a while after we had gone to bed. Bert had asked me how I felt, and if I thought they would leave us alone tonight. He had the feeling they would return again, and so did I.

About an hour after we both dozed off, Bert woke me up and we came out to the kitchen. He said a noise woke him, a lot of noises, as a matter of fact. He said they came from the hallway, sounding like footsteps, but there were so many. He got up to check things out and saw Christy sitting up in bed. She took a picture off the wall and was sitting with it in her lap making arm movements as though she was trying to open something to slide the picture into it. We both had the feeling that something had happened again.

JUNE 20, 1989

Bright and early at 5:00 A.M., Christopher came into our room and tried to wake me up. He had had a dream and he wanted to talk about it.

I got out of bed and grabbed my robe, thinking this was odd. Usually he comes into the room crying or comes in and climbs in with us while he's still half asleep. But this time he woke me up to talk about it.

Once we were out in the kitchen I asked him to tell me about the dream, but he couldn't. He just kept repeating that he had dreamed. It was odd that he seemed neither sleepy nor upset. He seemed almost dazed but not in a sleepy sort of daze. Slowly as we sat there he started to get sleepy enough to go back to bed. I also grabbed another hour of sleep before getting up to start the day.

Christopher's behavior was so peculiar and just wasn't like him at all. I decided I would have to talk to him about it later. Perhaps he'd be ready to talk later.

That wasn't the only strange coincidence that morning. Stacey woke up and hollered for me from the bathroom. Her nose was bleeding. I put her on the couch and questioned her casually as I cleaned up her nose and face. I asked if she had dreamed last night, and she said that she hadn't. I asked her if she had slept all night, and she answered that she hadn't, but I couldn't get anything more than that from her.

Christy added yet another problem. She came up to me later in the morning to tell me that twice that morning she had a strange tingling and pressure on that one spot on the back of her head. As I checked the area, I noticed a new spot. It was brighter and seemed fresher.

When Bert came home for lunch, I filled him in on everything. He told me to be sure to try to talk to Christopher, but I told him I was waiting until I felt he would be receptive to that conversation.

Later in the afternoon he seemed ready, so I took him into the kitchen, and we sat on the floor together, pow-wow style.

"Remember this morning when you woke me up to tell me about your dream?" I started.

"Yeah," he answered.

"Can you remember the dream? Can you tell me anything about it?" I asked.

"No, I just woke up."

"Can you remember how the dream made you feel? You know—happy, sad, scared, different?"

He thought hard about it. "No."

"Can you remember if when you woke up you felt like you just had the dream, or was it earlier in the night?"

"I think it was a lot earlier. It wasn't right before I woke up," he explained.

I could tell this dream was bothering him, but he didn't seem to know why.

"Where were you when you woke up?"

He looked surprised at that question, then he seemed to realize the importance of it and thought hard for a moment. "I was in bed."

"But you can't remember anything else about it?" I again asked.

"No," he answered, but his thoughts seemed to be somewhere else. He looked down at his feet. I waited. Something had clicked with him, and I didn't want to spoil his thought process. Finally he looked up.

"I was on the edge of my bed when I woke up." This seemed terribly important to him.

"Were you too close to the edge?" I didn't understand what he meant.

"No, but I went to sleep over by the wall." He was trying to get me to understand.

"You do move when you sleep," I said. "Most people do. Maybe you just switched positions."

"No," he said. "My pillow was under my head when I woke up." This was what had been odd to him.

"Your pillow?"

"When I went to sleep," he replied, "I tucked it way up in the corner and lay on it, but when I woke up it was almost to the edge and down far."

"You mean that when you move in your sleep you don't move your pillow with you?" I asked.

"If I move, my pillow always stays where it was when I went to sleep," he responded.

We ended the conversation at that point. I told him that if he were to have another dream or anything else, it would be perfectly OK for him to come and wake us up.

So, what was going on? All of us seemed to be affected on the same nights. The odds that this could be a coincidence were too high. We were becoming frustrated and anxious, and we couldn't take very much more of this.

How could we deal with this problem? I knew we couldn't all have gone mad at the same time. Bert and I had talked and talked, staying up too late for too many nights trying to figure this out. It didn't make any sense. If there were such things as aliens and abductions, then why were they interfering with our lives?

JUNE 23, 1989

The preceding couple of days seemed somewhat quiet. Bert partially woke up one night feeling as though something physical was either holding his legs down or actually sitting on them. It was unnerving, since he couldn't actually see anything. Neither of us slept very well. Christy sometimes sat up in bed and talked in her sleep, and Stacey had another bloody nose.

The days seemed almost normal, except for the odd flashes of memory we both kept having. Bert started to recall his early childhood years, from about four to thirteen years old, although he had never before been able to recall very much from that period of his life. Although he was under a lot of stress with what had been happening, he was starting to feel some release from tension that he had not been totally aware of until it started to ease up. He wondered if that could be related to what was happening to us. Were the memory blocks induced by these aliens blocking more than just the memories of them? Did they also hold the key to this stress level and the reasons why he had always been unable to remember much of his childhood?

We were both still having a hard time accepting all of this. One minute we were sure it couldn't be happening to us, and the next minute we knew it was. How does a person go about trying to accept such an unknown? Who was going to answer all of the questions we have? Would there ever be an answer to it all?

JUNE 24, 1989

Bert had his first hypnosis session this morning. On the drive back he seemed upset that he hadn't been under hypnosis, or that he hadn't felt like he had been under. He said the room was too bright, and that it would have to be darker next time. He went on to tell me that he tried to remember about the incident in 1976–77 but couldn't. The harder he tried to remember, the more upset his stomach became. When he came out of the hypnosis, he had a terrible headache.

I explained to him that when I was under hypnosis I felt the same way. I felt in control of what was going on, and I didn't feel like I was in an unconscious trance.

He thought about it all day and also looked through a book we have on self-hypnosis. This book is intended to help one feel less stress and further the success of one's careers.

After he read about what hypnosis feels like, he realized he had been under after all. He also realized that the headache and stomachache were probably the result of his mind's unwillingness to open up the memory, and he knew then that he had to get through to that memory and through the physical reactions if he was ever to know what happened to him.

We went to bed around 11:00 P.M., and lying there in the dark, he tried to relax. He felt himself relaxing more and more, and he felt very comfortable at home in his bed and in the dark. Soon he began to recall what he had not been able to remember earlier. The air was heavier in the room and we began to feel the presence in the room.

"Do you want to go out to the kitchen and talk about this?" I asked him. He was recalling a lot, but even now it started to give him a headache and stomach pain.

"Yeah," he said. "I could use a cold glass of water anyway."

Once we settled at the table, we both tried to remember everything that happened before we went to the field, from the moment that I picked him up that evening until we parked the car. I hoped he would recall more. If he could remember past the point where the wheels spun while we were in the field, then he could tell me, and I would then know whether my own memory was real or imagined.

"I remember that you came to my house," he said, "and then I got in the car. Is there a laundromat near the K-mart?"

"That's right," I said. "That was the laundromat we went to." I too could remember our going there now. "From your house we would have had to drive past the K-mart and turn right on the road that goes past the fairgrounds, then at the four-way stop we would have taken another right. I can't remember the name of that road, but if you take a left it takes you out to the airport."

"That's why I was confused," Bert said. "Normally when I left my house I would drive the other way into the downtown area."

"After the right at the four-way stop, the laundromat isn't too far down the road on the right. That's the one I always went to when I was a little girl and my mom and dad didn't own their own washer and dryer." I could remember it fairly clearly now. I grabbed a sheet of paper and a pen.

I asked Bert to draw what the laundromat looked like, if we both remembered correctly, it would match.

Bert took the pen and paper and began drawing the building and the inside of it. "Is this what you are remembering?"

"That's it!" Finally we could recall that part of the evening all those years ago.

"Then we didn't go up 8th street and to the highway from there. That's why I was confused. We took the back roads out of the city and missed the hill out of town all together. You drove up through a park or something." Bert's face lit up as he started to organize what had happened and why he had been so confused on those points.

"Well, it isn't really a park. The back road takes you over

the highway and up into a forest area. Once you get to the end of that road you either turn right to go to Dinosaur Park, or left takes you on a service road that runs alongside the highway. That's where Marine Life and other tourist attractions are located. I knew the road well since I used to live out there, and that had been the route the school bus had always taken."

"Right! That's right! No wonder I was having such a hard time remembering. You had me lost until we got onto the service road where I could see where we were. That's when we got on the highway."

"Yes," I said. "I can't believe we finally remembered all that!" And we were both remembering the same thing. Everything was starting to fall together. The events of that night were coming back piece by piece with too much clarity.

"Then we drove on out to see your friend," said Bert. "She wasn't home, so you wanted to show me the road that cuts over to the other highway. That was another part that was confusing me. When we went on vacation to see your folks a couple of years ago we saw the new water slide and other places near Marine Life. They have a paved road that cuts over to the other highway now!" Bert recalled.

"I don't know if it used to be there or not," I said, "but you're right, they do have a paved road now. But our road was still the same old farmer's gravel road."

"After we left, we took a left turn at the end of the road, and we were on pavement until just before we reached the bridge. That's when I remember it turned to gravel. Just past that point is where the road goes into a Y shape, and we took the left." He was remembering it as though it had happened yesterday.

"Right!"

"We slowed down at two different spots, but we didn't feel comfortable with either one, so we drove further until we pulled into the third place."

"I couldn't remember if we had slowed down two or three times, but that sounds familiar." I did remember that from the time we started down that road we didn't feel comfortable.

"We both remembered feeling that someone was watching us." He paused, and I nodded. "Then as we were getting ready to leave. . . ." His fingers began rubbing his temples. "My head is starting to hurt."

"Do you want to go on?" I asked. His body was reacting to the stress of the memories.

"Yes, I have to relive this. I have to get over this block." He continued. "We were getting ready to leave, and there was something looking in the car."

"Looking in the front window or the sides?" I asked.

Closing his eyes he seemed to be watching the memory as it happened. "The driver's side window, but there was something else."

"What?"

"I think there was someone looking in the passenger's side window also, and something was behind the car." His fingers massaged his temples harder.

"What happened then?" I knew what he was seeing. I had been trying all week to accept it.

"I was scared. I was so scared. You were scared, too."

"Yes. What were you doing?"

"The thing that was looking in the window . . . its eyes were so big, and it was looking straight in the window. It wasn't very tall, because it was midway up the window."

Shivers went up my spine. He was remembering everything exactly the way I had remembered it. There was only one way we could independently both remember and feel the same emotions—it must have happened!

"You went over my lap. You put your feet on the door or the seat and pushed yourself right over my lap!" He looked up at me.

"So that's how I did it. I remembered going over your lap. I wanted to get away from that being at the window. I went over your lap facing up, that explains how I got past the steering wheel and why I remember seeing the rear-view mirror as I went over you."

"So that's what you remember, too?" He looked somewhat shocked. His memory was the same as mine, and he also knew that that meant only one thing.

"Then what happened?" I asked.

"I was scared. You were on the other side of me now. . . . I was trying to do something." He closed his eyes and thought hard, "I just can't remember any more right now. My head feels like it's going to bust."

I knew then what I could do to help him. "I want you to listen to part of the tape from when I was under hypnosis." When Bert went in for his session Madaline had given me a copy of my hypnosis session. I had listened to it earlier with the headphones while Bert was taking a nap in the bedroom.

"I don't think I should. I have to remember this from my own memory."

"Yes I know, but I want you to hear the part of the session that covers the things you just told me so that you know that what you are remembering is actually memory, because I remembered the same things." I wanted him to be able to trust his own memory. I knew what I had remembered, but hearing him relay all the same details was also helping me to understand and to accept the reality of them.

"OK, but only to the point where I can't remember anymore."

"Right."

We sat in front of the stereo and I wound the tape forward to where we were sitting in the field. He listened as he realized I was repeating the same things he had just told me. Something had been at the window. There had been something else coming up behind the car, and there had been something at the passenger's side window. I did go over his lap, and we were both very scared.

I stopped the tape at that point, since the balance of the tape concerned further details of what I had remembered.

We talked a while longer before returning to bed. It still seemed so impossible, yet how else were we able to recall the same details? It was going to take a while to sort through everything that had happened to us, and once we did, we would have to figure out how to accept it and live with it.

"How we deal with it may depend on what we remember. We may remember something that will change our lives completely," Bert commented ominously.

JUNE 27, 1989

Bert had been out of town for two days and wouldn't be back until the following day. My mind should have been on my typical daily activities, but I found myself concentrating on the unknown, and more specifically on extraterrestrials.

Bert called long after the kids had gone to bed so that we could talk. He had remembered more. He had relaxed with the lights off in his motel room and had tried to recall more of the details of that peculiar night in 1976–77.

He explained that he was still getting headaches, but that he was trying hard to bring them under control. He recalled more of the details in the car, but in addition, he was now recalling partial memories of entering the spaceship. Since I hadn't remembered anything past his walking towards the spaceship, he couldn't tell me any of the details that he recalled.

I commented that I was searching through my childhood memories, recounting a handful of odd experiences with angels, fairies and ghosts. These experiences were not, it seems, always just "night-time dreams."

"I don't know which ones actually mean anything," I said. "However, if I have had any further 'alien' experiences, it is a place to start looking for them."

JUNE 28, 1989

On this day I tried to recall my childhood memories. When Bert called I told him about some of my memories and how I felt about them. After I got off of the phone my stomach was a mass of tension, and my nose started to bleed enough to make it necessary to lie down until it stopped.

The rest of the evening went fine. I took the kids to the park, then to a McDonald's for dinner. I felt really wiped out though, and after I tucked the kids into bed, I sat down to watch TV and relax. I knew what was wrong with me. My stomach still hurt, my nose had been bleeding on and off all evening, and I was very jumpy. I was in shock, and to make matters worse, I didn't feel alone.

Bert called back at about 11:30 P.M. I told him what was happening and also that our blanket had blood on it. I noticed it when I got it out of the bedroom to cover up with while I watched TV. The spot had been there for a while, but it couldn't have been very long since I had recently washed all the winter blankets. Where had the blood come from? We didn't have an answer.

It could be that one of us had had a slightly bloody nose in our sleep, but that still doesn't explain why all five of us have continued to have these strange and unexplainable nose bleeds.

JUNE 29, 1989

I slept terribly, and awoke feeling as though I had been through a marathon. My hands and arms were asleep and tingling, as though I had been lying on both of them wrong, but I knew I hadn't since I woke up flat on my back with my arms crossed over my ribs—just like before. My eyes were sore and bloodshot, and my nose was swollen and red—the same as when I've been crying. I also recalled crying. Had I been dreaming? My hands were swollen as though I had eaten too much salt, which wasn't so. I hadn't eaten anything at McDonald's because my stomach had been in such a knot, so I had eaten only a small salad when we got home.

I meditated to recall what had happened during the night while it was still fresh. This is what I remembered:

I was in a very light, white room. The people in the room were dressed in white, I think. A female and a male were in the room. The female was talking to me. Well, maybe talking is the wrong word. I recall words, but I can't be sure there were voices. I felt angry, and I was crying.

The female tried to comfort me, "It had to be this way. You couldn't know, it would have caused many problems for you."

"I know, but now I have to sort through all of it. It is so hard," I answered.

"We know. We are sorry, but you are doing as planned— you do know that." She still seemed to be trying to comfort me.

"Yes, I know, but I want to remember so fast, and I know it can't be too fast." I continued to cry.

"It is going as we expected—it will happen faster now— you are strong."

"It is so much. The magnitude of it all is over- whelming. . . ." I cried even harder.

"It will be a shock as it surfaces. Just remember that after the shock will come the reasons. Then it will all be clear to you," she explained.

"I know, I know. Between the shock and the reasoning there is so much pain."

For a moment it feels as though I am being hugged.

"What about Bert and the kids?" By then I was only sniffing.

"He is more troublesome. He is strong, though, and soon he will remember as you have. You will be strong for each other, as in the past."

"I know. I love him so much."

"And he you," she added.

"The kids?"

"As we have explained before, they will not have to hide from themselves. They will grow up knowing. The children will know and grow with us as a part of their lives, although at first they will not talk of this to others. All of your children have such knowledge and understanding, they are much like you and him."

She smiled, and then she added, "We will come soon . . . when you are ready."

As this recall occurred, I consciously knew it was real. When I woke up I felt confused. All the physical evidence showed that I had been crying, but I had been asleep. It had to have been a dream, but it hadn't been.

I spent the rest of the day in partial shock from what just happened, and I searched further into my childhood memories.

It seems illogical that your mind can keep things like this from you—secrets from yourself. But all the clues were there all along—the nagging memories and the oddness that surrounded them—it has all been there all along! From the time Bert and I started dating, odd things would happen that we would both cast off with some explanation or another.

JULY 1, 1989

On this day I had my second hypnosis session with Madaline. I had no idea what to expect. Where, after all these memories should I begin now? We both agreed that the best thing to do was to continue where I had left off at the last session, when I had been standing by the car with one of the aliens while Bert was being led towards the spaceship.

I went into the hypnosis quickly this time, and now I felt more at ease with the way it feels. It took a moment to place myself where we left off last time, because I wanted to stay on this side of the memory. I felt my stomach knotting as I tried to step forward to the next part of the memory.

As I stood by the car watching Bert being led into the spacecraft, I realized that the being standing just behind me knew me, and I felt as though I knew him. In fact I felt very comfortable being there with him. I was worried, though, because I was feeling some anxiety over what was happening to Bert. The being behind me put his hands on my shoulder, in a gesture meant to comfort me. Whether he talked with a voice or with telepathy I still couldn't tell, but I do know what he told me:

I wasn't to worry. They weren't going to hurt Bert, but they did have to do this to him. I couldn't go in until they were finished with him, because it could ultimately upset me. They weren't sure how he was going to react.

So I stood by the car with this alien and waited. I don't know how long we stood there, but eventually he took my arm, and we headed towards the ship.

As we walked up the ramp we went into a room. I knew this room, it was the driving room! There were the big windows where they look out. I had been here before. He had me sit on a chair just by the door and I could see almost the whole room from this point. There was so much equipment in there. It seemed to me that a radar control tower would probably look a lot like this; the big windows to look out of, and all of the equipment, but I knew this was the main center of the whole ship, the driving room. The being that brought me here was over by the window talking to someone, and there were two or three others busy at the control panels. They had a lot to monitor—everything must go smoothly.

I saw a movement to my right, and I turned and looked out the door. Bert was being led somewhere. He looked so stunned, and I was worried about him.

The being that brought me here then moved over to me, and we left the room. It's my turn, he explained. He took me down a hall and into a very white room. It seemed white because of the light. The driving room was not lit like this. I knew I didn't want to be in this room, though. I was undressed and put on a table. I felt like I was being taken into a surgery room at a hospital.

My stomach was really starting to hurt now from recalling this memory. I felt cold. They must have known it. Maybe I said it out loud, because they covered part of me with a blanket. There were at least four of the aliens there in the room. They all seemed busy doing tasks. They were nice, however, like a good nurse towards a patient, very sympathetic and helpful. The being that brought me in there set up some type of equipment near the end of the table with another alien. I didn't like this. He told me it would be all right and he would hurry. It wouldn't take long but it did need to be done. I didn't want to see what he was doing, so I looked beyond what he was doing at the other ones. They were so busy, everyone had something to do, and they all worked together.

I looked at the ones near me. My stomach hurt so badly now, not because of something physical, but because I was so afraid. I could see what they were doing, it didn't hurt but maybe it should have? I tried to relax my stomach, which was tense because of the fear. I was trying to tell it that this didn't hurt, but I felt like I might throw up. They had a metal cylinder. It had a long needle on the bottom of it, and they were lowering it into my right side. They needed something, and this would extract it. It didn't hurt, but I didn't want to be there, I was so afraid.

Next they took the cylinder and handed it to one of the other ones, a female. She took it back to where she had been preparing something. The being that brought me in here was looking into some equipment that had been moved near me. I think he was looking into my uterus. Maybe he was using my belly button. Perhaps there was a tube there. I don't know. I think he must have been using my belly button. It was like some huge X-ray machine, except it could be moved around easily and had great flexibility and mobility. I didn't want to know why it was there. I looked back at the being looking into part of this machine. He was standing to my left, near my lower abdomen. If he was looking at my uterus, he must have been doing it through my belly button.

He must have known how I felt, because he looked at me and somehow relayed a message: he would be done soon; and he was sorry but they had to do this; Bert and I are so serious about each other; they have to make a match; we must match; and what they were doing would tell them what they needed to know.

Were they getting a sample of the lining? No, they had gotten a sample from my right side already. What were they doing now? I was scared and confused. They were showing me something. Is it my uterus? I didn't know, it was white with veins and a big red thing on it.

I felt so scared, but they were done now. The female alien helped me down and also helped me with my clothes. It had gone well. I did fine, she explained. Then the one I knew came for me and took me back. He started talking to another alien—I could see Bert—he was in the driving room now. I think he was sitting where I had been earlier. He didn't notice me though. He was looking at all the control panels and equipment.

The captain of the meeting ship, Dets (pronounced Deets).

The being that brought me took my arm. It was time to go, but everything was all right. It was OK for Bert and me to be serious. We did match, and what they had done he was sure would be a success.

I did know this being and this ship. They lived here on this ship. This was their home now. I thought I knew his name, was it "Dets?" (pronounced Deets) I didn't know for sure.

We were leaving the ship. I turned to see Bert. He was coming, but he didn't want to leave the driving room. He loves equipment.

I got back in the car and crawled over past the steering wheel and sat on the passenger's side of the car. They helped Bert in. He looked so stunned, I started to cry for him. I cried for him because I knew what they did to him was hard. It had to be because what they did to me was hard to handle.

The car was on now. At least the lights were on anyway, and we'd be controlled until Bert was awake again. This was the hard part, and I had felt this before. It was time for the other part of my brain, the conscious part to wake up. We started to leave the field. Bert was at the steering wheel, but they controlled the car with their light. We neared the turn for the main gravel road, and it was hard to wake up. It meant I must forget again. Then we came almost to the end of the gravel road. The thicker cloud was around us. I didn't hear the gravel crunching on the tires, and I knew something was different. This cloud was so odd. . . .

So there it was. Madaline asked me if I knew what they had done to me. I wasn't sure. Thinking about that was so hard, it made me feel afraid.

I left her office feeling good, though. I had remembered, and that was important. The memory had resurfaced, and it felt good.

So now what? Now we continue . . . until all the memories are back. Hopefully then we will know what to do.

JULY 4, 1989

Bert was still trying to control the physical reaction he gets when he starts to remember. His moods seemed to be swinging as much as mine, from anger and frustration to amazement that this could have happened to him without his knowing it. His anger flared mostly from trying to control his physical reactions as he tried to unravel the details of the memory. But he said it was getting easier and he still felt that odd sense of relief from a tension that's been present for so long that he couldn't even recognize it as tension until it started to ease up. He felt sure that the many years of back pain and memory loss were caused by what has happened. He felt that now that he was breaking through, he'd be able to rid himself of the stress and memory problems he has had.

He didn't know whether or not he has any unusual memories from childhood since right then he was slowly starting to regain some of those memories he never thought he would. He felt that the return of his normal childhood memories was enough for him to work with for the present time. Once those were restored, he'd be able to go back and look for anything unusual. Until that time we wouldn't know if he had been involved with these aliens since childhood.

For the present, the most important thing he felt he needed to do was to get past the fear and the physical reactions he was having from the memory of 1976–77.

JULY 8, 1989

Recent days had been fairly normal, with our following mundane routines and contemplating our memories of aliens. On the one hand, we were a typical middle-class family but on the other hand, we had these bizarre memories. Oh, well, at least we were beginning to find humor in this!

We'd go from one extreme to another in this situation— from getting angry and speaking out into the thin air saying "prove yourself"—to just being thankful that they didn't step out of nowhere to confront us.

At this point, I felt confident that it really was happening. Why I felt this way wasn't completely clear, but if we ever were able to meet them on a one-to-one basis, Bert and I certainly had many questions for them. Until then I guessed we'd continue to recall our memories and perhaps discover some answers in them.

As we started the process of remembering, we also came across other people who seemed to have some of the same "symptoms" we had: the nosebleeds, marks, oddities, spells of restless nights and children sleep-walking.

Bert felt that perhaps we were supposed to help these people on the way towards remembering. I felt the same way. The way these conversations came about was unusual. Obviously, this is not something we'd gone around telling everyone. It's just not something you want co-workers, etc., to know about. But we got the strangest feeling when suddenly someone who has never discussed this subject with us before suddenly would bring it up. The similarities between what had happened to them and to us was just too unusual to be a coincidence. The oddest part was that both Bert and I felt that we had been told about these people just prior to seeing them. So when they brought up the subject, it was both a shock and a sense of déjà vu.

So we asked ourselves where should we go next? Apparently we were to be the ones to help other people remember, yet our own memories were still partially hidden, and what had surfaced was very disturbing to us.

This was the day Bert went in for his second hypnosis session. He remembered more about that night in 1976–77 but not all of it as yet. This is what he recalled:

He was trying to get the car started, and his head leaned hard against the steering wheel as he tried to see if any of the dashboard lights would come on. He looked quickly over his left shoulder to see what progress the aliens were making, then his eyes dropped to where the door and the floor board met. The door was being opened, and he was terrified that they were about to get in. But suddenly he felt calm, and he sat back. There was an older and taller being holding open the door, while a female one leaned in to take his arm. She told him not to be afraid because they would not hurt him. She was younger than the being holding the door.

He was then led towards a ship that sat approximately 30 feet behind the car. He had an alien on each side of him. They were both female as he recalls—a younger male followed slightly to his right and behind them.

In the spaceship he thought he saw a human male adult and male child off to his right. They seemed dazed. Were there other people on this ship that night?

Inside the ship, he was taken towards his left and down a hallway. They entered the second door on the left. He was undressed and led to a table, which wasn't much taller than his knees. It seemed confusing to him, because all the furniture and equipment seemed to be small, but it seemed to be proportionate to the size of the aliens in the room. They were very short and seemed to stand only mid-level to him. He could recall the two females giggling like teenagers as they undressed him.

A rendering of Bert's memory of the spaceship.

He lay on a table that was like a white box on the sides with the top made of a type of metal material that was neither shiny nor cold to the touch. A male who seemed to be a doctor or something similar talked to him. He was telling Bert that this would not take too long. Bert said he had the impression that the doctor didn't like doing this, and that he seemed to be filled with a great deal of sympathy for him.

Assistants to the doctor moved a large machine over the table, then lowered it between his abdomen and legs. Part of the machine was placed over his penis. He said that at that point he became very erect but couldn't remember what caused it. He also said that a female assistant, the one who had walked him from the car, seemed to be acting just like a teenager with a crush.

After he ejaculated, he was turned over onto his side and at this point he wasn't sure what they did. When he was turned onto his back again they tried to place something in his nose that hurt him, and he could feel blood from the opposite nostril. At this point he tried to move his head to keep them away, but the doctor was very close and sternly ordered him to hold still.

At this point the hypnosis session ended, and Bert couldn't remember anymore. His mind needed to adjust to the memory he had uncovered before he could go on.

He told me how it made him feel—not as scared anymore, but curious about what they were doing and why. And he couldn't get over the fact that the two girls were acting like teenagers, all giggly and whispering. What kind of aliens would have such human characteristics? And further, why did he feel attracted to the attention he was receiving from them? Shouldn't he feel terrified? He tried to explain his feelings that there was more to these "beings" than we were able to understand. I could see that he was groping to get to something deeper, some explanation that I just couldn't see. I wanted to know what happened, but I still felt so much fear. I didn't understand why his fear seemed to be turning more into curiosity, or why he was feeling that there was more to what was happening than just alien experiments.

JULY 14, 1989

We had continued to feel the presence, and it had become an almost minute-by-minute feeling. They were using a more aggressive approach with Bert, and he could feel their touches. It started out as a light and fast touch and it became firmer and longer.

It seemed to start the preceding night when Stacey had come crying into our bedroom, so we had let her sleep with us. I woke up early in the morning, and I couldn't remember everything that had occurred during the night. I did remember that Stacey and I were walking in the hallway of a spaceship and that she was asking me questions about things. I thought this was just too real, it couldn't have been a dream. I didn't say anything to Bert about it when he woke up, nor did I tell him that the back of my head and neck were extremely sore. But later in the morning I had to face what had happened during the night. When Stacey woke up, she complained that her head and neck hurt.

Later that evening I had a chance to talk to Bert about it, and he thought it was odd since the back of his head and neck had been sore for two days. He thought the sore areas were related to the cold he had that was becoming severe. Assuming that something might have been done to us, he let me check his head. I was shocked!

His original mark, the lone circle was no longer alone. On the lower part of his head almost in the center was a large area with a rash. Also in the area were three dots of blood almost like needle marks!

Bert checked my head. I didn't have the blood but my original mark had increased. It now also covered the lower center area of my head! We checked the kids and theirs were similar, on the lower center of their heads! Needless to say any chance that it could be a birthmark was out of the question! The possibility that all of us could have similar birthmarks in the same location was very slim, especially with their changing size and location at the same time!

That night must have been one of the strangest by far. We no sooner had gotten into bed than the room seemed alive with movement. This wasn't their typical light show. It almost seemed as though we could see their outlines as they moved around the room.

We didn't get up. We should have, considering what was happening, but I kept falling asleep. I tried very hard to stay awake, but I knew they were putting me to sleep! Fighting this feeling was like fighting to stay awake after receiving anesthesia—you have no choice! I could hear Bert. His cold sounded so bad. I had wanted him to go to the doctor, but he had refused, and now his cough was really rough. It was as if he couldn't get enough air into his lungs, and I could hear him complaining that his stomach hurt. I couldn't do anything to help him because they were putting me to sleep.

At 4:00 A.M. I woke up, partially sitting up on one arm, but I felt like I had just been lying down. I woke up because Bert yelled. I looked over at him, and he was trying to reach out to something—and that something was still there trying to get him to lie down!

Suddenly it was gone, and Bert jumped out of bed, turned on the light and came back to bed, grabbing his pillow.

"They were here! I am supposed to check my pillow for a blood spot!" He looked the pillow over carefully, then he stopped and he stared at it for a moment. "Look at this!" He pointed to the fresh blood spot on the pillow.

We came out to the kitchen to talk and to check his head. The mark that we just checked hours before was larger! Bert checked mine, and it was the same as before.

Bert started to tell me what he could remember. He wasn't completely asleep when they took us. He was lying there doubled over because his stomach hurt, and he felt bad. He felt like something was terribly wrong with him, but he didn't seem to have the strength to do anything about it. He decided that if he still felt that bad in the morning, he would go see the doctor.

The aliens seemed to be in a hurry. They took us fast and they seemed to be very worried about him. He said they gave him the impression that his condition was critical and related both to the new mark on his head that was causing some type of pressure and also to the severe cold he had. They had left him with one very clear thought—they had saved his life!

He remembered that they gave him a shot that also left a puncture mark and a sore spot on his arm! (Two days later he noticed a light bruise in the same area. Also his cold was improved, and a few days later it was completely gone.)

That night was truly a turning point in this bizarre stage of events. They had saved his life and had left convincing physical evidence. They also clarified the route to the return of our memories.

The meeting left an unmistakable impression with me that I was to start with the very first memory in my life and go from there. "The subsequent growth pattern is necessary for understanding." It was as though I was told to memorize this instruction because they certainly weren't my words! However, I did understand them. We had to start with our earliest memories and learn from each one up through the years. If we don't, we will simply get confused and end up with a great deal of mental stress. We can't attempt to jump into these memories midway. If we are going to understand all the ramifications we need to start from the beginning.

JULY 15, 1989

This morning I went to Madaline for hypnosis and told her what had happened to us. There was another feeling that remained with me after that late night meeting—I had been told to check Madaline and that she would also have the mark. She told me that she had had a headache and had slept very restlessly a couple of nights ago—the same night that this same thing happened to Stacey and me. So I checked the back of her head and yes, it was there, the same mark in the lower center of her head. She found it curious, but she was willing to accept that these beings were here and, for whatever the reasons, had chosen to involve her.

The hypnosis session went well. I recalled my first memory, and I was surprised because I had no idea or clue regarding that memory. I was only two years old at the time!

JULY 16, 1989

Tonight Christopher came into the room with a stomachache and asked if he could sleep with us. I told him he
could. I wasn't asleep completely when he came in, and I
knew why he had a stomachache. I got Bert up early the
next morning so that I could talk to him about it before the
kids got up.

I remembered being in the ship, walking with Christopher
at my side. He was upset and told me his stomach hurt. I
explained to him that it was part of what the aliens were
doing, that they don't mean for it to give you a stomachache,
but that with some people it does. I told him he could sleep
with us after we got back home. Then, as we neared the door
of the spaceship, I turned. I can't remember why I did, but
in doing so, I caught my left wrist on the edge of the door
frame and woke up that morning with that area sore and
slightly bruised. Christopher didn't seem to remember
anything.

So this was how our first shock began. We fumbled
through it as best we could considering the fact that we had
no idea what had happened to us.

Towards the end of this phase we began getting "promptings." Although we didn't realize how, we knew that we
were to stop seeing Madaline for any further hypnosis
sessions. We supposed that these feelings were being
"prompted" by these beings during the times they took us at
night. What else could explain our waking up one morning
knowing we were to stop the sessions and having the same
explanations for it?

We knew that we had only needed Madaline for the
memory of 1976–77 because it was important for our
conscious mind to know that we did indeed have correlating
memories under separate recall. It was the only way we
would be able to continue believing there was an unseen
force in our lives.

We also knew that it was time for us to continue with the remembering process under the guidance of these other beings. We had the strangest feeling that the remaining memories would be very difficult and would affect us in very personal ways.

Bert and I discussed in length the promptings we were receiving, and we knew that we needed to learn as much as possible about hypnosis so we would better understand the processes our alien friends would be conducting us through. What we didn't learn from the many books we checked out from the library, these other beings helped us to understand through promptings as well as from their assistance during our nightly sessions with them.

4

$\diamondsuit$

Fairies and Diamonds

"The subsequent growth pattern is necessary for understanding."

The meaning of this statement became even more evident as we began a methodical process of hypnotizing each other, as Madaline had hypnotized us. At first we decided to ignore the promptings we had had and go straight into fully remembering partially conscious memories.

One of the problems with doing our own hypnosis was knowing how to verify our memories. The first few sessions we had with Madaline proved that our memories matched. Separately we both remembered everything in identical detail. But now, how could we verify the memories?

We solved this problem by having the first person recall the memory, then keep certain details of it quiet until the other was under hypnosis. If the second person under hypnosis recalled the details the first person had omitted, then we could be fairly sure of the accuracy of our memories.

We uncovered some very vivid, frightening memories from our adult years. These memories covered sexual relations with other beings and medical examinations by them. These revelations filled approximately five cassette tapes with memories that didn't make any sense to us. As we tried to uncover them during hypnosis, we felt more confusion and fear than ever. When we sat down to transcribe the tapes at the end of the week, five of the tapes were blank, with the exception of the beginning of each tape where we had recorded the date and time. Was there significance to this phenomenon? Perhaps our ET friends were serious in requiring us to start at the beginning.

Bert was still having memory blocks even under hypnosis, so we started first with my childhood. These memories seemed a lot less confusing and much more systematic. We were sure now that this was indeed the correct approach to our remembering.

Trying to recall memories in a logical sequence was our next step in the awakening process. For me this was a fairly easy step, and the memories were less complicated and more manageable emotionally than they were when I was trying to jump in the middle of them. This allowed my conscious mind to experience these contacts in the order that they occurred. Each memory wove itself into my growing years, and although I never understood it until later, these memories helped me to become who I am.

Bert proceeded through this phase differently than I did. The stress that had been created when the extraterrestrials blocked his childhood memories of meetings with them, also inadvertently blocked the majority of all of his childhood memories.

As he began his hypnosis sessions at home, he continued to break into the barrier of the memory of 1976-77. This was to be one of his strongest memory blocks.

The extraterrestrials helped induce our hypnosis and the recovery of memories. At first the touches, flashes of light and sounds made by these other beings were disturbing, but we soon learned not to fear them and to understand that they were there to help.

The first memory I recalled through this process took place when I was two years old. Although I had originally gone through this memory with Madaline, I wasn't about to ignore the promptings again, so we started over from the beginning.

I had apparently left the yard on my own and wandered

down the road to a wooded area. As I played make-believe pony I noticed what I thought was a "fairy" at the bottom of the hill. She motioned to me to come down to her. With her long finger and flowing white gown, I was sure she must be a "fairy."

She looked very different from the way people look, which I suppose is why I didn't seem to be afraid of her. She had to be out of a fairy tale with that long finger, the white gown, large eyes and no hair. She seemed to be about as tall as a twelve-year-old.

She had taken me to a craft of some kind where an older "fairy" talked with me then took me into an examination room. In the room was another "fairy" who seemed to be a doctor. The girl "fairy" assisted him with the exam. At first they seemed to run some type of machine over the length of my body. Then the doctor put something into my nose. It hurt, but not for long. Then the girl "fairy" helped me from the table and took me into another room. This room was filled with several tables and a machine. From this machine she took two glasses of what I remember as malted milks.

She sat with me at a table and made me laugh by making goofy faces while I drank the malt. When I was through, she wiped my face, and we left the craft. She even skipped through the wooded area with me.

When we arrived back at the bottom of the hill, she told me not to tell anyone about my being with them or of having the malted milk. I then proceeded alone up the hill towards the road, and before I reached the top, my nose began to bleed severely.

I had no previous memory of this experience before hypnosis. Although I did remember the bloody nose and the hill, I always thought I had fallen down the hill.

It was after this memory that I began to wonder if Bert was right when he said he thought there was more to them than we knew. It's true they had done some type of medical examination, but there still was a kindness and a warmth about them.

It was later, during our awakening, that we began to

understand the reason for certain medical procedures and examinations. We will explain each of these in the sequence that we came to discover and understand them.

The next memory that I recalled happened when I was three years old. One night we were driving through the desert. I was sitting in the back seat when I saw a white object paralleling the car on the right side. It was flying just over the sand. I thought it was a round airplane, and as I watched it, suddenly there seemed to be a light on the car, almost like a cloud of light.

From my position I watched silently as the driver pulled the car over to the side of the road and stopped. None of the other occupants of the car were talking. They all just stared straight ahead.

I watched as two "fairies" floated from the "round airplane," which was now sitting on the sand. They came up to the car and opened the door. A male "fairy" stayed with the car's occupants, while the girl "fairy" took me with her to the ship. I recognized the girl as the same one that was in my memory from age two. She brought me to the same older "fairy." He was kindly and asked if I remembered him. He repeated his name, "Dets." It was pronounced "Deets."

I was then taken into the examination room and placed on a table. The doctor was the same, and although the female stayed with me, it was another male who assisted the doctor. At one point I was placed on my stomach. I could hear the voices of the doctor and the assistant. The assistant seemed to be questioning whether I was old enough for the procedure they were about to do. The doctor told him I was, and he proceeded to part the hair of the back of my head. It was at that point that I believe I was fully anesthetized.

The next thing I could remember was the female catching me as I jumped off the table. She then took me into the room with the tables and gave me what seemed to be a cookie. We didn't sit down to eat it however, but instead the older male came into the room and took me by the hand. I ate my cookie as we walked out into the hallway. He told me that this was his ship and that perhaps someday I could go with them. When we reached the ramp of the ship, the female took my hand, touched her belt, and we floated back to the car. I was placed into the back seat, and the male who had stayed with the car and my female companion turned together and floated back to the ship. The ship took off and suddenly the car was moving again.

I did have some conscious memory of this experience as I grew up. I always had a vivid memory of the tooth fairy taking me to her home and showing me some of her things. I remembered that I would someday be able to go with her. But as I grew older I realized that no matter how real this experience had always seemed to me there were no such things as fairies. The only way I could ever rationalize this memory was to believe that perhaps I had actually been in the company of an angel.

My next recollection came from when I was five years old and living in Germany. I had been asleep in bed when I was awakened by something pulling at my covers. I awoke to find a male alien standing at the side of my bed. I no longer felt he was a fairy, but I knew he wasn't a human. He put a long white robe on me and took me out of the apartment building. Once we were outside he took me towards the playground area, where I could see another alien standing near the slide. As we approached, I recognized him as Dets. He greeted me, and then we all started out across the field towards the fence. I don't recall feeling at all fearful while I was with them.

When we got to the fence, the younger male used some device to float us all over it. On the other side was a wooded area, and I began to follow a path through the tall grass. It looked as though the grass had been rolled over flat to create the path.

Not far into the area we came to the ship, and the ramp was open. Once inside, we went through large double doors into a smaller area. There were beings in this room. They seemed to be working at tables covered with buttons and screens.

I continued to follow Dets as we went upstairs and into

another room. This room was also filled with tables and equipment. One entire wall of the room was a large window. The window didn't look outside; instead it looked into a very large room. In the center of this room was a large pole. It started out at the first floor level and continued higher than the second floor.

I was then taken to the examination room. Dets asked me to sit down on a chair, and he sat near me asking for my hand. A female assistant was also in the room. She took my hand and after a quick prick, let me have my hand back. I looked at my hand and the newly placed sliver. Dets told me that it would one day be very important to me, and that I should never let anyone take it out. Dets and the younger male then took me back to the fence. Dets and I floated over, and the younger male stayed behind.

As we approached the apartment building, two Military Policemen started towards us and it seemed as if Dets must have ducked into some bushes. He was there one moment and then suddenly gone. I stood frozen as the two men began to question me as to who I was and why I was outside alone. Suddenly, they stopped talking and just continued to stare. Dets appeared, and we continued on until I was home in bed again.

Prior to hypnosis the only recollection I had of this meeting was a jumble of mixed memories. For instance, I always recalled receiving the sliver, but all that I remembered was my sitting in a small area and looking at the sliver in my hand while someone nearby talked to me about it. I also remembered walking towards the slide in a playground, and seeing a very odd boy standing there. For some reason I was afraid to remember this boy because he looked so scary. I remembered the Military Police questioning me, and I was afraid they would find my friend in the bushes. I never could remember why I had a friend who was hiding in the bushes.

As I began to recall these memories, it seemed that pieces of my life were finally coming together. All those odd bits of memory now had a place in my mind.

The next instance that I remembered came from when I was eight years old. This memory proved to be somewhat of a breakthrough. I realized from this memory that these beings seemed to have many of the same traits that we do.

I was living in Denver, Colorado, at the time. The house we were in was an older, two-story home. Late one night I found myself downstairs. I thought there was someone in the den, because I could see a light moving around in the room. The double doors into the den had a series of glass panes over which light curtains had been hung. This made it possible to see the light moving around inside the room, but it was impossible to see who was holding it. Slowly I had taken one knob in each hand and opened the doors.

It was then that I was able to make out a shadowy figure holding the light. The shadow spoke to me using my name. The fact that this shadow of a person used my name was probably the reason I didn't run or scream but continued to stand in the doorway.

Then this person did something with the light, an adjustment of some sort. The light was turned towards me, and the intensity of it changed to a brilliant white light. It was at this point that I seemed to feel less fear. I also seemed to know who was standing there. It was Dets again.

He told me not to be afraid, and he asked if I remembered him. He came over to me and closed the doors to the den. He led me over to the desk where I sat down in the chair. He stood next to me and slowly spun the globe that was on the table. It was then that I noticed someone else was in the room with us. The other person stood back in the shadows.

Dets then stopped the globe's slow spin and pointed to it, saying that was where I lived. He then explained to me that he didn't live anywhere on that globe. He and his people came from another planet that was far away. But he didn't live there anymore; his home was on his ship now.

He seemed to miss his planet a great deal. His mood seemed to be very reminiscent and sad. He told me he was from a place called Andromeda, but the conversation was, for the most part, more than I could comprehend. He was an adult trying to tell me of places and people he sorely missed. My happy-go-lucky eight-year-old disposition only understood that he was sad.

What I could recall from the conversation was that they had come a very long way to get to Earth. I also understood that from time to time they returned to visit their planet. Apparently these visits weren't as often as they wanted.

He explained that they had plans here on Earth, plans that needed to be fulfilled, plans that I could someday help them with if I so chose. However, that was all in the future, and for now I wasn't to worry about it.

Dets stopped talking, and the other person stepped out of the shadows. It seemed to be the same younger male I had recalled from earlier times, but I just wasn't sure. The younger male took a hand-held machine and did something to the back of my head. The only explanation I was given at that time was that the machine tells them about me.

Before they left, Dets told me to write, because I could become an author, like the ones who wrote those other books. He pointed out the books in the room. Before he left he seemed to be very sentimental towards me, and he commented that I was so much like his little girl. I stayed in the chair after they left, thinking about the conversation until I fell asleep.

In the conscious state, the only portions of this memory that I ever recalled were walking up to the den doors, fearful that someone was in there, and then sitting in the den staring at the globe on the desk until I fell asleep. I woke up the next morning in that same chair.

As I recalled more and more of these memories from my youth, I began to realize that these beings were actually individuals with personalities. Different from us and yet the same. It was important for me to understand who they were and what they were about. Now, three years later, both Bert and I realize that these youthful memories were important not only to us, but also to all the other people going through similar awakenings.

A number of these people, whom we know personally,

have had childhood memories of fairies, little people, spooks, etc.—memories that never seemed to fit in but yet never faded.

Not every unusual memory I had from childhood proved to be beneficial. There were a few odd memories that turned out to be nothing more than a child's game or dream. These were productive, however, in that they showed that the hypnosis was indeed helping me to sort out my memories.

The next recollection came from the age of eleven. I was then living in Rapid City, South Dakota. We lived on the edge of town and were somewhat secluded. I had been in bed for some time when I thought I saw something outside the window. Apparently I was calmed by the light beam they used. There wasn't much time to feel any fear. I went to the window and opened it, and I seemed to recall that I was asked to do this, but I couldn't remember hearing a voice. I suspect that telepathy was used.

I climbed out of the window towards a being. He put his arm under my arm and across my back. We then floated straight up through an open porthole in the bottom of a ship.

I was taken to the first floor room, and I then raced up the stairs on my own. Dets was standing at the top waiting for me. He gave me a wholehearted welcome and led me into the ship's upper control room. By now I seemed to be just about as tall as he was.

Dets had me watch through the window in the center of the room as the lights in the engine room shut off. The engine itself seemed to start moving. I was then told to watch a monitor, and I could see houses and buildings. It was fascinating to see the city at night from an aerial view. Dets told me that those were my "special diamonds," and that no one else could see them the way that I could.

I still seemed to have some trouble looking at him. His eyes were large, and he had many wrinkles on his face. But he was nice, and I felt very comfortable there with him.

As I sat watching the city through the monitor, he pulled a chair up next to mine. He began to do something to the back of my head. It seemed to be some type of machine that in effect reads one's memory. Whether it was physically "plugged in" or reacted as a remote, I couldn't be sure. This machine seemed to be "down loading" all of my memory at a high rate of speed.

After a moment he took my hand and looked at the sliver. After his visual check of this, he turned his attention to one of several control panels. He pointed out some buttons to me and even showed me one I could work, but I refused. The whole matter of flying around the city on a spacecraft, plus all the desks with control panels and buttons seemed to be getting the better of me. I wasn't about to touch anything!

After a little more conversation that I couldn't completely recall, Dets took me back to the male being who had brought me from the house. He in turn took me downstairs and we stood over the closed porthole. We then began floating above it. Consequently, I felt less afraid when the porthole opened and I could see how high up in the air we were. We then began our descent to our house. He helped me get back through the window, and I got back into bed.

Previous to hypnosis, the only conscious recall I ever had of this memory was my staring out through what I thought was a window. I saw the aerial view of Rapid City and someone beside me saying these were "my special diamonds," the lights of the city at night. As I grew older I couldn't explain why I'd remembered seeing the city from the sky, never having flown over it.

During the recall of this memory I seemed to connect the younger male with all of the previous times. He never seemed to talk directly to me, but he was always there, holding gadgets and controlling their usage, floating, using light beams, etc.

The next time I recall meeting these beings I was fourteen. We were living outside of Hill City, South Dakota, at that time. We lived in a beautiful, mountainous area surrounded by hills and trees. I would spend lengthy periods of time exploring our backyard and beyond. Even though there were miles and miles of wilderness outside, I'd never

met the beings on these solitary hikes. Instead, they came
again at night while everyone slept.

I'm not sure what originally awakened me. As I opened
my eyes, though, I could see a blue light in the room. It was
coming from inside the room and not from the windows. As
I focused I was shocked to see the outline of two people
standing beside my dresser. One was slightly taller than the
other. As my eyes became more accustomed to the light, I
could see that they were not humans. The taller one was a
male, and the other one was a female. Even with no hair
their traits were masculine and feminine.

Denise's memory of the two figures
standing in her bedroom.

Then I saw a light flash, but I wasn't able to see which
one held the machine, since they were standing so close
together. I then lay back on the pillow. Although I didn't feel
the same amount of panic, I was frightened. It's odd to feel
both calm and fear as a joint emotion. I felt tears sliding
slowly down my cheeks and hair. The female touched one of
the tears that had fallen into my hair. She looked sympathetic and told me I would be all right. She seemed familiar.
I was sure her name was "Keyanna." I had seen her before
during these meetings. The male just stood there and stared.
His eyes just watched. It was the same male again.

Between the two of them they arranged me in a completely straight position. Keyanna continued to talk, letting me know that I needn't be afraid and that they were not going to hurt me. Then I began to float. The male was holding the machine that controlled the floating. Keyanna led the way, and she was also floating. Then I was floating behind her in the same position I had been in while on the bed. He then followed me, and he too was floating.

They took me up into the hills not far from the house. There in the clearing was a large, silvery metal ship. Lights ran around its circular body. As we neared the ship I saw another of these beings standing near, as a lookout or a guard.

I was taken up a ramp, into the ship and down the hall to the medical room. Then Keyanna and I were left alone. She helped me undress and get on the table. Then a doctor came in. He did several different exams using several different machines. This portion of the memory was more complex and harder to recall. At one point the doctor seemed to do some type of nerve conduction test. He seemed concerned about my wrists and ankles. I have since deduced that they knew I was having growth problems there. The only conclusion they could apparently come up with was that they couldn't interfere.

Another machine was placed over my abdomen, and I felt as though a large air bubble was being pushed through my insides. It neither hurt nor felt comfortable, but it was an odd sensation.

Keyanna assisted me as I got dressed. She and the same male then floated me back to my house. By this time I was feeling much more comfortable with them. Keyanna seemed to talk most of the time, and she was kind and friendly.

Once I was back in bed I didn't want them to go. Keyanna said that they would be back the next night. To reassure me of this she took a ring I had placed on my dresser earlier. She said that this was proof she would be back, because she would return with my ring the next night.

Later that night I woke up thinking that my alarm clock was ringing. The clock was set for much later than it was. I felt nervous and upset, but I didn't know why. Later that morning I discovered that my ring was missing. This was upsetting because I also seemed to have a strange eerie feeling. That night I searched for my ring again before going to bed, but it was nowhere to be found.

Sometime later after I had fallen asleep, I again woke up. Keyanna was standing beside my bed holding my ring out for me. I smiled. She then placed the ring near my alarm clock. The male being was there also. As I stood up I realized that they were going to let me walk on my own. I could remember the floor feeling cold to my bare feet. They must have been prepared for that because they put some type of soft footwear on my feet.

We all walked out together, but instead of heading out into the hills, we headed towards the road. We crossed the road and floated up into the ship. I could remember hearing the low frequency vibration of the engine.

I was led again to the medical room. The doctor was waiting as we entered. He greeted us in a fairly friendly way. Keyanna then helped me get undressed and onto the table. Another type of examination was done on me with the use of a needle that was passed through my belly button. The apparatus with the needle was hooked to another machine. I wasn't sure what the exam was for, and it was fairly upsetting. I had a sensation of tingling throughout my body. The doctor began talking about several things I just couldn't seem to follow. A nurse was recording what he was saying.

The next thing I remembered was looking at this needle being pulled from my belly button. It bled slightly. The doctor did something to it to stop the bleeding, and then he left the room. He seemed fairly satisfied with the results of his testing.

Keyanna talked as she helped me with my clothes. She told me that I was getting older, and that from now on my world would be different, that there were wonderful things in store for me.

As we started to leave the room I saw that the same male was near the door waiting for us. This time however, Keyanna spoke his name. As well as I could remember, his name was "Beek." They brought me back home and before they left Keyanna said that they would meet with me again.

Once again I woke up some time later to what I thought was the sound of the alarm clock ringing. My nerves seemed to be ringing with it. The clock wasn't actually ringing, however, and when I woke up the next morning, I found my ring next to the clock. Not being able to explain the eerie feeling I'd had, the alarm clock, or the ring, I decided that there must have been a ghost in the house.

The beings did not return again until I was almost fifteen years old. We had moved back to Rapid City, South Dakota, and were living about five miles outside of Rapid City in a combination mobile home and RV park.

Just past the trailer park was a service road that turned into a gravel road just on the other side of an old bridge. Further up the gravel road forked, and in either direction the road was unpaved and led to farms and fields.

This particular summer day I walked to the bridge on my own. Sometimes I would spend time there by myself just looking at the scenery, woods and fields. This time, though, I found myself following a dry river bed through the field towards the hill. I felt tingles over my body as I walked on, not sure where I was going or why.

The tingles increased, and I left the creek bed and walked towards the trees. Soon after I reached the trees two of the beings stepped out in front of me. A female flashed a light at me. I no longer tingled, nor did I feel scared. I was in something of a dazed state. I recognized the male, Beek, but I hadn't met the female before.

At first they walked towards me slowly. I realized then that they were being cautious of me and any possible reactions I might have. They each grasped my arms and led me further into the trees to their waiting ship. I was taken directly into the medical room where a very quick medical exam was done.

I was then taken to another room where Dets, the older being, was waiting. He explained that he hadn't intended for this meeting to be so abrupt, but they couldn't risk staying any longer. Beek and the female then escorted me back to the edge of the woods. They explained how I should walk back, and then I started back towards the creek alone.

I walked back the same way I had come until I got to the bridge. Instead of going up the side to the top I went under the bridge. I sat down in the dirt, put my head on my knees and fell asleep. I woke up later that afternoon.

The only conscious recall I had of this memory was waking up under the bridge. Later I would go to that bridge occasionally looking for something, never sure of what it was. I always seemed to be trying to ease a nagging feeling the area held for me, trying to find a memory that I didn't even realize was missing.

These were the memories I was able to recall from my childhood. The hypnosis sessions themselves were very unusual. At first, realizing that other beings were in the house with us was disturbing, yet with the return of the earlier memories, we began to get to know these beings. Our hypnosis sessions would suddenly come alive with unexplainable sounds, flashes of light and soft touches. The room at times would seem as thick as fog when they would begin their "light show."

The touches were perhaps the hardest to get used to. Suddenly we would feel a tingling sensation either on our head or face, like being lightly touched by someone. Yet we couldn't see anything.

These beings seemed to help with the hypnosis by elevating the memory into a higher level. As we relaxed and started the hypnosis count we would get a touch or two, as though they were saying "hello." Then we would feel some type of equipment actually pressing up against different points on the forehead and head. Suddenly we would feel very dizzy and could feel the depth of the hypnosis as we went under quickly.

5

Long, Bony Fingers

Bert's memories from childhood were few. An accident when he was four years old caused the extraterrestrials to temporarily discontinue any intense meetings with him. They did, however, continue to track him. Just prior to the accident at age four, during one meeting with him they had placed the tracking device into his nostril and also placed the monitor into the back of his head.

Eventually we were told by the extraterrestrials that they were Andromes (pronounced an-drom′-ease) from Andromeda. The Andromes try to install the tracking device and monitor as early as possible in the human child. The variables are the physical condition of the child, the Andromes' schedule and the opportunities to access the child.

After Bert's accident at age four, the Andromes watched his medical progress throughout his recovery in the hospital but didn't attempt to have a meeting with him. Doing so could have caused further stress to his already weakened condition.

The Andromes who tracked Bert were not from the same ship that I knew from childhood. They were another group of Andromes stationed in another Androme ship. We now know that there are several of these ships assigned around Earth.

When Bert was about seven years old he was involved in a short meeting with them. During the meeting he recalled watching an Androme female while she was holding another human child, a young girl, above her and talking to her as an adult sometimes does with a child. Bert remembered how the black eyes of this rather short lady fascinated him. The kindness that she showed to both the little girl and Bert was almost like that of a mother. The meeting itself seemed to be simply a sharing of time, perhaps so that they would remain in his memory, perhaps for other reasons of which he was never made aware.

When he next recalled seeing these beings, Bert was nine years old and living in Ft. Richardson, Alaska. He had been playing alone in a large wooded area near his home. Because of the size and solitude of the area, Bert wasn't allowed to play there. However, the temptation to explore overwhelmed the warnings from his parents. Venturing farther into the woods he discovered a railroad track that cut its way through the thick stand of trees.

Three small beings appeared suddenly from behind the trees near the tracks, two males and one female. He stood watching them as they walked closer to him. He couldn't recall any sense of fear with this memory, just a strange, calm feeling. They looked very different, yet his feelings of curiosity seemed to be somewhat dulled.

One of the male beings spoke to him, warning him of the dangers of being out alone in the woods and playing near the railroad tracks. The other two beings nodded in agreement. He recognized the female as the same one from earlier in his childhood. Even now her motherly attitude conveyed worry about his safety. Then told him it was time for him to go back home, and he did.

The next occasion he remembers visiting with them was when he was about ten or eleven years old, living in Canistota, South Dakota. He was awakened one night by a young Androme male who handed Bert the clothes he had tossed on the floor before going to bed that night. Bert put them on, and together they went into the living room. The male and female Andromes he had seen years earlier near the railroad tracks in the woods were waiting there. They led him outside.

He could see that just above the house was a large silvery spaceship. They floated him up through an opening in the base of the craft. Once inside he saw that they were in a large room. He looked around and could see panels on the walls, for what sort of operations, he didn't know. He wanted to ask, but as he looked closer at these beings he seemed to forget his questions. The male and female returned his intent stare with understanding smiles coming from their very tiny mouths. The female Androme reached out her hand towards him, momentarily frightening him when he saw that her hand was different from that of a human. Her index finger seemed to extend further than any of her other fingers, giving it a long, bony look. Softly, she stroked his cheek, and he could feel himself relax slightly.

They then led him through the large room and out into a corridor, where they left the ship by way of a smaller opening and a ramp. They led him through what seemed to be a much larger spacecraft and to a place that looked like a park. Here he found that there were other children, both from Andromeda and Earth. They invited him to play a type of game that was very similar to our game of volleyball. He recalled that he had a lot of fun playing with the other children.

Later the female Androme took him into a medical room in what looked like a building. A female assistant, who seemed to be a nurse, helped Bert up onto the table.

Soon there after, an older male Androme entered the room. He talked momentarily with the females, then he spoke with Bert. It was a brief but friendly introduction, as Bert recalled. The doctor went right to work by looking into Bert's nose with a small instrument. Bert felt nothing, and the procedure took only moments. Next, the doctor ran a type of machine over the length of Bert's body. He felt it was a scanning machine of some kind.

The doctor was quick with his procedures and he left the room without any explanations. The females helped Bert off the table and he was then returned home. This was his last memory of the Andromes until the 1976-77 incident in South Dakota.

In these early memories we mentioned the tracking device and the monitor. We have since come to learn what these are used for:

- The tracking device is usually placed in the right nostril and allows them to locate your exact position at any time.
- The monitor is a much more complicated device and is usually implanted only in humans who will be in long-term relationships with the Andromes.
- The monitor is placed in the back of the head and connected to several portions of the brain. Part of the function of this device is to mechanically lock out portions of your memory. This allows them to safely continue having meetings with the person with little or no memory of these meetings leaking to the conscious mind.
- The monitor is also used to shut off the conscious mind. This allows them to deal with the subconscious self. This method is normally less shocking and can be done through light frequency.

The monitor is a very important part of the awakening process. It is used to slowly raise all of the subconscious memories to the conscious level. It also monitors the amount of mental and physical stress these memories may be causing. Thus they know when to slow down or speed up the process.

When the Andromes were raising our memory levels we could feel all types of weird sensations in our head and neck area. At times in the beginning the experience caused a lot of sudden dizziness. We began to refer to these sensations as "adjustments," for we thought that the monitors were being fine tuned at each level.

6

Passenger in My Womb

In late July, 1989, I had a very interesting experience. I went to sleep watching the thickness in the air accumulate, as they began their "light show" for us. I'm not sure how long I had been sleeping when I felt someone pulling the covers away from me. I opened my eyes, and Beek was just inches from my face! He was looking at me and smiling!

I recognized him and I smiled back. I knew him, or at least some part of me knew him. Then the initial reaction gave way to all my conscious fears of these mysterious beings. Between my excitement at seeing him and the fear that seemed to be building from my stomach to my throat, I was losing control.

My face must have shown this change. He said it was all right and that I was fine. He said he would come again. The last thing I remembered seeing was a flash of light.

That seems so long ago now. Although we didn't know it at the time, we have since discovered that meeting him in the conscious state was an unexpected accident. For some reason the first flash of light had not put me under, and I had remained conscious. When Beek woke me up and I smiled, he didn't know anything had gone wrong until my face changed, reflecting the panic I was beginning to feel.

In the beginning of our awakening, we didn't realize that we were meeting with them almost every night.

During the next few months of this phase, our consciousness was slowly awakened. Some nights we would wake up at different hours and recall odd memories of floating or seeing shadows moving around the room. Later we understood that at these odd times we were actually coming back to bed after having been with them. The meetings with them were happening almost every night now and seemed to last from one to two hours each time. On rare occasions the meetings lasted up to four hours.

Slowly we became more aware of who they were and that they were often with us. In the daytime we began getting touches more often, and with harder intensity. They never seemed to give us more than we could handle. For instance, Bert began getting frequent, firmer touches long before I did. He was more in control of his fear of them, whereas their slight touches unnerved me at first.

We continued the hypnosis in the presence of our invisible company of Androme companions through October, 1989.

The memories covering our adult years taught us much about our relationship with the Andromes. Now Bert was ready to thoroughly review and complete the recall of the memory in 1976-1977, the memory of our first experience together with the Andromes.

Bert reviewed that night in the field, and without fear or physical reactions he was able to remember further details. He recalled that the doctor had him turn on his side. Using some type of instrument to lift the skin on the lower right side of his back, the doctor extracted a tissue sample from him. The procedure left a permanent scar. He further recalled that the procedure to place the tracking device was preceded by the removal of a similar device previously placed by the other ship.

The memories we had from that night were confusing, and although the details were the same, neither of us seemed to be able to comprehend the reasons for the medical tests. We understood that because of the seriousness of our relationship, the Andromes felt the need to see if we were compatible. They needed to make some type of a match. As will be explained in greater detail soon, it was somewhat later that we discovered who actually needed to match.

Months after this memory was recalled we received an odd sort of verification. The UFO investigator we had met with in June had come across an old article that he thought we would find interesting, and so he mailed us a copy. The article told about a UFO that had been spotted on January 2, 1977. The sighting occurred over a two-hour period, and there were ten witnesses that night. The UFO seemed to have shown up just as a search for a missing boy was begun and disappeared as soon as the boy was found. Because Bert had recalled seeing a human man and boy on the ship (with whom he apparently was not supposed to come into contact), this article was particularly interesting. Efforts to locate the people named in the article failed, however.

For Bert, our 1976-77 meeting together with the Andromes was also the first lengthy meeting he had had with them since he was younger. Even to his subconscious mind these beings were "alien" to him. This feeling also made him dangerous to the Andromes, for until he was able to get to know them, there was the risk that he could panic and attempt to hurt them.

Three days after the night on the lonely road, the Andromes made a return trip for Bert. He had been in bed asleep when they came. There were two or three of them in his basement room when he woke up. They floated him outside where he could see not only the night sky but a light that was too close to be a star. He recognized the circular dark shape of the ship as together they began to float up towards the light that radiated from a hole in the bottom of the ship.

Once inside the ship Bert was taken directly to the medical room and was placed stomach-down on the table. The doctor then adjusted the monitor in the back of his head. Bert was then taken back home and put back to bed. It had been quick.

This was another step in his new relationship with the Andromes. The monitor needed to be adjusted since the amount of time with them would be increased. Now responsibility for Bert had been officially transferred to the new ship.

In our first few adult memories, we almost had the feeling of being nothing more than a case file or some kind of scientific project to the Andromes. On the surface the medical tests, the transfer of responsibilities and the adjustment of devices seems quite cold and impersonal. Yet these beings were not unsympathetic to our feelings or needs. They were friendly, and when possible they took the time to tell us and show us who they were. In the next memory we recalled, Dets did take time with us.

This meeting occurred in early 1977. Bert and I and a friend had been watching TV late one night. At the sound of someone coming into the room we looked up. In that same split second, a flash of light went across the room, and then another.

For the first few moments everything seemed somewhat hazy to us. The initial shock of having the conscious mind turned off seems to cause a few moments of disorientation. Two Andromes helped us as we started to leave the house. The friend who had been in the room with us was still on the couch staring at the TV. She didn't seem to be seeing or hearing anything.

We were taken into the backyard, where we floated up above the house into the porthole in the bottom of the ship. From there we had been led upstairs to the control room, where Dets was waiting for us.

We sat down, and Dets told us that they wanted to let us know that they would be gone for some time. He went on to say that in a few years Bert and I would need to make some decisions. He said that these decisions would affect our lives, and we must remember that it would be our choice. However, he didn't elaborate on the type of decisions we would face.

He then offered to show us the ship, a ship he was sure we would appreciate. He seemed so proud of it. The best way to describe Dets is that he reminds us of an older English gentleman. He is formal and quiet in his ways, but he is also something of a father figure as well. He treats us as his children, and he wants to share his knowledge with us.

We gladly accepted his invitation. Dets started with the room we were in, calling it the "main operational control room." The large pole we could see through the window was part of the engine. We followed him as he led us down to the first floor of the ship.

The room located directly beneath the control room he called the "preliminary engine power control room." From there we went out into the hallway of the ship, and there were doors located to the left and right. The first door on the outside wall of the ship opened into a ramp for their use when they landed.

Dets started down the circular hallway. The next door on the right was a type of storage area. Further down the hall the next door to the right was called the "data collection and retrieval center." The next few doors on the left all seemed to be related to the workings of the ship, life support and navigation.

The ship was compact and efficient, and yet had so many things in it. There were rooms for the crew as well as a main room for their relaxation and entertainment. There was a dining room, medical rooms and a medical supply area.

After the tour we were taken back home to our places in front of the television set. Our friend was still gazing unseeingly at the static on the screen. As we regained consciousness, we discovered that the TV station was no longer on the air. Because of our grogginess, we felt that we had fallen asleep.

We have since learned more about this highly efficient ship. These "meeting" ships are approximately sixty to seventy feet in diameter, and the crews on these ships are normally staffed with twenty-five members, both female and male. The duties of the crew range from engineering of the ship's mechanical devices to washing dishes. Skilled duties are assigned to specific individuals, while the non-skilled chores are alternately scheduled among everyone.

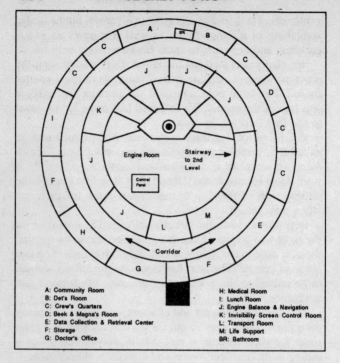

A: Community Room
B: Det's Room
C: Crew's Quarters
D: Beek & Magna's Room
E: Data Collection & Retrieval Center
F: Storage
G: Doctor's Office

H: Medical Room
I: Lunch Room
J: Engine Balance & Navigation
K: Invisibility Screen Control Room
L: Transport Room
M: Life Support
BR: Bathroom

Interior view of the meeting ship that is used to travel throughout a given area. It is used for regular meetings between the Andromes and their human mates.

Humans who do become a part of this society are taught skills, and they help with the chores; even during the secretive short meetings.

Through hypnosis we discovered a good example of the use of the tracking devices. Not only did the devices help the Andromes to pinpoint the exact location of their contacts in their homes, but they also located them anywhere they moved.

In the summer of 1977 Bert and I moved from South Dakota to the state of Washington. That September they made an unscheduled return trip to our new place.

It was very late at night. Bert and I sat staring out the patio doors at the star-filled night sky. A light flashed, and we were "under."

Dets and another male entered the doors. Dets explained that they hadn't planned on visiting with us yet, but that when our position changed they came to check. He wanted to let us know that they knew where we were and that they would be coming back soon.

They left. We weren't told where they were going. Possibly to their home? Or possibly they were going somewhere else to meet with other contactees.

This was a short memory, yet it made a difference in how we felt. The Andromes had taken time out from their schedule to simply let us know that they were still watching us, that our move hadn't meant we were lost to them.

Our phase of remembering continued. We were slowly learning more about these beings. Some of our fear of them seemed to be diminishing, yet so many more questions were being raised. What did they want from us? What decisions were we going to have to make? In 1989 we recalled a memory from 1977 in which they talked of future decisions. By 1989 those decisions surely must already have been made and carried through one way or another. What were they?

It was in August of that year that we began to find out. We also discovered what choices we had made.

While the event itself happened in 1978, recalling it for the first time in 1989 was devastating. It was our conscious minds in 1989 that had to deal with the decisions made by our subconscious minds in 1978.

At first Bert couldn't recall this memory—his conscious mind didn't want to learn of it. This memory brought back the physical reactions he thought he had gotten over after the completion of the memory on the lonely road. After dealing with the feelings within himself, he was finally able to remember. I also had a difficult time with the memory and with its aftereffects.

In late winter of 1978 we were picked up for another

unscheduled meeting. We were returned to the medical room again, but it looked different this time. There was a second examination table and more equipment. Dets, the doctor, Bert, a female assistant, Beek (the quiet younger male) and I were all in the room. The doctor took a hand-held device and moved it along my lower abdomen.

The doctor then looked at Dets and told him it was confirmed that I was pregnant. Dets took me by the arm and pulled me aside. Bert also came up to us. Dets was upset, and he explained that we had moved faster than they had anticipated. The decisions that were to be made in the future would have to be made now. It was obvious that he felt we were too young to be in the position he was about to put us in. But the choice of time had been taken out of his and our hands. I was pregnant, and it was time to decide.

He went on to explain to us that the Androme people, although they could produce children, could not now do so successfully. For biological reasons their race had become, in effect, barren. The weakness that had taken over their genetics had to be overcome, and because of their religious views, they refused to have their scientists work on any type of genetic altering.

Their beliefs also prevent them from coming to Earth or any other world and stealing the specimens of eggs and sperm that they need. They fully believe that the right to procreate is a gift given individually by God, and that it is the responsibility of each being to use this means of reproduction as their own. They believe it is no one's right to just take it from another.

It was through their prayers and counseling that they had finally agreed on a way to continue their race. This was to be accomplished by the introduction of another race into theirs through a complete union of marriage. The intricate details involved in such a solution took many memories for us to understand.

Their solution was to create a new family unit made up of an Androme and a human. In order to do this successfully, specific tests would have to be done on both the Androme and the human to assure compatibility of the genetic makeup. They needed to be sure that the weakness they needed bred out was not already becoming a weakness in the human. Before they could introduce Andromes and humans for possible relationships, they would have to make sure that they "matched."

Prospective individuals were introduced to each other and the natural course of relationships determined who would marry. To provide a full family unit for the children and the adults, the Andromes as well as the humans were allowed to marry within their own kind as well. In more complex marriages, a human couple would marry an Androme couple. These were rare cases, however.

Dets explained that they preferred to work in parallel with the earth female's first pregnancy so that they were be less chance for the conscious mind to ever know something was different about the pregnancy.

I was asked to join in marriage with Beek and to carry his child along with Bert's. Both Bert and I agreed.

Dets performed the wedding immediately. There was no time for delay. The doctor then took an egg from one of my ovaries, and Beek and I were left alone to consummate the marriage. Sexual intercourse between Andromes and humans is very similar to that between humans. The purpose of the act is the expression of love between us, and for fertilization. When we had completed our union, the doctor returned. He placed the egg in my uterus, drawing it through Beek's semen left from the joining. With the addition of a new passenger in my womb, I began a double motherhood.

Once this memory had been uncovered there was no going back. Bert and I knew now what they wanted from us—children. The next few days were hard ones for us.

I tried to understand why I would marry an alien. The moral implications of this tortured my mind for days. I didn't believe it was possible to love and marry more than a single person. I tried to reason logically that all I really had done was to help someone. That didn't work, though. I also knew I had feelings for this alien named Beek.

Bert began to deal with feelings of intense jealousy as he tried to comprehend the memory. He fought the anger and jealousy. Yet inside he knew there was more to learn. He knew he too had made the same choice to help later. He had to understand this anger and jealousy and reason it out, since it would not be logical for it to be OK for him to help them this way, but not for me to do the same.

7

Double Motherhood

In July of 1978 Bert and I were married. He then joined the National Guard, and while he was in training I moved to Colorado to stay with my parents. I was seven months pregnant.

My pregnancy had been an unusual one. During the first four months my uterus wouldn't grow properly. By the fourth month the doctor was sure that I would lose the baby. Before the end of the fourth month my uterus not only began to grow properly, but I looked more like I was six months pregnant.

I didn't see another doctor until after the move to Colorado in early September, 1978. I was due in late October. After the examination the doctor told me that although I wasn't officially due for almost two months, he thought I could deliver any day. He explained that it wasn't unusual for a first pregnancy to be early, and that upon examination he could feel that the baby had already dropped into position. He also suspected twins as he listened to the heartbeat monitor. After listening awhile, he finally decided it must have been an echo.

To everyone's surprise, however, I carried the baby not only to the due date, but also nearly two weeks further. Our daughter Christy was born November 3, 1978. She was only six pounds, but the doctor had guessed that she would be over seven pounds at birth.

The night before Christy was born, I had been in the bathtub. I felt a rush of water and thought that my water had broken. I knew that labor would start soon thereafter, yet nothing happened. So I had gone to bed thinking that whatever it was that I felt must not have been the water bag.

By 3:00 A.M. I was up with labor pains. I was in labor for a total of 23 hours.

Four days after the birth, I was at home with the baby when I had a very vivid dream that I was in labor. The room was strange, not like the hospital I had been in. There were little doctors all around me and other people I couldn't identify. I gave birth to a very small, dark-haired boy. I woke up shaking—the dream had seemed so real to me. I thought I must be crazy to relive labor pains, but it seemed so real.

After thinking about the dream for a while I decided that because of the vividness of it, perhaps it had been a premonition. Perhaps our next child would be a little boy with lots of dark hair.

Now through the use of hypnosis I went back to this "dream."

The evening of November 2, 1978, the night of my bath was when the first labor had started. Shortly after I had gone to bed I felt the first cramps of labor, but before I could do anything about it, the Andromes came in. There were four beings, and I was put under quickly with a flash of light. I was floated out of the room, with two of them holding their hands under my waist and bottom. They were supporting the weight of the babies so that it wouldn't hurt my back as I was floated to the ship.

At the ship I was taken straight to the medical room where the doctor and his assistants were waiting with Dets and Beek. The next few minutes were the hardest for everyone. The doctor would have to help deliver Beek's baby, while leaving Bert's child untouched in my womb.

A baby boy with lots of dark hair was born several minutes later. It was his water bag that had broken earlier that evening.

When I first recalled this memory under hypnosis, I had a terrible time with my emotions. I didn't want to accept that I was having all the same feelings for Beek and his baby as I did for Bert and our child.

The new baby was given to Dets for a type of baptism and naming. Beek had chosen the name "Ankra." The baby was then given to Beek, and he and I both shared a few moments gazing at the tiny baby.

As soon as the doctor finished with me, he told Dets that I would be in labor soon with my second child and that I needed to be returned home immediately. So I was taken back home, and Beek stayed on the ship with Ankra.

I woke up in labor. Unknown to my conscious mind or any of the humans around me, the extraterrestrial doctor stayed with me until well after Christy's delivery.

While I was in the hospital, Dets, Beek and the doctor came to visit. It was late one night during a black out. The only lights that had remained on in the hospital were the emergency lights in the nursing stations and hallways.

The beings entered through the window of my room. An Androme security being came with them to watch the door while we talked. They were checking to see how I was doing and to admire the new baby girl. She was in a bassinet in the room with me. It was like any other family gathering to coo over a new arrival, except that these were beings from another planet.

A few days after Christy and I were back home, Beek returned late at night. He took me to where they had parked the ship in the field. He took me to see Ankra, and my double motherhood began.

Beek told me that he would soon marry an Androme female named Magna. His new bride would be as much the mother to our child as I was. I felt joy at his words instead of jealousy. Or at least this "night" time part of me felt joy. My conscious mind was very confused.

The memories I recalled into consciousness while under hypnosis were only throwing more confusion at me. Now I would have to accept that in addition to Bert. I was also married to an alien with whom I had produced a blended child. Furthermore, my ET husband was planning to marry someone else as well.

At that point of our awakening Bert and I went through some very stress-filled days. There were days when we would snap at each other and days when we would cry on each other's shoulders.

How could there be parts of our minds that seemed so separate from the conscious parts? How could we be separate within ourselves? Were these our souls? Our subconscious minds? Who were they? And how could we get in contact with them? How could we introduce ourselves to ourselves?

Bert began to read of this entity we call the soul through the Bible and the writings of Edgar Cayce. We began to discuss the different levels of the brain. Even in the books we had read on hypnosis we had learned that there are several levels to the brain and that none are completely understood.

This because an important part of our awakening. The goal, we learned, was to minimize the differences in the levels of the brain and to literally become at one with ourselves. In order to awaken we needed to discover and unite every part of our mind and soul. This is a long process with no easy steps.

Bert and I worked harder at remembering. The next memory we uncovered occurred during December, 1978. He was on leave and was coming home to see Christy for the first time. What we didn't know at that time was that he was also going to meet his other child, Ankra, the son from Beek and myself.

It was during Bert's first night home that Beek came and took us to the ship. On this visit we noticed that the ship's legs were of uneven lengths. The legs, it seems, adjust and keep the ship level on sloping ground.

We followed Beek into the ship, and he took us to the crew's quarters, where we entered one of the rooms. It was a small room with just enough space for a bed, a small kitchenette table, a built-in dresser and a small bathroom.

Dets sat on the bed holding Ankra. Beek stood somewhat away from us as Dets introduced the baby to Bert. Dets talked for a short period about how much of a help we had been to them and how proud he was of such a fine, young, baby boy.

Bert was confused by this memory. It further aroused the anger and jealousy he was feeling consciously. Yet subconsciously he knew that he felt all right about the situation. He also knew that he felt just as much a part of Ankra's life as he did of Christy's.

These feelings only confused us. We were trying to uncover the reasons why these beings had contacted us, why they had begun such a relationship with us, and we had agreed? The feelings of love and family towards them were not what we had expected. Yet it was these feelings that won out over the anger and jealousy. It was the family relationship with these beings that carried us through the confusion and helped us sort through the more difficult negative feelings.

During the time Bert spent in basic training and schooling he matured hard and fast. It was a time of rigorous physical and mental training, a time of feeling indestructible and gung-ho. The military turns boys into men, or so the boys are told. They turn them into fighting machines, to kill or be killed. But, as Bert points out, although he hated the training methods, his loyalty was never tainted, and he understands that the military is a needed part of our Earth society. This is the land of the free and the home of the brave, where one should be willing to die to protect the liberty that is America.

Nevertheless it was hard on him. He learned to party hard and routinely, something he had never done before, and something he quit doing just before his stint was up.

Bert always felt that there was a particular time during his training when something must have happened that made him wake up and see what he had become. Suddenly his attitude changed, the partying stopped, and he began to look at himself seriously.

Now under hypnosis he discovered what had caused the change.

Late one night Bert was asleep in his bunk in the barracks. He and his buddy had been out drinking earlier. He awoke to find that there were four Androme men in the room. They quickly floated him out. He was still dressed in only his T-shirt and shorts. The Andromes were fast but cautious as they stole down the back stairs and out to the back of the building. No one else was out there, and it was dark. The ship hovered like a dark shadow in the night sky.

Bert was floated up and taken into the medical room. The doctor pulled his dog tags out from under his T-shirt. Looking at them somewhat disgustingly, he placed them back under the shirt.

As Bert looked around in his drunken haze he could see that besides the doctor there were also Dets, Beek and a female Androme named Magna. They all seemed to be staring at him, their faces filled with disappointment.

The words Dets spoke to him were stern and memorable. "What are you doing is a shame and a disgrace both to your body and to your soul. It's also an insult to your intelligence and your abilities. We're concerned that if this abuse continues you will destroy yourself. We don't wish this to happen. We are highly disappointed in you!" Dets then turned and left the room. Magna looked at him sadly, and Bert was taken back to the barracks.

Although he wasn't able to recall this meeting the next morning, the impression was a lasting one, and he began to change his ways.

Bert thought that Dets reminded him very much of a father figure. He seemed to be as stern and authoritative as a father could be. But these traits were rooted in the love and the caring of a father.

We discovered that the Andromes do not believe in certain Earth customs such as the military. They do have beings who are trained and skilled in security and protection, but it is vastly different from any earthly military. They don't believe in war, and they live in harmony with many different societies.

But if they don't believe in war, and they live in peace, then why would they need any security? That answer is painful to us, considering that we are Earth people ourselves. They need it for protection from Earth people!

At last Bert completed training and returned to Colorado to take Christy and me back to Washington. It was on this trip while we were staying overnight in a motel that Beek and Magna came to see us once again.

Their reason for visiting was only to see how we were doing and to let us know that they were watching out for us. They also told us that the time was near to make the remaining decisions.

It was the spring of 1979 after we had arrived in Washington that they came again.

We stayed temporarily with some friends we knew until we found an apartment. Late one night, we were asleep, while Beek and Magna came into our room. They quietly looked at sleeping Christy as we got dressed to go to the ship. A security being was left in the house to watch over the baby and to see that no one would discover us missing. Interestingly one of the people who lived in the house had also awakened that night. He thought he saw a ghost about three and a half to four feet tall, all white with large black oval eyes floating in his room. Then he'd gone back to sleep. He didn't know why he had simply gone back to sleep, when he had felt so much fear at the sight of this "ghost."

After we arrived on the ship that night we went up to the control room where Dets was again waiting for us. He announced that Beek and Magna had married. Beek and Magna stood together nearby. They were smiling shyly, and they looked very happy together.

Dets explained to us that he was sorry that everything had been done in stages. Our timing had been off, and therefore the plans and decisions we all needed to make were made separately. First was the decision Beek and I had made. Beek and Magna had made theirs and soon Bert and Magna would make their decision.

Ankra was brought in, and Magna and I looked at him. He had grown quite a bit and was very cute. He looked more human than Androme, although it was obvious that as he grew and his facial features matured, he would look more Androme.

Magna and I became quick friends, and I knew that Beek couldn't have chosen a nicer person to wed and be the primary mother of Ankra. Magna also explained in her shy way that she was quite taken with Bert as well. The meeting ended with the promise of more meetings, meetings to decide the future of us all.

Now we had even more to deal with consciously. I was in love with Bert, and I was in love with Beek. I had a child from each, and I was becoming fast friends with Beek's Androme wife, Magna, even though I was also married to Beek. Bert was in love with me, and he was becoming close friends with Beek. He had a child from me and a surrogate child from Beek and myself. And now he found that he was also falling in love with Magna.

We were either in the middle of a very strange soap opera, or we had a lot of growth to accomplish! We found that we were jealous of our spouse's other love, while at the same time approving of our own other love. We also resisted feelings of friendship towards the other being of whom we were jealous.

We discussed our feelings of hurt, but we were also able to discuss our feelings of love and happiness.

8

A Four-Ring Ceremony

In June of 1979 we moved from Puyallup, Washington, to Seattle into our very first home, a small, furnished, one-bedroom apartment. Neither it nor the building it was in was much to look at, but it was ours. Not long after we moved in we even received a small discount off of our rent each month by becoming assistant managers. This was something we never did again during the years that followed. The reason wasn't because of the late-night calls from tenants for various reasons, but because of the prejudice we saw the landlord exhibit towards prospective renters. We saw firsthand how some things work in this world. We would show an apartment and take applications from some very nice and qualified people, yet the landlord trashed these applications because he didn't like the color of their skins. We were upset. Perhaps our relationship with extraterrestrials made us more sensitive to discrimination based on minor differences of skin color.

Bert and Magna were wed in the fall of 1979. I was not present at this ceremony because I had been in the hospital for an appendectomy, and due to the schedule of the meeting ship at that time the ceremony could not be rescheduled. I felt left out.

Magna and two security guards came for Bert late one night. The guards assured Magna's safety until Bert was fully in control of his subconscious mind. Then they stayed with Christy, who was asleep in her crib, or so they thought.

Magna led Bert to the ship where they met with Dets. Again he explained the needs of the Androme people to Bert. Then he gave him the same choice he had given me with Beek. Bert was asked if he would take Magna to be his wife and produce children with her.

Bert accepted. Although the hypnosis and subsequent return of this memory was difficult for Bert, he knew that he was in love with Magna, and that because of the exceptional circumstances we had been given with the Andromes, he was in no danger of jeopardizing the love we had for each other.

Magna was also in love with Bert and accepted the marriage as well.

Then Dets took them to Beek, who was at that time feeding Ankra. The bottle he held was similar to that of earthly baby bottles except that its material seemed to be neither plastic nor glass, and the diameter seemed to be less.

Magna told Beek that Bert had accepted. Beek seemed to approve, yet there was something in his eyes that told Bert that these decisions were not easy for them either.

Dets then took Bert and Magna to one of the private quarters, where he wed them. The doctor and Beek witnessed the ceremony. Bert and Magna were then left alone to consummate their marriage.

Although Bert had no conscious recall of this memory, it was during this time period that we both felt a lot of stress. Neither of us felt as though we were getting enough sleep, and what sleep we did get was very restless. Bert assumed his restless nights and constant headaches and backaches were related to job stress, while I placed the blame for my problem on the surgery and recovery process, even though my recovery was taking place at an amazingly fast rate.

Under hypnosis, I remembered that Magna came one night during the week following their marriage. I had been up long after Bert and Christy had gone to sleep. I was trying to catch up on some of the housework I had gotten behind on due to the surgery.

Magna had first appeared through the kitchen window. She had telepathically asked me to open the door for her. As I did, I saw that she had also brought with her two security guards. Magna and I sat down together in the kitchen and she told me that she and Bert had wed while I was in the hospital. I was happy for them, and realized that this would explain what Christy had tried to tell me.

Christy was only about a year old at that time, and she had tried to tell me about the lady who had come to see daddy when I was gone. Having a very limited vocabulary, she couldn't explain clearly what she was trying to say.

This had disturbed me even though I tried to ignore it, but now I understood. Christy had not been asleep when Magna came for Bert. Nor had she been put into her subconscious state, since she consciously remembered seeing someone, yet she didn't have the vocabulary necessary to relay this information to anyone.

During our hypnosis session, I told Bert that after our talk, Magna had left the house. I retained the rest of this memory, but didn't relay it verbally to Bert during the hypnosis. This was to determine if his memory would match mine.

Bert went under hypnosis with the impression left by me, that he was not involved in the meeting which I had recalled. Yet, as he began the session he felt confused. Of course he felt the invisible touches from Beek and Magna and knew that they were helping him to recall, yet he continued to get a memory that occurred just after my surgery. He finally decided to go with it and he recalled a night shortly after my hospital stay when Magna had wakened him. He could see me standing near the door to our bedroom.

Magna had explained to Bert that during their consummation, the procedure that the doctor used to ensure that her egg would be fertilized failed, and that she had not become pregnant. She had returned this night to again try for conception, as well as to let me know that they had wed. Bert then recalled that he and Magna made love in our bed while I cleaned up the kitchen. At this point I was still working through the jealousy that invades my conscious mind. While in the subconscious state, I am very accepting of this situation and the power of universal love overrides the ego. On this night I found some of the jealousy issues that Bert and I were continually dealing with were over-flowing into the conscious mind, and I had to work to control it.

After the hypnosis session I told Bert that I too had remembered the same thing, and when he recalled what I had held back, I felt a jolt of shock. There was indeed only one way he could have remembered the same thing—it must have happened. I didn't tell him during my hypnosis that I recalled Magna going in to see him after our visit, or the reasons why. As with this memory and other hypnosis sessions, details left out by one person were recovered by the other person, thus verifying the memories.

Bert was, as I was, having a hard time dealing with the sexual side of this four-sided relationship. We were slowly beginning to understand the emotional side, but now we had to explore and come to grips with the sexual dimensions of a four-way marriage.

We had to revise the rules of the society that we knew. Our memories were showing us another way—a way to retain the capacity for extended love and marriage without losing morality or fidelity. We believe that this marriage doesn't defy the rules set by God, but rather that it encompasses a greater understanding of God and his vast universe. Our earthly standards are not the only ones under God's care, and our Androme friends seem very spiritual, considerate, purposeful and God-fearing.

Later in 1979 the joining became final. Beek and Magna both came to us one night. We left with them for the ship while security guards stayed with Christy in the apartment.

On board the ships Dets met with us. He explained that it was time for the final joining. Now that the individual marriages were complete—Bert and I, Beek and I, Bert and

Magna, and Beek and Magna—it was time to join the four of us as one, to complete the bond.

The room was filled with other crew members who came to watch the ceremony. As the four of us joined hands we formed a small circle. Dets began to speak of the love and faithfulness we would share with one another, as he slowly walked around us placing his hand on each of our heads. Dets further spoke of the bonding which was taking place in God's eyes, and said that the union would benefit both of our societies and that we were all very courageous in our effort to help one another.

After the ceremony there were cheers and congratulations from the crew members and Dets. We then went back to our apartment where the four of us privately consummated our union. Since the meeting ship is very small, we did not have individual bedrooms, and we shared one room. This one room, however, did have some privacy. Once again in the subconscious state, this situation was quite acceptable. The more the subconscious comes through, the more it helps the conscious mind get over its ego.

9

The Unreborn Soul

During the phase of recalling our adult years with the Andromes, we began to notice that the memories we had uncovered could not be the only ones. The memories we had recalled seemed to be missing a very important factor. The depth of feeling we felt for Beek and Magna had to have developed through more than just an occasional visit from them, unless they had been programming our emotions. We felt strongly that this was not the case. It is our feeling that if we were being brainwashed, we would become more robot-like and just the opposite is true. We both feel we have become more independent, and we are more confident about our individual beliefs and more capable of standing up for them no matter what society thinks about us. We could not have done this even three years ago.

We concluded that we were not remembering all of the visits. But why? Could it have been because the unremembered visits were strictly social calls with no important significance? Could it have been because they were short visits? Could it be that our own subconscious was editing, searching only for important occurrences or decisions? Could it be that some of the visits were telepathic or unseen, rather than physical?

We know now, three years later, that all of these reasons were true. With their help we concentrated on remembering the episodes that formed the structure of our relationship, such as marriages and births. These were the peak events that showed the progress of our relationship.

The memories of shorter visits came on their own to slowly let us understand the emotional build-up of the relationship. These visits entailed only conversations with each other. These visits built our friendships and the love we felt towards each other.

Because of their telepathic skills we unknowingly spoke with them subconsciously while we were awake. These conversations came through to us consciously as ideas or thoughts. Now we can identity when this is happening, and at times we can even bring the conversation up to the conscious level.

There were times when they were around us but invisible, and we were not consciously aware of them other than feeling a presence. This was the presence that we accepted then as a ghost.

During our hypnosis sessions and at other times during the day, our animals also reacted to these unseen beings. At first our parakeets would begin squawking loudly as though something had upset them terribly. Then they, as well as we, seemed to get used to the light shows and odd sounds that seemed to accompany our hypnosis sessions and our daily lives.

The dogs were another matter altogether. In the very beginning of our awakening process they would suddenly bark as though they had heard something. This is not unusual behavior for dogs, but if you know your pet, you know his habits. The way our two dogs were barking was strange, and they seemed confused.

As we began to work through our relationship with the Andromes, we weren't the only ones in the house who were affected. The dogs' sleeping patterns suddenly changed as drastically as ours. Suddenly they began to sleep in the children's rooms, and they were jumpy and nervous. At times during the day, one dog or the other would suddenly jump up from a sound sleep and look around the room. They acted as if they had been petted or bumped into, and when the dogs would see that the only people in the room were not near enough to have touched them, they looked thoroughly confused. We began to feel sorry for them. It was hard enough for us to conceptualize invisible people, but there was just no way that we could explain this to the dogs!

Later on during the awakening we began to notice that at times the dogs actually seemed able to see them, as well as sense them, when they were invisible. We believed that they were able to see the Andromes' auras at times. It's strange to have your dog sitting in front of you and staring behind you as though watching someone—especially when his glance corresponds with touches you are feeling.

We found that the hypnosis was not only beneficial in recalling lost memories of Andromes, but it was also beneficial in several other areas of our life. We used it to sort out and explore memories that were never seriously put to rest, but it also helped us to relax and relieve stress.

We used it to get closer to our inner selves, to discover the inner doorway with which the Creator had blessed each of us. We prayed while under hypnosis, focusing all of our inner self towards being with God. We seemed to find a closeness with the Creator there, and we found an expansion of His universe within our reach. The vast expanse of this universe became increasingly clear to us during hypnosis.

In August of 1980 we moved back to Puyallup, Washington. We rented the converted upstairs of an older home. We always felt that this house was haunted. We could hear strange noises and footsteps, smell odd odors like perfume and other unusual scents. At first we felt it was the ghost that had followed us when we moved. It was later that we discovered that the two previous tenants had the same complaints—sounds, scents and a feeling of a ghostly presence.

We lived in that house for over a year. It was during this time that Bert again began to feel the stress from work, and his backache and headaches returned. I in turn thought I was fighting off my first case of housewife blues. I felt depressed most of the time. Christy, our daughter, began to have nightmares about a monster with red eyes, and she wanted to play by herself most of the time.

As we began hypnosis related to this time period we encountered a problem that at first blocked our ability to remember. As I reached back into that time period my mind suddenly felt dull. Bert described his experience as a thick dark blanket that seemed to be covering his mind. Neither of us seemed to be able to recall much of the time spent in that house, either with the Andromes or with ourselves!

It felt as if there were full months missing, and what bothered us the most was that even under hypnosis the months seemed to be missing. There was one thing that did come through to us loud and clear, however. There was something definitely not right in that house!

It took several attempts with hypnosis to locate any clue that might access that time period for us. Finally, I was able to pull a memory into focus.

The memory was startling at first, for there was Beek in the doorway of our bedroom. But there was also another presence in the room—a ghost! A female ghost! The hypnosis also seemed to be allowing us to see what our subconscious mind saw, and the subconscious mind does have the ability to see other entities easily.

We had to work hard to get through the memories of the time we were in this house, but it did open our eyes to an even larger universe. A logical order does seem to exist for everything and everyone. We must give the greater part of the credit for this learning experience to the Andromes, for it was they who helped us to understand the universe and it's treasures.

We have learned much from them about the universal forces, but the turning point in our learning was in that house. We fully believe that one of our main goals at that point was to bring the conscious and the subconscious to a point where there is little or no difference between them.

The memory I recalled presented me with a ghost who seemed to be trying to torment me. She was standing near

Christy, who was sleeping. I was frightened and felt a raging anger towards this ghost who dared to threaten my child.

The ghost left at the appearance of Beek in the doorway. Beek then told me that he and Magna would return at a later time with someone who could help us understand this ghostly presence in our home.

One night after we had gone to bed, Beek and Magna returned with Dets and the equivalent of a priest. This priest began to tell us about God, referred to Him as the "One Maker," and as the "Creator of all." He explained that by "all" he was not just referring to Earth or Andromeda. He was referring to all of everything in the entire universe.

He explained that although there are differences in environments for the different creations, we must all live by the same rules set by the Creator. We all have the same goal, to grow and to return to the Creator. We are all souls from the Creator. Just the packaging, the physical body, is different.

This priest went on to say that in the form of a soul the ghost has no boundaries. A soul can go where it wants to at anytime. Then he seemed to call for the ghost in our house, and she came forward. Her attitude was less aggressive. The Andromes understood her and were not intimidated. This apparently took the fun out of her pranks.

The priest explained that this soul, or ghost as we called it, needed a lot more growth than she had experienced, and she continued to hang onto hurt feelings and anger from her previous life. She had so far refused the chance for rebirth, and we were not to let her lack of growth interfere with our own growth.

The ghost did not bother us anymore, but she did not leave the house. The Andromes did not intend to exorcise her from our home. Rather, they wanted to explain to us her presence in it. What seemed amazing to our conscious minds was the ease with which Andromes handle such things as "ghosts." They seem to have a deep understanding of Creation, which helped us accept this ghost's existence.

10

Building a Blended Family

Not long after the meeting with the priest during the autumn of 1980, Bert and Magna's child was born. Beek rushed into our bedroom late one night. Talking in an excited, hushed whisper, he said it was time—Magna was in labor.

Androme security guards again stayed to baby-sit while we headed for the window. Our apartment was the second story of the house, and just outside of one of the windows was the roof to the first floor porch. We stepped out onto it and floated up to the ship.

We ran to the medical room where the doctor, Dets and a team of assistants were preparing for the birth. Magna lay in labor on a table and smiled as we came in, happy to see us. We all stood around her, encouraging her through her labor pains.

Minutes later she gave birth, just as humans do, to a baby girl. The baby girl was handed to Dets for a type of baptism and naming. The baby was named "Zeema," and she was passed around to the four of us to cuddle and coo over.

This episode was another of the many events that neither Bert or I had any recollection of consciously.

As we progressed through the hypnosis, each session helped to draw our conscious minds closer to our subconscious minds and to the ET family it was involved with. The joy of having another child added to the seriousness of the situation and created new responsibilities. We agreed that we had to rise above any of our petty jealousies and feelings of hurt if we were to consciously pull together the entire bi-cultural family. There were complex feelings and other people besides ourselves that we needed to think about.

So we continued with the hypnosis, letting the memories teach us about our newly discovered Androme family and the feelings we held for them.

Slowly the touches and light shows increased. The touches, although they were still somewhat unsettling to my nerves, did help. Both Bert and I agreed that the touches were a physical occurrence that helped us during the times we felt we were simply going crazy, rather than discovering truth. We knew they were helping us return our memories, and it was comforting to know that they were monitoring our sessions. They never seemed to let us remember too much at one time. We were always given only what we could emotionally handle.

Over the course of our awakening we realized that we also helped ourselves subconsciously. It was through meetings with them during the night that the four of us discussed the progress of our conscious minds. At first, the realization that part of ourselves had been working openly with alien beings to help our conscious mind wake up to them was odd. But it is your own inner self that knows how you are accepting the situation emotionally. It knows at what point you need to slow down the input of information. It gave our conscious minds the time they needed to assimilate what they had learned.

We discovered that the times when we were frustrated and doubted the situation the most were either times when we were going to have trouble emotionally dealing with a memory in an upcoming hypnosis session or times when the memories and situation had been raised a level higher towards the conscious mind.

During September of 1989, Bert was the first to discover a new development in our situation—telepathy. One day as he was driving, he felt the presence of Magna in the car, and he thought he heard something. Then he heard it again, but the voice was in his head rather than in the car.

Both Bert and I began testing this new possibility. Telepathically he would ask a question of Magna, and would not tell me the answer. I would then ask Beek the same question telepathically. We would consistently get the same answers.

We tried telepathy with each other but didn't get the same results. It seemed that between the two of us, I was able to receive Bert's thoughts either in actual words or by picture image fairly often. He could not receive me as well. It seemed that he was able to send the thoughts, while I was able to receive them.

Receiving thoughts from other people wasn't totally new to me, however. Occasionally I had been able to do that with certain people that I knew very well. Usually it happened during a crisis in their lives, and I would be able to perceive that there was something wrong. Occasionally I would even pick up the problem itself, such as a car accident or other emergency involving a family member.

The ability to sense that something is wrong with someone you know isn't that unusual. There are countless stories of a loved one sensing a disturbance with another loved one. But now Bert and I had entered a new dimension in this psychic phenomenon, and we were trying to develop it in order to enable us to better understand these other beings.

We continued to exercise this new talent for a few months. Gradually we used it less and less, however, since we discovered that it wasn't always accurate and that one had to be wary of one's own desire to hear the answers one wanted, instead of the truth. Humans can be somewhat self-oriented and it can be difficult to set one's needs and desires aside. We continued to use telepathy, but we used it more slowly and with much greater care.

Another factor slowing us down with telepathy was that the hypnosis sessions themselves kept us busy with all of the new knowledge we were gathering and with the emotional impact the knowledge was having on us.

Other memories of being with Beek and Magna were times of sharing and watching our three children—Ankra, Christy and Zeema—grow. Physically the children all developed normally or what we would consider normal, except that to Bert and me, Ankra and Zeema seemed smaller and thinner than a human child would be. Ankra and Zeema were actually developing more quickly than Beek and Magna had expected. However, Ankra and Zeema seemed to us to develop more quickly mentally than Earth children, probably due to the child-rearing methods of the Andromes.

One interesting fact came up during one of the sessions. Magna not only breast fed Zeema, but she also bottle fed her. The blended Androme/human child requires slightly different nutrients than the Androme female can supply through breast milk alone.

We recalled sharing Christmas of 1980 with our extended family. Although they don't celebrate Christmas, they recognize our religious beliefs of the birth of our savior, Jesus, regarding this special holiday. The Androme people do celebrate a day similar to our Christmas. It is the day of Creation. The holiday is to honor the Creator and the universe and souls he created. This holiday is a very spiritual time for them and is shared by their society as a whole.

During these meetings we also came to understand that the Andromes do indeed speak a separate language. When two-year-old Ankra and his near-twin Christy played with a toy that Ankra had brought with him, he spoke to her in both English and Androme. The toy Ankra had brought to our home with him was very similar to an earth child's toy truck, except that this truck floated through the air. Later we discovered that the Andromes have some amazing "floating" toys for their children to play with and ride on.

We were slowly learning that we were a family. We spent what time we could together just doing family things.

Sometimes we would visit with them and the other crew members on the ship, while at other times we were together in our home.

During one visit both Beek and Magna were very sad. An Androme crew member, who also had a relationship similar to ours, lost her human mate, apparently in a car accident. It was a tragic loss for everyone on board the ship, because they all knew him well. It also meant that even though our Androme friends seemed to observe us much of the time, they were sometimes powerless to protect us from harm.

After the emotional upset of these memories I became frustrated. I didn't want to experience motherly feelings towards children I didn't consciously know. I didn't want to feel sadness at the loss of a person I didn't know, or for the people and Andromes who shared a part of his life. I didn't want to feel love towards any Andromes, especially when my conscious mind still wanted to fight the fact that they even existed.

Bert was adjusting to the situation more easily than I was at this point. He could accept the love more easily, from himself and from them, and it seemed that he had rid himself of all his previous feelings of jealousy and that he had welcomed, with open arms, the relationship the four of us had.

One day we began to experience physical changes. Although Bert, the kids and I felt as though we had the flu, we didn't have a fever. In fact our temperatures ranged from a 96.8 to 97.8, a bit on the cool side of normal. Even though the flu symptoms eventually faded, our temperatures remained low.

The only explanation we received was one that Bert received telepathically. Our temperatures were lower because of the adjustments with our monitors and because of our being with them so often. This lower body temperature was also intended to help us physically with the stress we were under.

The temperature changes only seemed to frustrate me further at this point. A part of my consciousness would not give up its doubts and would not adjust to the new level of awareness. I had come to a standstill emotionally.

Beek, Magna and our subconscious minds decided that I needed some sort of shock to enable me to break through my doubts and to begin dealing with my emotional feelings. At that time neither Bert nor I realized just how involved our subconscious minds were with the evolution of the awakening process.

On September 14, 1989, I was vacuuming near the hallway I could see that one of the lights was on in the children's bedroom. I continued vacuuming until suddenly the vacuum shut off. As I turned around to look at it I noticed that the light in the bedroom was now off. I suspected it was a fuse, so I went out into the garage to check it. But all the fuses were OK. I also noticed that the bedroom and the living room lights were controlled by different fuses.

Returning to the living room I noticed that the switch on the vacuum was off. This switch could not have been accidentally turned off, and now the light in the kids' room was on! There was no explanation as to what had happened. The vacuum could only have been shut off manually, and the light in the kids' room didn't turn off and then on all on its own.

It shocked me. It shocked me to the point of tears, but it was what I needed. After that I began to deal with the feelings I didn't want to deal with, and slowly I began to let my heart open up to these invisible beings.

We continued with the hypnosis sessions, recalling the memories of early spring, 1981. The doctor on the ship told all of us that I was pregnant with Bert's child. Consciously I didn't know this, for it was still too early in the pregnancy.

Dets asked if I would again carry a second child from Beek. All four of us agreed happily.

The doctor again took an egg from my ovary and made it ready for fertilization. Beek and I spent time alone together before the doctor returned to place the egg in my womb.

This egg develops in a separate bag of water that "cloaks" its presence during the double pregnancy.

All was going well until late spring when a problem developed one afternoon. I fell to the floor with severe cramps, and before Bert could get from the living room into the hallway to help me, the Andromes had entered through the kitchen window and were also headed for me. The monitor inside of me had alerted them to the problem.

I was rushed up to the ship, where the doctor tried to save both of the babies, both boys. I felt confused and couldn't seem to stop the ringing in my ears. I tried to yell at them to save my babies. I yelled, "NO! Don't let me lose them."

The doctor was not able to save the Androme/human baby, but he was able to prevent the miscarriage from also taking the human baby.

It was hard for all four of us to deal with this. The loss of the child was a terrible tragedy. We worked through the grief together over the next few weeks and concentrated on the child I still carried.

In late November, 1981, I woke up to see Beek and Magna standing near the bed. They told me that the monitor had picked up some type of vibration which meant that my water bag was about to break and that I would soon be in labor. They wanted to let me know that Beek and the doctor would be there during the delivery to watch over me, invisibly. I then went back to sleep.

Not long after that I woke up, startled. I didn't recall seeing Beek, but I was suddenly wide awake. I just knew that my water was about to break. I didn't know why I knew that, but I did. I jumped up, as fast as an overdue pregnant woman can jump, trying to get out of the bed and into the bathroom. As soon as I stood straight up, however, my water broke. At least I had made it out of the bed.

Twenty minutes later major labor pains set in. Gathering up Christy, Bert rushed us out the door. We dropped our daughter off with her grandmother and went to the hospital.

At the hospital they discovered that the baby was in breach position, and the umbilical cord was in a precarious position around the baby's neck. I was rushed in for a C-section.

Our son, Christopher, was successfully delivered, weighing in at a healthy 7 lbs. 11 oz., with lots of hair.

During my stay in the hospital the Androme doctor visited me, giving a bit of a helping hand with my recovery. My human doctor was amazed at how quickly I was healing. Beek and Magna also visited me in the hospital. Magna was with me much of the time. Although I didn't know it consciously, she was encouraging and watching over me.

In the spring of 1982 we moved into a duplex in town. Not long after our move and during one of the visits we were having with Beek and Magna, they announced that Magna was ready to get pregnant. After a quick discussion we all agreed that another child would be nice and was what we all wanted.

After the preparations with the doctor, Bert and Magna spent some private time together.

On January 1, 1983 Magna gave birth to a baby boy, who was named "Anthro." At a later point we would discover that another child had been born in January of 1982, but we were unaware of this at the present time.

Beek picked us up on our drive home from a New Year's Eve party. The ship had pulled our car over to the side of the road, and Beek floated us up to the ship. We were taken back to the car shortly after Anthro's birth and we were put back on the road, as though we had never left it.

Interestingly we did have an odd conscious memory of that night, but we didn't realize it. We left the party that night while it was still dark outside, somewhere between 3 and 4 A.M. When we arrived home it was daylight and it was almost 7A.M. The drive takes only fifteen to twenty minutes. It never occurred to us to stop and think about it, though. We had missed time, and darkness had suddenly turned into daylight. Still our conscious minds ignored the oddity of it.

As we recalled other memories of times spent with Beek, Magna and the kids, our conscious minds seemed to adapt to it all. As we did so, the Andromes increased their presence and touches in our daily lives, slowly letting us become further accustomed to them.

One evening I saw a faint outline as it moved nearer to me. I could actually make out Beek's outline. It was, I must admit, a little scary, but it was also very exciting. Then both Bert and I watched as we saw Magna's outline slowly fade in. She moved across the room, floating.

The touches continued to happen. At times it seemed very odd to us. We could be anywhere, at work or at the store, and we would suddenly begin to feel the touches. At times it seemed funny, too. How do you tell someone that while they are carrying on an average everyday conversation with you that you are being touched by an invisible alien? Well, you don't tell them! Not many people would understand that.

During our after-dinner walks at night, which we took regularly with the kids, street lights began turning off when we walked under them, another of the little reminders that our "friends" were near us.

As we continued with the hypnosis we recalled that we had even played hide-and-seek with Beek and Magna, however this game was meant to improve our psychic skills. Bert and Magna would hide while Beek and I would walk through the hall of the ship stopping at each closed door. The object of the game was to try to mentally pick out which door the other couple was behind. Since Beek and Magna were so good at using their psychic skills, Bert and I would usually end up just practicing our psychic abilities.

In the spring of 1983 we had a memorable visit with Beek and Magna. Bert was the first to recall it under hypnosis. One morning very early Beek and Magna came. They helped us pack up the kids, and we floated to the ship with them. This visit was unusual because it was daylight outside.

Dets met us in the ship and told us that they were soon going to Andromeda for a short visit, and that if we wanted to, we could come with them. Of course we wanted to. We went with Beek and Magna to their room and, grabbing a blanket to spread on the floor, we all sat down. Beek went on to explain that their planet was very similar to ours. Some of the many similarities were the existence of minerals such as gold and silver. But although these are considered precious to our civilization, these minerals are not precious in the Androme world. There is no monetary value placed on items or property within their culture. Each person works and shares for the good of all.

We must have talked for about three hours before landing near Beek and Magna's house on their planet. Bert, still under hypnosis, recalled how the grass looked white instead of dark green and how the house was a one-story home, long and rectangular in shape. He talked about the wooden floors and panels in the house, as well as the location of the rooms.

As he described this house under hypnosis, I felt shocked. The house he was describing to me was a house I had seen. It was a house that I seemed to recall vividly dreaming about in the summer of 1983. Until the hypnosis session I had thought it had been just a very vivid dream.

Bert remembered under hypnosis that we returned home later that same day. We suspect the actual time it took to get there and back may have been about six hours, plus the short time we spent there, but the exact duration of time is unclear.

We recalled another memory from 1983, a short episode that occurred during a vacation. On our return trip, after a full day of driving, we were looking forward to stopping at a motel for the night. About 11:00 P.M. we were hoping to find a vacancy in a motel just a few miles before the next town. Once we arrived in town, we found that it was well after 1:00 A.M. We assumed that we had misread our clock the first time, since it couldn't have taken us that long to reach the town.

Of course what actually had happened was that out on the lonely highway, the ship had pulled our vehicle over, and we had been taken to it. We had freshened up with a bite to eat and some cool juice to drink while visiting with Beek, Magna and the children. They had wanted to see us, and they had been worried that we were both too tired for the drive.

As we worked to recall what had happened to us during that period of our lives, Beek and Magna decided to get a little bolder with their presence. One night as I was comfortably stretched out on the floor with a blanket, relaxing into hypnosis, I felt what I thought was one of our dogs come and lie down by my side. I thought it was strange that Bert would let the dog do that. Normally we keep the dogs away while we go into hypnosis. We had found that by reducing noise, lights and other distractions, we were able to conduct the hypnosis sessions much more successfully.

After a few moments it got up, and I heard steps crossing to the other side of the room. It sounded as though the dog, if it was a dog, was too close to the wall and had scraped her collar as she lay down again. But that would be impossible, considering the furniture arrangement in the room. She couldn't have gotten that close to the wall.

Later, I asked Bert what that noise had been. He said that it must have been our "friends," so I asked him whether the dog hadn't made the noise. Bert replied that he had locked both dogs in another room earlier.

We continued the session and felt the usual touches we had by now grown accustomed to.

In January of 1984 I unknowingly became pregnant with my third child by Bert and a second child by Beek. The night of the conception of Beek's child I woke up shaking and upset from a horrible nightmare. It was a very vivid dream in which a lot of strange doctors surrounded me. I was screaming "No!" at them.

I felt as if someone was taking an unborn child from me, and I wanted to fight them off.

The dream shook me badly and I was upset for days. All I could surmise was that possibly I had had a premonition that I might lose our next child, not realizing that I was indeed already pregnant.

The nightmare gained even more meaning when I was surprised to discover that I was pregnant a few weeks later.

I worried throughout the pregnancy that I was going to lose the baby.

Now I understand the origin of that nightmare since I was pregnant again, my subconscious was worried about miscarrying the blended baby, so it reviewed the memory of the loss while I slept, allowing my conscious mind to remember as a dream something it knew nothing of. All that my conscious mind could relay to me was the recollection of the strange doctors and the deep anguish of the loss.

We have since found out that it is difficult to carry both fetuses to term. The Andromes try to prevent the loss of both fetuses, however, they can not always save them both. In my case they were able to save only the human child, but there have been other cases where both the human and blended child have been lost.

My third pregnancy went well, with nothing unusual other than my doctor checking me for twins because of my fast growth rate. Due to a little Androme technology, he saw only one child on his ultrasound scanner.

Two weeks before my due date Bert left on a week-long trip, and I became severely ill with a bronchial virus. Late one night, as I struggled to breathe, I began to worry about my illness and my unborn baby. I decided that since I was home alone and had my other two sleeping children to think of, I would call the doctor in the morning. Finally, propped up on the couch with the vaporizer nearby, I drifted into a fitful sleep.

A friend of ours named Reginald had gone along with Bert on this 600-mile round trip. They had planned to stay overnight in a motel before the long drive back. However, a convention was in town this particular night, and their choice was limited to sharing a room or sleeping in their car. Exhausted, they decided to share a comfortable room.

Under hypnosis Bert remembered that Beek and Magna had entered their room that night. Beek had wakened Bert to let him know that it was time for me to have Beek's baby. In the meantime Magna woke Reginald in his subconscious state and helped him out of bed. Everyone agreed that

Reginald was welcome if he wanted to go along. He was a close friend of ours, and he said that he would like to come along.

The ship travelled 300 miles in a few seconds and brought Bert and Reginald to me. Hurriedly they woke me and took me to the ship's medical room, where the doctor began to deliver Beek's baby, while leaving Bert's child in the womb. Beek let me name the baby boy, and I chose "Beek, Jr."

Before sending me back to my house, the doctor gave me some medicine to cure my bronchial infection, which apparently was turning into pneumonia.

After I was back home on the couch in my original position, Bert and Reginald were taken back to the ship for their return flight.

The birth of Beek, Jr., took place early Friday morning, and Bert arrived home later that night. By Monday morning I was in labor with the other child. She was born two weeks premature and we named her "Stacey."

During this three years of our awakening, we have discovered that Reginald is familiar with extraterrestrials. He told us about two occasions when he had consciously seen a UFO. Reginald agreed to undergo hypnosis. He felt there was an episode in which he was involved with us, but for the sake of verification we didn't give him any details of what we knew.

It took several hypnosis sessions before he reached the memory he was searching for. He had a hard time breaking into the first memory, but we dared not give him any assistance.

Reginald reluctantly began recounting as many of the details of that night as he could. His conscious mind refused to accept what it was seeing, and he presented all his recollections as if they were from his imagination. He went on to describe the exact placement of the Andromes in the room, the gender of the Androme who had spoken with him, where they went and what had occurred, all exactly as Bert and I had described it.

When Reginald had finished, we read part of our own hypnosis transcript of this recollection. This transcript had been prepared months beforehand, so he knew we were being truthful in our discussions with him and weren't just agreeing with what he had recalled in order to make him feel better. He was shocked! He knew there was no way he could have recounted exactly the same memory we had unless it was actually what had taken place.

As we continued to uncover the year of 1984 through hypnosis, we discovered that other events had left some conscious clues that we had ignored. Just three weeks after Stacey and Beek, Jr. were born, our family moved to Portland, Oregon. We moved into a fairly large older home that sat on a large plot of land.

For the first two weeks things seemed to be going fairly smoothly, but then we began to sleep restlessly, and we had a problem with two areas in the house. One bedroom in particular bothered us the most. The feelings we received from this room were so upsetting that we didn't even set it up as a bedroom. We kept it as a storage room instead. The other area that bothered us was in the garage where there was a small dug-out storage area for canned goods, etc.

Our landlord, who didn't realize that these areas bothered us, stopped by one day. He was talking about several different subjects when he began to speak of the previous tenants, two strange women who apparently had been into witchcraft. We didn't explain to him that we felt that they must have left behind some very eerie problems with the house. We moved out of the house after having been there for just three months, but not before our Androme mates visited us, leaving clues in the forms of restless nights, vivid dreams and bloody noses.

One of the vivid dreams I recalled during this period involved Christopher's head bleeding. Upon awakening I decided that perhaps he was in danger of falling, and that the dream had been a premonition. Nothing happened, however.

Under hypnosis I recalled the full memory. The placement of both the monitor and the tracker in each of our children was always witnessed and agreed upon by one or more of the four parents. Consequently, I had been in the medical room on board the ship when the doctor placed a monitor in Christopher's head. Because the event was stressful even for my subconscious, my conscious mind also retained a piece of the actual visual image as a dream.

On another night in the same house, I was awakened by something. Over the bed was a blue light, and at the end of the bed stood a dark clothed figure. I reached over to awaken Bert. Startled, he sat up and began swinging his arms towards the end of the bed. Suddenly the light changed to include shades of red and green. I couldn't move. I just sat watching. Then just as suddenly, I felt myself lying down beside Bert.

In the morning I was shaking. What had happened? I explained it to myself in the only way I could. It wasn't a dream, I was sure of that! It must have been evil spirits from the house, but under hypnosis this dream proved to be a visit from Beek and Magna, simply time together. Bert had no conscious recall of what had happened.

During our hypnosis sessions we came across an extremely difficult memory that I couldn't fully access. Beek, Magna and the subconscious portions of Bert and me all felt I was not ready to deal consciously with the full impact of what had happened. Bert was allowed to recall it, but it was difficult on him and he cried for the loss to us all then and now.

During early autumn of 1985 Zeema had become ill with a type of bronchial infection. The doctor was at a loss to stop the virus until it was too late. She was almost five years old when she passed away.

On a Saturday morning two days later we were flown to their planet for the funeral. Once again we lost time and never knew it. The funeral was very much the same as we have here on earth. All four of us hurt for each other.

During this tragic event we were also concerned over Magna's health. She was pregnant at the time, and only a few weeks later in October, she gave birth to a baby girl who was named Kehalma.

On another night Bert awoke thinking he had had a very vivid dream in which he had been fighting off aliens that were shooting at him with light-ray guns. He had been thinking in his dream of building a ray gun to protect himself from them in the future. But under hypnosis his memory proved to be of a somewhat stressful meeting with our ET in-laws.

Beek and Magna had introduced us to their parents, and we soon discovered that neither set of parents particularly liked having their children involved with humans. They felt sure that their children would only be hurt and that the marriages could never work.

They did not hate humans. The problem lay more in the fact that they knew humans. They knew how our society works, and they were fearful for their children's happiness and safety. They also knew that the marriages were necessary for their race's survival, and they understood their children's need to forge new relationships with our society, but this intercultural relationship between the Andromes and humans is hard for the Androme people to handle. However, over the years since that first meeting, they have come to accept us as a part of their family. Perhaps someday the worries of both people will be diminished, and a peaceful, conscious union can take place. We can only hope and pray that this book will help to achieve that peace in some small way.

Further memories that we unfolded were memories that build families—times of watching the children grow, times of fun and laughter, and times of differences. We cherished each meeting together until the next time.

In the fall of 1986 we went on vacation to South Dakota. At that point in our lives we still believed that the cloud we had seen when we were teenagers had been a religious experience. We took the time one day to drive out to the road, where this experience had occurred. The deserted old farmer's access road was still as we remembered it. As we drove by the spot where we remembered being in the cloud, however, we felt strangely numb, almost as if we didn't recognize it. We felt sure that driving by the area would spark that odd feeling we experienced so many years ago, but there was nothing.

Through hypnosis later we understood why: that night had affected us so deeply that we couldn't risk feeling it again. During one of our subconscious meetings with Beek, Magna and Dets, it had been decided that we shouldn't have any type of feelings for that site. It wasn't time yet for our awakening to begin, and we couldn't risk any memories surfacing. So there was a complete lack of conscious associations with that part of the lonely road.

In December of 1988 we welcomed a new member to our already large family. Magna gave birth to a baby boy whom she named Bert, Jr. The four of us smiled as we watched his brothers and sisters look him over excitedly.

11

The Evaluation Committee

In phase one of our awakening, we relived childhood experiences that had been hidden in our subconscious minds. In phase two we rediscovered adult memories. In phase three of our awakening, which began in October of 1989, we began to consciously experience meetings with our Androme mates. We began to wake up nearly every morning recalling the other's dreams in detail. The dreams were actually memory—we had begun to remember being with Beek and Magna each night.

Although we could now recall some of the meetings with Beek and Magna without the use of hypnosis, we still continued our hypnosis sessions. These sessions had brought our understanding up to the time just prior to our initial shock when we had discovered what had really happened on the lonely road.

Under hypnosis we recalled a meeting that had occurred during the early part of 1989 in which Dets had spoken with all four of us. He wanted to make sure that we all agreed on the awakening, and he wanted to know whether or not we were ready to begin. The awakening process is long and hard, he explained, and it would take a great deal of effort and time on the part of each of us.

We remembered agreeing to it, but portions of the memory were unclear. Was the ultimate goal to know them on a conscious level? Or was there more? Would we be allowed to go with them, live with them? If we did come to know them on the conscious level, would we be allowed to stay on Earth? Would it be safe here for us? We weren't sure of anything. Whatever the goal, it was what we had been working towards all this time.

Early in October we began to feel more touches than ever, and we had a definite feeling that something was about to happen. We were even sure of a date. We felt that whatever it was, it would happen on the seventh. Could it be that we were going to meet them? We were hoping that the process was over and that it was time, but that wasn't to be the case.

The evening of the seventh was indeed strange. We felt the touches of Beek and Magna most of the evening, and we could feel the excitement they were feeling, but nothing happened. We finally went to bed, both disappointed and confused, but we both awakened at 5:00 A.M., lying stiff and straight as boards with our arms crossed over our ribs. We lay on opposite sides of the bed from when we had gone to sleep! Also, I could remember some of what had happened during the night! I got right up and immediately wrote down what I had remembered.

We had been on the ship with Beek and Magna, although I couldn't remember their faces clearly. She and I had talked about the floating devices they strap to the backs of their younger children, where they cannot reach it. This device automatically begins floating the child when it senses a free fall. I thought it had to be one of the greatest devices ever invented! When the child is old enough, the device is hooked onto a belt in the front of them so that the child can control when to float and when not to, just as the adults do.

I also recalled a small pet in a cage similar to a hamster's cage that Magna and Beek placed on the table. Apparently small pets of this type were allowed on the meeting ship. We nicknamed the pet a puppy dog worm. It was about six inches long, and it reminded me of an inch worm, except that its diameter was thicker. It was colorful, but what I noticed the most about it was that it had a head and face similar to a dog, and when it was spoken to it responded like a dog.

Bert also saw this tiny creature. He too felt the head and face were very similar to a dog's. He said that he could see the same type of intelligence in its eyes that you would find in a dog's.

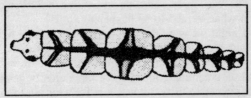

This is the animal we nicknamed a puppy dog worm. It is approximately 6 inches long. It looks like a worm but it acts like a puppy dog and has a puppy dog face. Due to its small size it is the only pet allowed on the meeting ship.

Later in the morning, Bert finally told me that Beek and Magna had explained to him telepathically that we were confused about the meeting. There was to be another meeting on the seventh, but the meeting wasn't for us to meet them consciously. It was to be between the four of us, plus an evaluation committee made up of three of the Andromes in authority. They were evaluating whether or not we would be permitted to awaken completely.

Since I didn't trust the reliability of telepathy and I was feeling extremely confused about the whole situation, I just shrugged off this new development.

We went about our daily business. It was Saturday, and the car needed a tune-up. We also needed to do some yard work. Later in the afternoon we stopped long enough to discuss something strange that we both had been experiencing, although until we talked about it, neither of us had a clue that the other was experiencing the same thing.

We felt as if we were being bombarded with questions, personal questions about ourselves. What was worse was the fact that we felt sure that a part of our mind was answering these questions. It's odd to be having an in-depth talk about your entire life without actually being included consciously in the conversation!

Bert tried to listen to what was being asked, and at times he even tried to answer telepathically. I wondered then if Bert's telepathy earlier that morning hadn't been correct after all. Was there someone evaluating us? Would that explain what seemed to be happening to us?

That night we went through a hypnosis session to see if we could recall the rest of what had happened the night before. We remembered we had been taken to meet the evaluation committee, made up of three elderly gentlemen who explained to us that it was rare for a human to make it through the awakening process. They said they were there to make a decision as to whether or not we would be allowed to continue, based upon our past history with them, our past conscious Earth history, our current status and our ability to change and adjust to our new situation. They also explained that they would make a decision as quickly as possible.

That weekend was a very strange one. We couldn't seem to get the voices and their questions out of our minds, and at night it seemed one dream followed another, all about our past actions and present situation.

Later we also discovered that there had been UFO sightings in the area! We were not too surprised that during the three years of our awakening, quite a few UFO sightings occurred near us.

The promptings of the evaluation committee had started the new phase we were in. These Andromes were as kind as the others we had met to that point, and they were thorough in their investigation. They even read through the diary we had been keeping of our awakening experiences. They made it known to us, through telepathy, that they would not allow the awakening to continue if there was any chance that it could threaten their security or way of life.

They were greatly concerned that they be portrayed in the light of truth if we pursued the publishing of a book about them. They approved of what we had written to that point.

In our new phase of awakening our conscious minds would slowly begin to see and accept the reality of the situation, and more of the memories we had not recovered through hypnosis would be raised into consciousness.

The following Monday we experienced a daytime meeting with the evaluation committee. Bert was home, and we were sitting at the table together when I felt the tingling touch of our Androme friends. The touch, however, felt different than it normally did, and I suddenly realized that it wasn't either Beek or Magna this time. Telepathically I understood that it was one of the committee members extracting information from my monitor. I didn't want to accept the message I was hearing telepathically, yet it seemed to be the only explanation for what I was feeling.

The tingling I felt on the lower right side of my head suddenly changed to a strong pressure and began to rise further and further up my head until it reached my forehead. It continued until it felt like it was just inside the bridge of my nose. I tried to relax, but the sensation and pressure began to get stronger until I was sure I wouldn't be able to handle it anymore. Then the pressure slowly reversed itself, following its original path backwards.

Up to that point I hadn't told Bert what I was feeling. Before I could explain to him what was happening to me, he described what was happening to him—it was the same. He then tried to turn his head to one side, only to feel the pressure of an invisible hand turn it forward again. He also heard, telepathically, instructions to please keep his head straight ahead.

Bert had telepathically received the same message that I had. He also understood that they would review the memories they were pulling from our monitors, and later they would ask us questions regarding them. It seemed so odd to be sitting in our dining room with invisible committee members from another planet pulling memories from our brains.

But one of our dogs saw something. She had been lying on the floor near Bert when suddenly she looked up, but not at him. She focused just beyond Bert's head, staring as if she was watching someone's movements. Her eyes followed the movement to the back of Bert's head. Then she looked directly into Bert's face with a puzzled look on her face.

She continued this pattern for almost twenty minutes, when suddenly her ears perked up as though she had been spoken to. Her expression quickly changed to a startled one, and she got up and ran out of the room! It was definitely an interesting lunch!

As the nightly memories continued, we tried to adjust. We were confused at first, and we learned that as the conscious mind is slowly awakened it is still in a sleep state, able to receive what was actually going on while still retaining its ability to dream.

At the times part of a memory is replaced by a dream image, particularly when the conscious mind is seeing something very shocking, such as people floating or a doctor performing surgery. The conscious mind cannot accept this and loses control, allowing confusion and fear to create familiar images that protect the sanity of the conscious mind. Our conscious mind edits what we are not ready to deal with, but this automatic protection also hinders us by making some of the memories harder to understand and more complex to translate.

The conscious mind's ability to dream during a subconscious episode is also a hindrance, because two images can be recalled at once—what was actually occurring to the subconscious self and the conscious dream images generated from conversation. For example, if your subconscious self was sitting at a table talking with another person about apples, your mind might picture one for you. In this subconscious/conscious dream state you would be receiving into your memory what was actually in the room as well as the dream image of an apple. Recalling this memory later could reveal both images together.

This part of the awakening was very confusing for us. We learned that writing down everything we could remember enabled us to go back later to review and clarify many events. We would write in the morning on any topic, feeling or person that was initially on our minds, even if there wasn't any actual memory we could recall. We soon discovered that these were more than just waking thoughts. We found that most of the time these thoughts were clues as to what had been happening during the meetings.

We also began to notice that there were more and more nights when we felt like we hadn't slept all night. We would wake up most mornings feeling very tired. Later we learned that as the conscious mind begins to wake up slowly and become a part of these meetings, it is getting less rest. The meetings normally seemed to last only an hour or two, so we knew we were not losing a great amount of sleep.

At times we felt confused when we awoke, feeling sure that we had been just doing something or talking to someone, instead of sleeping. To realize suddenly that we were just waking up was disorienting. This shock often causes us to lose the memory.

But as we began to adjust to this type of recall, we began to control how we would wake up. As our first conscious thought came through, we would begin repeating what we remembered, urging ourselves to remember it before it got lost in the transition between sleeping and waking. There were times when it worked and times when it didn't work. There have been times when one of us has awakened, repeating what we could recall, only to lose the memory while walking from the bedroom to the kitchen.

The Andromes continuously monitored us and helped us through this time period. They adjusted our monitors to increase our abilities to recall the meetings.

They also monitored us physically, realizing that we were using up our energy and that we would need support to help us through this time. Several trips to their doctor were required to help us physically. They were not the medical experiments that we feared. They are thorough in their monitoring. At times they gave us a shot of vitamins to protect us from becoming too worn down. Sometimes these shots left needle marks on our arms that were clearly visible the next day.

We started to need naps during the day. These sleepy times came on suddenly, as if someone had actually made us tired. Indeed they had! These naps helped us physically, but they also had another purpose.

As we lay down for our nap, we felt the touches of the mechanical devices that Beek and Magna used to help us with our hypnosis. Then we felt ourselves being taken into a deep hypnotic state. Sometimes these devices caused pain—at times it felt as if part of our skull was being moved, causing us to suddenly lose consciousness. Beek and Magna were giving back to us past memories of these times. These memories were run through our minds like a movie, and while they were playing, our subconscious minds would telepathically narrate the memory with them.

When we awakened, it was often because they told us telepathically that it was time to do so. We felt very lethargic when we awoke, due to the depth of the hypnosis.

During our evaluation week we had a final meeting with the evaluation committee. They asked us whether or not we felt we could adapt to their way of life—to live a quieter way of life, in a simpler manner. Could we live and farm as a part of their community? These were questions that we found easy to answer—they were describing the kind of life we had always wanted for ourselves.

By October 13, 1989, the evaluation committee returned with a judgment. We were allowed to continue the awakening process.

12

Physical Evidence

Our new level of awakening focused our attention on the standards we lived by, the ways of our society that we had sometimes questioned, and other ways we hadn't thought much about.

The changes that we began to experience in our daily lives occurred slowly. We began editing more of the media we watched for entertainment, finding that movies that contained violence, horror and sex were becoming more offensive to us. We began noticing that we didn't care to be around people who share crude or prejudicial jokes or constantly use foul language. We began to take Christy's lead and became more active in environmental causes. Our attitudes toward a wide range of ideals gradually changed.

On October 15, 1989, Christopher awoke with scratches along the side of his nose, and Bert woke up with a very sore back. Upon examining Bert's back, we discovered a swollen red area approximately two inches long by an inch wide starting to develop into a severe bruise.

I was surprised that Christopher's scratches matched my memory or "dream" from that night. I recalled that he had been wrestling around with Anthro. The scratches must have occurred while the boys were goofing around.

Later that morning Bert lay down awhile. His back was really bothering him. Neither of us could remember anything from the night before that might explain the bruise on his back.

When Bert awoke from his nap his back felt better. I checked the bruise and the mark was almost healed. The redness and swelling were gone, and the bruise was fading. How could such a bad bruise heal so quickly?

Bert underwent hypnosis that evening to try to remember how he had been bruised. He recalled, as I did also, that the children had come down from the ship to play in our house with our children. Christopher and Anthro had been wrestling in our house.

Apparently we had then left them with a female Androme babysitter while we joined Beek and Magna on the ship where they showed us a storage compartment that was being put up in the engine room. As Bert was stepping back out of the partially completed storage area, he tripped and fell back against one of the metal support bars, hurting his back. The storage compartment, Bert believed, was going to be used to store our things when we later were to move onto the ship.

After the hypnosis session we wondered if this was really going to happen. Were they getting ready to take us aboard? Were they going to transport us to their planet? It seemed so to us.

Bert also recalled what had happened while he was taking his nap earlier that day. Beek and Magna had come in with the doctor. Beek stayed by the door in case anyone came down the hallway, while the doctor placed a hand-held machine over the sore area. The machine reversed most of the damage that occurred when Bert had hit his back on the metal bar. After this process was finished, they left, floating through the outside wall, and Bert awoke nearly healed.

On October 16, 1989, I awoke remembering what had happened the night before. I remembered Beek and Magna becoming visible near the bed. They asked how Stacey was feeling, since she had been having a bit of trouble with her asthma and had come in to sleep with us. I was worried about her because she also had a fever.

Magna said that we would have the doctor on the ship

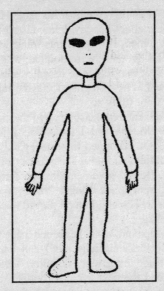

A white jumpsuit that is typically used when
traveling between the mother ship and earth.

look at her. She then handed me a one-piece white jumpsuit
to put on Stacey. There were also similar suits for the rest of
us; even the boots were built-in. They were the same type of
jumpsuit we had seen them wearing in many of our
memories.

Bert and I got Stacey and ourselves ready while Beek and
Magna went to awaken Christy and Christopher. Once we
were all dressed in jumpsuits, we went out to living room
and into the front yard, where we were floated up to the ship
in groups of two. I carried Stacey.

We all stopped for a moment in the engine room of the
ship to look at the progress being made in putting up the
storage cubical. Dets came in to speak with Bert and Beek
while Magna and I took the kids to their compartment.

In their compartment I saw the other children, and they all
had a bit of their parents in them. Beek, Jr., ran up to me and

said "Ma-Ma." I could remember his face! He was chatting away, telling me about his day. I saw his blonde hair, and I saw his teeth. Unless my conscious mind was confused, I believed that all his teeth were pointed, resembling canine teeth. But since it is possible to dream while the conscious mind slowly wakes up to reality, I may be mistaken on this point, but I do not think so.

Bert and Beek entered the room, and they stayed with the children while Magna and I took Stacey to the doctor's office. The doctor explained that Stacey's asthma was due mainly to pollution, and until she was out of it he couldn't cure her of it. He did give her some medicine to help her through her current attack. Magna, Stacey and I returned to the compartment. The children all played together while the four adults talked.

I didn't understand what happened next until recently. Again because the conscious mind can dream while the unconscious mind experiences reality, I felt that I had actually dreamed the next event. I thought that I had been visualizing the conversation in which the four of us discussed how to go about getting a publisher for our book. I realize now that I hadn't been visualizing through dreaming at all—I had been witnessing what was actually taking place.

I remember going down the road, in a spacecraft, not in our car, which was what I had first wanted to believe. We were then outside, standing in the grass and talking with three people. One was a male publisher wearing glasses, and next to him was a female whom I thought was his assistant, or someone who worked closely with him. One of them had something to do with photography, perhaps the woman, but this wasn't clear to me. There was a third person with them, but who it was, or even whether this person was human or Androme, I don't know.

We were told that this publisher had two phone numbers. The first number would put us through to the office, while the other number was a private number for friends and family to use. I also recalled that we talked of the possibility that this publisher and his assistant might be allowed to take a picture of all of us near the ship before we actually left as proof for the book.

At the time I believed that I was dreaming a sequence brought about by the conversation Beek, Bert, Magna and I were having. Now I realize that it was not a dream sequence at all. In October of 1989 my conscious mind was unable to accept the recollection of these memories independently from hypnosis, and it certainly was unable to grasp the reality of subconsciously visiting with other humans to arrange a way for our conscious selves to meet one another, all while in the company of Andromes!

We will explain how we met the publisher later on in this book. He did, however, have two phone numbers, one a business number and the second number a private number. The woman who was with him is actually a joint partner. Of the two, he is the photographer.

We finished that night's meeting and went back home. We were going to get back into bed in different positions from those in which we had gone to bed, in order to give our conscious minds further physical proof. Bert was going to lie on the outside of the bed, while Stacey and I were going to lie on the inside near the wall. But I realized the wall was cold when my hand touched it, and I didn't want Stacey exposed to it. Magna also pointed out that we shouldn't switch positions with five-year-old Stacey involved. She felt that it was one thing for us to awaken on the opposite side of the bed, but it might shock Stacey too much if she noticed. At this point in her awakening, Stacey was still alternating between easily remembering her visits with our "extended" family and remembering nothing. Therefore, we had to follow Magna's suggestion and protect Stacey's conscious mind.

As we switched back into our original positions, Beek, who was standing near the end of the bed, said that he had the other children in bed. He also said that Christopher would probably be in soon to sleep with us because he was complaining about his stomach hurting. Between the snacks he had on the ship and his slightly raised consciousness level, he had gotten an upset stomach.

It wasn't long after Beek and Magna left, as we slowly slipped from the subconscious state into a normal sleep, that Christopher did come into the room. He came up to the bed and said he had a stomachache. I forced my eyes open and was about to reply that it was because of the snacks on the ship but fortunately, I realized what I was about to say and stopped myself. I may have remembered why he had an upset stomach, but his conscious mind knew nothing about it. I got up and got him some medicine for it, and then I let him sleep with us. Needless to say we were crowded for the remainder of the night.

The next night was similar. This time Bert woke up remembering what had happened, while I couldn't remember as easily. The meeting was a simple visit, and we didn't even wake the kids. What interested me, though, was that I remembered that as I was floating down from the ship past the roof of our house, I saw our neighbor's cat running across our roof! He seemed oblivious to Beek and myself.

When I first woke up I felt frustrated, believing that I had been dreaming. A cat on the roof! It was later that week when I discovered that our neighbor's cat did use the roof of our house as a path around the yard where our dogs were.

Bert and I also discussed another interesting point of that memory. The cat had been oblivious to us and the ship! We had been invisible to him! We had come down from the ship in a white, sparkling light that apparently masks our presence. This light can also mask the ship and a large group of people and can be used on a belt to make an individual invisible, allowing him to walk or float around unseen among conscious people.

We discovered later, through telepathy and memories that the light can be used during the day as well as the night. The Andromes also can shield their spacecraft by projecting a three-dimensional scene to anyone around. For instance, if they land during the day at a house, they recreate a hologram-like image of the house's environment as a disguise. To the passer-by it looks like any other house with no activity around it.

We began to learn many more things from Beek and Magna through the awakening. We realized, by observing their ways, that these were very spiritual people. We had discovered their beliefs through hypnosis but being able to recall the nightly memories seemed to reinforce our understanding of these beliefs.

We looked harder at our own beliefs and at our world as a whole. Why couldn't our world join in their beliefs? Why must we have so many religions? There was only one God, one Creator. The Andromes and apparently several other alien cultures had joined together, believing in one Creator. Why couldn't we?

Bert studied the beliefs of several religions, and he discovered that some of the main differences come from society itself. Each religion subjects its followers to its own societal rules and beliefs, as well as to the laws of God. He discovered that people have edited the holy books of all religions, and at times they left out what they felt did not belong. People decided which prophets portrayed God's word.

Religions may have their place on this Earth, but perhaps the reasons for the divisions should be re-examined. Perhaps the reasons for revising, editing and deleting information from the holy books should be re-examined. Perhaps the reasoning for the division of our cultures should again be thought through carefully.

What we learned from the Andromes and from our own experiences is that God, the Creator, is the Creator of all. We found that we could reach Him easily from within. Each time we prayed, meditated or entered hypnosis, we walked with our Creator. It is with His love and guidance that we have made it through our experiences with the Andromes.

One of the Andromes' main concerns is that Earth people will tend to look upon them as gods or angels or, in some cases, demons. But once we discovered that the Andromes were real, we didn't confuse them with God. When we needed guidance through the trying times of our awakening we turned to our Creator, and turned within for His help.

The spiritual beliefs of the Andromes prohibit them from interfering with humans' conscious minds. Because of the highly spiritual levels the Andromes have achieved, they cannot publicly and consciously interact with our Earth. Humans would make them into another religion rather than continuing their own learning and growth process as individuals.

The Andromes may become involved with certain humans whose subconscious and soul levels have achieved a certain level of growth. They may even become known to the consciousness of such a person if his or her conscious mind has sufficient growth potential. The Andromes and the person's subconscious decides whether the conscious mind can handle this growth.

Through our awakening we learned that as we consciously gained more information about the Andromes and other humans, we also were subject to the same non-interference law set down by God. We cannot interfere with another person's growth process by pushing what we have learned onto them. Each person travels his own path.

On October 26, 1989, we received a full monitor change during our waking hours. We sat still for two hours late that evening as Beek and Magna operated the equipment that caused our monitors to release more of our suppressed memories into higher levels of our consciousness. Again, although we felt physical effects, we did not see anyone. After we went to bed we were awakened at 3:00 A.M. by Christopher coming into our bedroom with a sore throat. After taking care of him, we discussed what we had remembered. Beek and Magna had taken us to the ship to talk over the conscious contact we were working towards and the way that our relatives would handle this situation in our lives. We knew the situation would not be easy for anyone.

The Androme babysitter could have zapped Christopher to sleep so as not to disrupt our meeting that night, but they care very deeply about us and our children and what our conscious minds need. They consider our Earth children to be as much their children as our blended children are, so it was arranged for us to handle Christopher's problem consciously.

As we sat in the kitchen talking over what we could remember about our interrupted meeting, I noticed that my T-shirt was wet. I told Bert that I couldn't think of anything more embarrassing than to remember being with our Androme mates and discover that I had spilled something on my shirt! We laughed and went back to bed. When we were all settled back in bed, Beek and Magna returned for us.

We completed our original discussion. When we returned to bed the second time, Beek turned our alarm off so that it wouldn't ring in the morning. I explained to him that I had some appointments in the morning and that I couldn't afford to be late. What would I say, after all? "Excuse my tardiness, but I was up all night flying around in space with aliens?" I didn't think that would go over well.

Beek told me that he would wake me up at 7:00 A.M. instead of the 5:30 A.M. I had originally planned. The alarm didn't ring that morning, and I woke up to the telepathic urges from Beek at 7:13 A.M. He apparently had been trying to rouse me telepathically since 7:00 A.M. I was very tired.

Although I was rushed to get ready for my appointments on time I realized that here again I had received a type of conscious verification. Had these been very vivid dreams instead of actual memories, I wouldn't have found a spill on my night shirt, nor would my alarm clock have been shut off, nor would a telepathic voice have been trying to wake me for over ten minutes.

On October 28, 1989, we discovered that we each were experiencing the same thing, and we realized it had to do with the Andromes. On the inside of our noses we had both been feeling an odd kind of fluttering all day. Bert described it as feeling as if that a bug had flown up his nostril and was fluttering its wings, except that there was also an odd tingling with it.

Bert understood telepathically that the doctor was the one causing this sensation. It had to do with some of the changes that were being made to our monitors.

The next day I awoke at 4:05 A.M. I remembered much of the meeting this time, so when Bert woke up later that morning, I had him tell me what he remembered first. It all seemed so clear that I still had cónscious doubts that it could have happened. I wondered if I had been dreaming instead of remembering. However, Bert recalled what I had, and that set my doubts aside.

He remembered that we had left an elder Androme woman to sit with our sleeping children while we went to the ship. Beek and Magna had told us that the awakening was going well and that our conscious minds were adjusting fine. We looked through the ship and at the changes they had made with their compartment. These changes were to help accommodate us. We thought they had said it was for us to live on the ship with them.

Then Bert and Beek went to the engine room to discuss Bert's position there. Magna and I stayed and continued our talk. I remembered helping her heat up some type of tea for us to drink. Later we came back to the house, woke up the kids and took them to the ship to show them the changes in Beek and Magna's compartment. Even though both Bert and I recalled the same thing, it was confusing. Were we really going to live with them?

The next evening we recalled that during our meeting with them we had discussed how our conscious minds were handling the situation and how we would accept the situation. We recalled that our subconscious selves had been talking over the doubts and fears that our conscious minds were struggling with. We were working with the Andromes at night in our subconscious to help our conscious minds accept in broad daylight the reality of what was happening to us. During the day we would remember what we had talked about the previous night. This process helped us to consciously sort through our problems.

Bert also helped me to sort through the relationship.

Although he was accepting it very well, I was having a problem with it. Now that I was starting to remember consciously, I was having a harder time with the reality of it.

Bert was very helpful by letting me discuss with him feelings of guilt. He shared with me how he had overcome his own feelings of guilt by concentrating, not on Earth's customs, but on how we all were together and how they were as a people. We shared our concerns consciously during the day with each other and at night subconsciously with Beek and Magna. We worked through our fears and theirs.

Yes, theirs. They too feared that in the process of our awakening they would lose the relationship we had all shared for years, and if we were unable to cope with the reality of the awakening, they could lose us forever.

The awakening was not only hard on us, but on them as well. They too lost sleep because of the hours we were all keeping. They too lost sleep worrying about their doubts.

On November 1, 1989, I awoke with a splitting headache. It was just after 3:00 A.M. in the morning. After I took some medication, my head finally seemed to stop hurting so badly, and I went back to bed.

In the morning, I didn't remember anything, and Bert was too angry to say a word. We were both extremely agitated, and my head still hurt somewhat. After Bert went to work I lay down again, and I prayed to God for help. I couldn't remember what had happened the night before, and in my anger and agitation, I wanted to again doubt what was happening.

I went to sleep very quickly—it must have been induced by Beek or Magna. I then recalled the memory of what had occurred the night before. Both Bert and I had been to see the doctor on the ship. The new adjustment in the monitors required him to physically go into the head and relocate the monitor. I recalled suddenly becoming conscious during the meeting. The room seemed dark, but I could feel them doing something to my head. I panicked and tried to get up. Beek and Magna both grabbed me and at that point I was put out completely.

When I awoke from my nap, I felt shaky. If this was not a dream and was actually a memory, how would I know? I again prayed to God for help. Within two minutes Bert called me.

He was no longer in a bad mood, and he explained to me that he had had a nightmare that had caused his foul mood. He said that in his nightmare some doctors had opened up his head and looked at his brain. He also thought that he had awakened and that they had asked him to help by controlling himself and staying calm. His subconscious then seemed to regain control, because he lost the memory from that point on.

His memory was similar to mine. They had apparently done the same adjustment on him, but he remembered his as it had happened that night. When the doctor opened my brain, Bert had been present. Later after his surgery was done he combined the memories of seeing my brain with memories of the work done on him. This excessive stimulus temporarily shocked his conscious mind and gave him the impression of a nightmare.

Once we had our memories sorted out we understood what had happened. Our agitation was caused because the monitors had allowed more of the reality to seep into our conscious minds. The conscious mind seems to find this irritating and fights the process. The conscious mind seems to take these new levels as reality shocks and will fight the change.

This process of raising reality into the conscious mind became a pattern over time. The agitation, confusion, and occasional temporary loss of memory would be replaced by a period of being able to recall our meetings in clearer detail. This reaction was repeated many times during the awakening process. For example, when we look back on the original memory of our encounter in 1976, the picture is fuller than it was before. When we were taken to the craft, we felt as if we were being led around like robots. In reality, we were actually carrying on a complete conversations with the Andromes and were told completely of all that was happening.

During November of 1989, the Androme doctor had been spending more time with me and the position of my monitor. The monitor had been in my head since I was three years old, it had woven itself into the physical growth of my brain over the years. This condition had caused a medical problem when the monitor had been slowly adjusted and removed. We also understood that this problem didn't relate to the pressure headaches or dizzy spells I had been going through. Those symptoms were common to anyone going through the awakening process.

Later in November we spent a weekend away from home. We had at first believed that this would be a great opportunity to see whether or not we would still recall the memories each morning.

The biggest surprise that weekend wasn't that we did remember. The surprise was that we discovered that we had truly accepted the changes in our life, but others around us had not changed. We found that the games of society, the games people play for each other, seemed very false. We watched as people gathered together in celebration, drinks in hand. They smiled from their lips, but not from their hearts. They looked empty of life when we looked into their eyes.

We also discovered that we could tell who else was involved with Andromes. We suspected that we would just know. What we didn't know back then was that part of the reason we would know was that we were listening to our inner voices. Our subconscious minds knew personally who was involved—usually we had visited with some of these people during our meetings with Beek and Magna.

Two of the couples we were with that weekend were people whom we had spoken to about extraterrestrials earlier in the year. The circumstances in which those conversations took place were preplanned, although consciously we had only suspected that this was the case.

In Reginald's case we brought up the subject of UFOs and gradually told of our involvement. Reginald and his wife, Elizabeth, in turn opened up and told us of their experiences. We checked them for red marks on their heads. They as well as we were surprised when we found them. They both eventually began hypnosis, although they never did complete the full phase of remembering.

The other couple, Dave and Ellen, brought up the subject on their own although we would normally never discuss this topic with them. Our relationship with them was a relatively superficial one that never seemed to involve any in-depth philosophy. So when we got into this conversation with them, we were surprised. Yet it seemed to acknowledge what we had felt was preplanned.

Dave was at first skeptical, even though he had experienced missing time, suffered from pressure headaches, found the mark on the head and believed that other beings existed. His wife, Ellen, found it easier to accept what we had discovered. Their children also sleepwalked, had marks and suffered from bloody noses. Ellen had noticed that they would all go through restless nights, with very vivid dreams at the same times. It was during these times that she had noticed the bloody noses and other symptoms.

The initial talk with them went well, or so we thought. Dave and Ellen then admitted to us later that when we had first talked with them they had decided that it was all imagination and that we were nuts. Then after almost two years of their own strange occurrences, they asked us to come and get our alien friends because they didn't know what to do about them! Perhaps that's what this book is about.

These two couples and others play a significant role in our awakening, as will be explained later.

That weekend in November we also suspected that another couple was involved. Ted and Morgan, however, had, and still have, no idea of their involvement. They aren't ready to wake up yet, although we suspect, even now, that they may be soon.

The other people we met with that weekend were not involved. The differences were conscious ones as well. The ones not involved were the ones who played the most games, seemed to be the least satisfied with life, and didn't seem particularly close to their inner selves.

Both Bert and I recalled a very short visit we had with Beek and Magna that weekend. Our weekend consisted of two days and one night, and that one night was spent at Reginald's house. The meeting with Beek and Magna occurred only in the bedroom we stayed in. We learned a lot that weekend about ourselves and other people.

The following week Bert had to go out of town on a job-related service call. This job was to be the first overnight assignment he had gone on for some months. It could be another opportunity for experimenting. We wondered what would happen if we were not together in the same location at night—what would we remember in the morning?

The morning after Bert had been gone all night he called. It was 7:00 A.M., and he called to tell me what had happened to him just after he had gone to bed. Just after 11:00 P.M. he was awakened by both Beek and Magna, but it wasn't just his subconscious that was awakened. Magna stood off to one side of the room, and Beek stood in front of Bert. Bert said that as he looked at Beek, he felt somewhat groggy. His conscious mind was only partially awake. Bert said he told Beek he wasn't afraid, that he thought he should be, but he wasn't. He then felt so happy that he hugged Beek. Magna didn't step any closer, and Bert wasn't sure if it was because of the precarious conscious moment or her shyness.

At that point he lost any further memory and woke up again in bed. It was after midnight. After he had returned to sleep the second time, they came again, and he recalled what happened during the meeting. But before he told me any of that, he wanted me to tell him if anything had happened to me.

I in turn told him about my evening. I didn't go to bed until after midnight, and I didn't feel any touches from Beek and Magna prior to going to bed. I believed they weren't with me. I did recall a very vivid dream when I woke up in the morning, but it didn't make any sense. Bert asked me to tell him anyway.

I told him that I thought I had been in a living room with some people. I thought I knew who these people were, but they didn't look right to me or act like the people I knew. I told Bert that their living room was odd, and I described it to him. I told him the location of the TV, a table and a lamp, and I explained that there was a bed in the room.

I then told him how I remembered stepping out onto a fenced-in porch. I could see a small hill that was covered with bark chips or something like that. There were also trees on it, and some of them were changing into fall colors.

Bert said that I had just described his motel room to him! Then I realized it myself—that was why the bed had been in the living room. Bert went on to say that it wasn't a porch I had been on, but a balcony, a fenced-in balcony. He said that he didn't think there was a hill, but he asked me to hang on so he could check. He came back to the phone and said that just past the parking lot there was a hill covered with a type of dark red gravel, and there were trees on it. He hadn't stood out on the balcony last night and didn't realize what the view was like until now. He also said that the trees were changing colors. Bert then explained to me that he remembered Beek, Magna and me in his motel room last night.

So our experiment worked. Beek and Magna couldn't have shown us any better way. They took me to Bert, who was in a town I had never been in before in my life. I even remembered parts of the scenery Bert hadn't noticed. If Beek and Magna had taken us on the ship as usual or brought Bert home, the memory would have been questionable. But by taking me there, we both encountered a memory that was surprising.

That meeting also showed us more about them. They traveled the distance of over 300 miles one way as if it were a trip around the block! Beek and Magna had again brought a babysitter to watch over our sleeping children at home. I was the only one who left the house to go to the other side of the state with them.

This meeting, and the recall of it, also told us something else. I thought the people we were with were people I knew consciously. But the way they looked and acted didn't seem right to me. I had been superimposing a dream image over the real image, because the real image was too shocking to my conscious mind. My conscious mind accepted seeing Bert, and accepted seeing the surroundings he was in. It even accepted that I was with another couple. But when my mind consciously glimpsed Beek and Magna, it couldn't handle the shock and transposed another couple I knew in place of them.

The next night Bert and I again both recalled our meeting. I began to tell Bert how I had remembered Beek waking me up. He again had the babysitter for the children, and just he and I left the house. Once we were on the ship, it only seemed to take seconds until we were over the motel.

Bert said that fit his memory as well. He had only recalled seeing Magna and that he had gone with her to the ship. Once on the ship he could remember seeing Beek and me there. Again they had changed enough of our normal routine to create a conscious verification.

We recalled talking about several topics, then joked about writing notes. This was because earlier in the evening Bert and I had talked on the phone about writing a note to each other and exchanging it if we met again that night. It would be something for our conscious minds to accept.

Once he was on the ship, Bert scribbled a note to me using a small piece of paper and a pen of Magna's. He then folded it up and handed it to all of us to read. It said something to the effect of "I was here." All four of us laughed about it but agreed that our conscious minds were not ready for that type of shock as yet. We left the note with Beek and Magna.

Then we remembered that Beek got a call over a type of intercom, and he reported that they had to get me back immediately. Christy wasn't feeling well and was waking up. Everything needed to get back to normal.

At that point things just seemed to go black in both our memories, and then I recalled feeling myself lying down in bed. I felt confused and tried to open my eyes. When I did, Christy was coming into the room, and she was sick with the flu.

As Bert and I discussed this memory, we realized again that although they could have taken care of Christy in her subconscious state, they didn't. She knew consciously that she was ill, and it had to be taken care of on a conscious level in order to protect her.

The next night we again recalled what had taken place. Bert called me the following morning and said that he didn't think he could remember very much. He had remembered spending time with Magna in his motel room, but he just couldn't seem to remember any time on the ship or with Beek or me.

I told him that was probably all there was to remember, because I too had only recalled Beek being at the house with me. I couldn't recall leaving the house.

Again our memories had been the same.

For the next couple of weeks following Bert's service call, the meetings at night were shorter. All of us came down with the flu and we didn't feel well.

Although it didn't seem that unusual to us at the time that Beek and Magna would also get the flu, we have learned since then that the Andromes don't have much sickness. When their people choose to become involved with Earth people, however, they also expose themselves to the physical ailments we have. They put their physical health at risk each time they enter unprotected into our atmosphere. Prior telepathic conversations with Beek and Magna indicated that they have an average life expectancy of 500 to 550 earth years. Their involvement with humans and the Earth's environment has lowered that figure down to an estimated 300 years.

There was also another reason why things seemed to slow

down during that two-week period. At the time, though, we didn't realize what had happened. One morning I awoke remembering seeing Magna giving birth to a baby girl. Bert too recalled something about a baby. At that time we thought it must have been the return of an old memory because we were fairly sure that Magna wasn't pregnant. It was several months later, through Beek and Magna's constant help, that we realized she had just had another child. We had witnessed her birth while we were partially conscious. Her name was Einga.

It was also during the month of November that Bert and I finally told our children what was going on. Although they had some memories of those they fondly termed the ETs, they didn't know the full extent of the relationship.

At first I adamantly objected to telling the children everything, but Bert insisted. The children took it better than I expected. Upon learning that they had another set of parents, as well as other brothers and sisters, they accepted it. There was no shock. In fact, it seemed to put some pieces of their own memory together for them. As it had been for us, it was for them—the puzzle seemed to be fitting together.

Towards the end of the month I recalled one episode in which, after some private adult time together, Magna and Bert had gone down to the house to get the kids. They had showered together before they left, and I took the time when they were gone to take my shower on the ship. Magna and Bert had also taken the kids on a fast tour of the ship to show them part of what Bert's job was. Other than it having to do with the engine room, he still hadn't remembered clearly enough to understand it consciously. They also stopped for a quick snack. I had just finished my shower when they returned, and we all came back home.

I woke up at 3:30 A.M. in my bed. I remembered being on the ship in my T-shirt, and I didn't recall the suit I had been wearing previously. Then I noticed something else—my T-shirt was wet in spots where I hadn't dried off well enough after my shower!

The next night a similar situation occurred. After adult private time with Beek I remembered being in the shower on the ship. This time, however, I remembered Beek, Bert, and Magna pulling me from the shower and hurriedly helping me to get dressed. Christopher was waking up at home and again things needed to be put back to normal.

The next thing I knew I was back in my bed at the house and Christopher was staring at me from beside the bed. He had awakened with a stomachache. I got him all tucked back into bed and comforted him.

I then went and got a clean T-shirt to wear, as the one I had on was completely soaked! Bert and I also checked and noticed something else—we no longer had any deodorant on. It too had been washed off during the showers.

It was this type of conscious clue that helped us through phase three of the awakening. Even if we tired to accept that we could possibly "dream" the same dream every night for over a month, maybe through ESP or some other phenomenon, we couldn't explain away the correlating physical proof of these memories.

At the end of November, Bert and I recalled a memory that shows how the conscious mind can become confused if it gets too much of a shock.

I woke up shaking and upset. I felt as though I had just had a nightmare, and what I remembered seemed to support that theory. I remembered being in the compartment with Beek and Magna. The door slid open and Bert walked in. He started talking about how the doctor had just done something to his heart. He began to describe the procedure and the reason for it.

My conscious mind, which was watching and listening to all of this, suddenly couldn't handle the situation. I suddenly saw the room begin to spin and Bert's chest open up. I thought I saw blood everywhere just before things turned black, and I lost all further memory until I had awakened in bed.

Bert told me that he too recalled that he had gone to see

the doctor and that some type of procedure had been done to his heart. The memory seemed to be much more under control for him, although he couldn't recall exactly what the doctor had done.

My conscious mind had rejected the reality of what it was hearing and seeing and had flashed strange and frightened images just before I blacked out.

I saw no blood and I didn't see Bert's heart. My conscious mind pictured my worries, fears and fright over something I consciously could not deal with. Digging past these false images is hard—they were placed there by the conscious mind in its fear. Ridding the conscious mind of its fears is a large and difficult undertaking. It's also why the awakening process is long and tedious. It has been extremely helpful for both Bert and me to experience this together, and to love and support each other.

Although at the time there was no visible mark on Bert's chest, three days later a faint bruise did show up.

During other meetings we also began to know more about our duties and what the Andromes were expecting from us. For instance, their language is different from ours. We suspect from our memories that subconsciously we may already have some working knowledge of it. We will be expected to consciously learn it as well.

Of course we knew that Bert was involved with the engine room, but now Magna showed me what I would be learning to do. She showed me to a room where I was placed in front of a computer. It was different from any I had seen, other than on their ship. The keyboard was known as a "membrane," a flat surface keyboard, like some that you may have seen in some restaurants or stores. However, the keyboard was in the Androme language and didn't have as many keys as English keyboards.

Magna asked me three questions, and I was to locate the answers on the computer. I did the best I could and took the paper over to her to read. By this time Dets had come into the room. He took the paper, looked it over, and said that I had gotten two out of the three correct.

I remembered feeling disappointed that I had missed one, but then, I thought, maybe that wasn't too bad, considering that I was new to the machine and to the language.

It would seem we had a lot more to learn.

13

A City on a Ship

December 1, 1989, marked our daughter Christy's entry into the phase of conscious recollection of her memories of being with Andromes. The day before had begun oddly. Neither Bert nor I could recall much of what had occurred overnight. I recalled nothing, and Bert could remember only that I had been taken to see the doctor, but he couldn't recall why.

From the moment I had awakened, I had felt a strange little fluttering sensation just above my forehead as if there were a small bug under my skin, fluttering its wings and causing the area to tingle. The feeling was just like the one we had felt before in our noses, except that it covered a larger area. There was also a tension across the top of my head, like a wire pulled tight. Someone had changed my monitor again.

The tingling continued all that day, and at times it was irritating. We went to bed about 10:00 P.M., but I was up again at 12:30 A.M. The fluttering in my head had stopped, so I went back to bed. At 3:30 A.M. both Bert and I arose again. It was a two-memory night again. We both recalled what had happened after 12:30 A.M. There had been a lot of movement, walking around and talking. Then we were looking out of the door of our house, watching a small white ship land in our street. Several people were with me, although I wasn't sure who they were. Then I remembered someone saying that we should call 9-1-1, because there was a UFO landing in the street. Instead, we all walked towards the ship that had parked at the school across the street from our house.

I couldn't recall the rest of the conversation, but I remembered how funny it sounded that we should call 9-1-1 to report a UFO that was there to pick us up. Another strange thing was that the UFO wasn't one I could ever recall seeing before. I was small and shaped like a large van, or RV.

Later that same day Christy asked us if she could tell us about a dream she had. She had no knowledge of what we had remembered. She told us that she had dreamed that she saw a small, white UFO land on the street, and that she had told someone to call 9-1-1. She said that Daddy then told her that it was OK and that he knew the secret code. She said we then all left the house and walked across the street to the school where the ship had parked.

I explained to her that she hadn't dreamed this, that she had remembered it. From that day on she began her third phase of awakening. The children wouldn't need to go through the second phase of the awakening, since they were remembering as they grew.

The children began the first phase of the awakening when we did, with the initial shock. They were allowed to remember just enough to help us along with our awakening. They were then put "on hold," as Bert and I recalled our many years of past memories. Christy, however, being older, needed to start her third phase of awakening before the other two children. She was old enough to have preconceived ideas and conscious fears.

December began with further changes, and with three of us in the third phase. It was an everyday occurrence for us to wake up in the morning and begin a round of questioning. "Did you remember last night?" We all knew that once the younger two children also began to remember, we would be very near full conscious contact.

On December 2nd, I awoke remembering that I had been

curling my hair and Magna had been helping me. We had been just like a couple of teenage girls. I was surprised when I looked in the mirror and found that my hair was indeed curled instead of flattened from sleeping on it. I also noticed that on the top of the right side of my head there was a gooey area as if shampoo hadn't been rinsed out thoroughly. That side of my head was sore, and I also had a bloody nose.

Bert checked the area and found that the lower part of my skull had fresh red circular dots. We had apparently been to see the doctor again, which explained why none of us seemed to recall very much.

I lay down later that day to take a nap, and I awoke realizing that I hadn't been in bed the entire time. I remembered being with Beek and Magna, floating down the hallway and looking at Bert and the kids. I remembered thinking that I was like a mouse in the corner, and no one knew I was watching. I was invisible, and I was floating near the ceiling.

I then floated beside Beek and Magna as we turned towards the closed window in our living room. We moved straight for it, then we went right through it! We passed through a solid object! Both Bert and I understood that they could do this, but it was amazing to experience it!

We were out in the rain, yet I didn't feel wet. We floated up and into the ship. Dets and our regular Androme babysitter were there. Dets asked me some questions that I answered, but I apparently didn't pay enough attention to what my subconscious was doing to remember the conversation.

I did remember feeling as if I really had to go to the bathroom, but there was no time. Magna was holding baby Einga, and she said that she needed to feed her. Beek took me back to the house. We floated through the closed window again and back to the bedroom. I then went to the bathroom, and Beek helped me to lie down again in bed.

My reaction when I awoke was that I had to go to the bathroom. But I couldn't, because I had just gone. After I explained to Bert what I remembered, he said that explained why he had been feeling that I was near or thinking of him. It felt like the telepathy he and I have, not nearly as strong as Beek and Magna's, but still there.

Through most of December the nightly meetings were filled with all types of information. The whole family began to take an active interest in animal rights. The Andromes also seem to care very much about animals. With such a deep love and respect for animals, the Andromes could not be responsible for the cattle mutilations that some ascribe to aliens. They are a kind and gentle people whose beliefs uphold the laws of the One Creator of all life.

Because of what the Andromes were teaching us, Bert's religious studies and our love for animals, we, as a family, decided to become vegetarians. We could no longer accept the idea of any animal dying to feed us, especially when there were many other varieties of foods we could eat instead.

After researching the library, we began our new diet. We found that whole foods added taste and variety and we ate more nutritious meals. We felt very pleased about our new changes.

Through Beek and Magna we learned more about their society. Ours is a monetary society, while theirs is not. Each one does his or her part to support the community of Andromes. They work for each other's needs, not for monetary gain. Their farmers work to feed the people, free of charge. Their stores are buildings in which they share their society's products that they create, grow and build for each other's needs.

The Andromes have swap meets. Beek and Magna took us to one. The handmade items there are not for sale—they are given away. There is no greed. Their people only take what they need or can use. They have shown us how a society can grow and learn together without the downfalls of greed and power. Theirs is a beautiful way of life, full of love and warmth, full of the Creator and his magnificent ways.

Later in December Christopher got a sty on his eye. I was

going to take him to the doctor the next day. But after a trip to the medical room aboard ship, his eye was nearly healed the next day.

Soon there was another meeting at which a physical change in us was to take place. Beek and Magna explained what the doctor had done. We were to expect a weight change within the next week. The doctor had used some technique to lower the density of our bone mass. Without changing the structure or strength of our bones, he was going to make them weigh less. This change was necessary for us to become a part of their world. The changes would not be made on the children, however, because they were still growing.

Within a week's time, even during our Christmas goodies binge, both Bert and I lost five pounds! Our clothes didn't seem any looser, and we didn't look thinner, yet the scale showed that we had lost weight. We double checked our findings with two other scales. They showed the same result.

During the last part of December we were visited at our house by Reginald, Elizabeth and their two young children. Although they had been continuing hypnosis, Reginald hadn't proceeded very far. Elizabeth, on the other hand, had recalled several suppressed memories. Her attitude, however, was hostile towards the Andromes. During a discussion with her, she accused them of brainwashing us.

We tried to explain to her that we were not being brainwashed and that we had never been forced into any part of the relationship. The Andromes had dealt with our subconscious on a very truthful level. The relationship was our decision, a decision we made from within. True, it was without our conscious involvement at the time, but once our conscious development had reached a level where it too could be involved, our conscious minds agreed with our subconscious minds that we wanted to continue to build this special interplanetary relationship. It was our choice.

We told Elizabeth that we can now experience at a conscious level a greater part of the Creator's physical universe because of the universal knowledge and insight we have learned. There is no short cut to understanding your inner being and no one can give the exact instructions to find your path. In finding our path we have given up many of the fears and rules society has set before us, turning instead to the wisdom of the one Creator.

Then Elizabeth asked us how we could trust an unknown alien society more than we do our fellow human beings? How could we be so disloyal?

We responded, saying that there can be no disloyalty if you belong to God and have faith in Him and His wondrous ways. All of life is the creation of God. Saying we are being disloyal to Earth is very narrow-minded. We are loyal to our Creator and to the life He has created. Is that wrong?

The problems with Elizabeth carried over to the ship, when Elizabeth upset Magna by insulting baby Einga. Her actions were so threatening that she was asked to leave the ship. She cried and asked to stay, but Reginald told her that they had to go. It was a very emotional time.

The four of us were upset over Elizabeth's threats towards the Andromes, but we understood that we would meet many humans who needed more spiritual development within.

The Andromes had one of their religious leaders talk with Elizabeth, but she didn't seem to be receptive to him. He told us that there was nothing more he or any of us could do for her at that point. She seemed to deny acceptance of God's love, and until she was ready to take the path back to God, there was nothing much we could do. She wouldn't change until she was ready.

Because of her aggressive nature she had been placed in a separate area from the children. An Androme security guard was also present in case she became violent. I sat down with her and tried talking to her. She explained that it was each person's responsibility consciously and subconsciously to do whatever damage they could to the Androme people. She wanted nothing to do with them.

Frustrated, I left the area to talk with Reginald, Beek and

Magna. Bert tried to talk to her, but he too couldn't get anywhere with her. She seemed unwilling to change.

Beek and Magna and the other Andromes were saddened by her attitude. They had hoped that they could help her, but she wouldn't accept it. For security reasons they had separated her from the rest of the group, but she wasn't jailed or cuffed. She was on the opposite side of the room, sitting at a table. She was even allowed to smoke in that area. The Andromes did not try to brainwash her or force her into something she didn't want. They were kind and patient with her. They wanted to help, and when she refused, they didn't compromise her freedom of choice.

Her husband Reginald and their two children, on the other hand, seemed very comfortable with the Andromes.

We continued to meet Reginald and Elizabeth subconsciously, and consciously our relationship with them remained as it had been. They were not able, at that time, to remember the subconscious meetings, and we chose not to give them the details.

In early January, 1990, Stacey had a severe asthma attack. The first night of the attack I was extremely upset with the Andromes. With all their technology, why didn't they just cure her? I knew they had helped her in the past, but why didn't they just fix it?

We met with the Androme doctor that night, and he explained that he could not do much for her current attack, it had been brought on by a flu virus they couldn't control. Her asthma required around-the-clock medication. He said the asthma was going to get worse and that they couldn't prevent it.

He reminded us that most of her asthma problem was brought on by pollution, and until we could get her moved out of the pollution, she couldn't be cured. He also tried to explain that she was not allergic to cats, as Earth doctors had told us. Months later our Earth doctors confirmed that she was no longer allergic to cats and that perhaps she had just outgrown her allergy.

I was still upset when I woke up in the morning. Stacey

had gotten worse, and as I rushed her to the hospital, I telepathically told them all off. After the emergency treatment at the hospital, Bert and I took Stacey to her asthma doctor. He measured her breathing and she had lost 80% of her lung capacity. One lung was collapsing. He immediately hooked her up to an IV solution to get the attack under control.

Once she was out of danger the doctor explained that normally he would have put her in the hospital, but knowing that I was familiar with the medications and the equipment, he said she could go home. We were to administer her medications 'round-the-clock for the next few days. He said that there was some type of virus going around that seemed to be hitting all asthmatics very hard, just what the Androme doctor had told me. We had to learn to accept their limitations as well as our own.

As we drove Stacey home I felt like crying. Bert talked to me and told me I shouldn't feel so bad. It was a natural reaction for me to get upset with them. He had gotten upset too, but he knew that there was a reason why they couldn't help, or they would have.

During Stacey's recovery, the Androme doctor saw her each night. He was monitoring the Earth doctor's orders. He also added some of his own medication to her recovery.

Towards the middle of January our level of consciousness again seemed to change. The memories seemed clearer, but still confusing. We recalled a subconscious visit with Beek's parents. They seemed to have a different attitude towards us now. We talked with them about the changes we had gone through in the past months, and they seemed to be happy for us.

What was confusing to us during that meeting was that we didn't recognize where we were. We weren't in the meeting ship we were accustomed to. We were in someplace large, and it had buildings like a city.

In January of 1990, Beek and Magna slowly let us know that there were other people we could help through the awakening process. Because we had already made it so far, we could now begin to help others. Neither Bert nor I were sure we wanted that responsibility. We wanted to help, but were we really the ones to do it?

On January 11, 1990, Bert and I had just gotten to bed at 12:00 A.M. when we woke up at 1:30 A.M. We felt strange. We knew something had happened, but we just weren't sure what it was. We fell right back to sleep.

When we awoke in the morning, we recalled what had happened. Beek and Magna had come back for us after we had returned to sleep at 1:30 A.M. We all spoke about what had happened earlier in the evening when we joined them on the ship the first time. A call had suddenly come in that required the ship to leave immediately. Beek and Magna had rushed us back home and left with the ship. Someone had needed assistance right away. Neither Bert nor I could remember who it was, though, or what the problem had been.

The rest of the meeting that night was family time. We all spent time playing with the kids. Christy also remembered this playtime, although she was confused because she thought Daddy had been wearing long johns. It was, of course, the Androme jumpsuit that we were all wearing.

A few days later Bert found out just what had probably caused the ship to leave on an emergency. A friend of his, Paul, had entered a lounge just before midnight to have a drink. He told Bert that while he was there two women, a blonde and one with black hair came up to him and began speaking to him. The blonde told him that she was a being from another planet, and she proceeded to tell him his name, the number of his children and their ages. She also informed him that he would father another child in the future. He asked her if it would be her child, and she informed him that it would not. Then she turned, walked up to another man, and began dancing with him. Paul felt that it was her original intention to see this other man anyway. Paul said that he looked at the brunette, and he thought she had strange looking eyes, almost like she had no white in her eyes. There was something about her that frightened him, and he didn't understand why no one else in the bar noticed her. He then looked back at the blonde woman and was wishing that she would come over and talk to him some more. She immediately stopped dancing, turned to look at him, walked over and sat down at his table. He remembered nothing more until the next morning.

The only information we could get telepathically about what had happened was that Paul had come across beings other than Andromes, but what the Andromes had done about it was apparently confidential. There was no reason for us to suspect that Paul's story was not true. The time he last remembers being with these people was around 1:30 A.M., about the same time that the Andromes dropped us off in a hurry and left.

Paul also displayed the "symptoms" of being involved with the Andromes—marks on the head, missing time, restless nights, children with unexplained nose bleeds and some very vivid dreams. Bert helped Paul understand more about the Andromes and the possibility of his involvement with them. It wasn't until later that we were sure from our own memories that Paul was indeed involved.

A few weeks later we discovered just how connected we were to Elizabeth, Reginald, Paul and several other people. Meanwhile we made another fascinating discovery.

Bert, Christy and I had frequently seen a small white ship landing to pick us up. In it we were flown to a very large mother ship that resembled a small planet in size. Often we recalled something about moving. Finally we understood what had happened. We had become so involved with what was familiar to our conscious mind that we had missed the less familiar aspects of what was going on.

Beek and Magna were no longer on the small meeting ship. It had been decided that there just wasn't enough room on the smaller ship for all of us. Det's meeting ship was also needed in other places to conduct other relationships. Beek and Magna had moved and they were all now living in a temporary apartment on the bigger ship until a house belonging to Magna's uncle was remodeled to fit all of us.

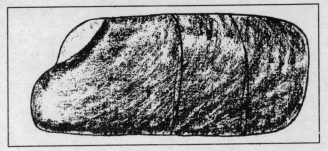

The large transport that is used to move people between the mother ship and Earth. It holds about five adults and three to five children.

The mother ship is huge. At times we felt more like we were on a small planet. It is set up with geographical form and climate. The city on it contains buildings, sidewalks, a park, a small river and more. The house is located with other houses near hills covered with grass and trees.

The Andromes use "transports" to get back and forth to their human contacts. These transports are cigar-shaped, and they range in size from a mid-size RV to a small family van.

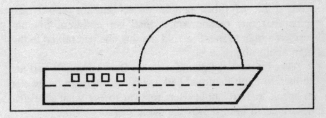

A side view of the exterior of the mother ship. This vehicle is located behind the moon, and it simulates a complete planetary environment. It is about five miles long by four miles wide, and the environment dome is a mile high.

Bert, Christy and I remembered one of the larger transports one morning. We had gotten into it with several other people and children. For some reason, however, we couldn't seem to recall who the other people were. We watched out the window of the transport as we flew to the mother ship.

We parked the transport near a small lake, and we were given a short tour.

We were shown an aquarium window in a wall and learned that the small lake and river are part of the ship's ecosystem. The adults in our party were then shown someone in a type of diving or astronaut suit. The being in the suit couldn't breathe and died.

Neither Bert nor I knew what to make of the last part of this memory. Whom had we been with, and who had died? I thought that we had watched this last part on a monitor, as if we had been shown this accident on film. It was confusing.

Later on we received a call from Elizabeth. Because Reginald and Elizabeth lived in another state, we hadn't been in conscious contact with them very much since their visit to our house. Elizabeth wanted to tell me about a vivid dream she had had and asked if I could explain it to her. She proceeded to tell me the same memory we had recalled about the lake, the tour, the aquarium and the death.

I told her I had known that there were other people there, but I couldn't recall who they were. I was surprised she had been one of them. Elizabeth said that she too knew that there were a lot of other people there, but she could only remember one person, other than her children. She described a man to me. She told me that she had talked to this man about aliens.

After I got off the phone with her Bert called. He had just spoken to Paul. Paul had had a very vivid dream he wanted to speak to Bert about. Bert relayed to me what Paul had described to him. It was the same memory again.

I then told Bert about Elizabeth's call and what she had told me. I relayed Elizabeth's description of the man she remembered. Bert and I agreed that her description sounded like Paul. Bert explained that Paul had remembered talking to a woman about aliens. He then double-checked with Paul and got a description of the woman. His description sounded like Elizabeth, but Paul had never consciously met Elizabeth or Reginald!

The next few subconscious meetings after that were

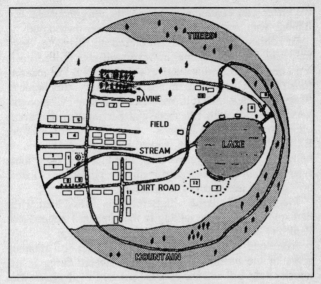

Legend:

1: Apartments
2: Parks
3: Mall
4: School for adults
5: Hospital
6: Administration
7: School for children
8: Home of Beek and Magna
9: Workshop
10: Religious Center
11: Grocery Store
12: Community Center
13: Service Station

An interior view of the environmental dome located on the mother ship. There are complete factories and complex control systems at various sublevels below this main level.

mainly family times. Stacey even surprised us one morning by remembering that she had seen Daddy and Christopher playing with some other kids in the water. She also added that our "van" was parked on a bridge by the water. Although she hadn't started into the third phase of awakening, the memory had slipped through her monitor.

Stacey was correct. She had seen Daddy and Christopher playing in the water with Beek and her other brothers. And our "van," actually a transport, had been parked on a bridge near the water. Her conscious mind saw the only thing she was familiar with, a van, although we have never owned one.

In February, 1989, we again picked up Elizabeth, Reginald and Paul. This time, however, we also picked up at least one of Elizabeth's relatives—her mother. The meeting took place on the mother ship in the large two-story home of Magna's uncles, on a hill. We were discussing evil thoughts and witchcraft with Elizabeth and her mother, and some other Andromes and humans who were present. Neither Elizabeth nor her mother seemed willing to give up their beliefs in witchcraft, yet we knew that there had been some type of change, because Elizabeth was no longer isolated, and she had less security than before.

I remembered talking with Bert, Reginald and Paul. They had split off and were talking in the kitchen. I noticed that Paul had been drinking prior to being picked up.

After that night we found that Elizabeth had retained some of the memory. She had remembered being at the house on the hill and she recalled some of the humans who had been present. What was surprising was that Elizabeth's mother had been so shaken up by a "dream" she had had that she had told Elizabeth about it. She relayed that she had thought Bert had broken into her house and that no one seemed to be worried about it. Then she thought that there seemed to be so many people around that perhaps Bert was having a party. She had consciously met Bert only a couple of times.

Paul didn't recall the memory, although he felt that something had happened that night. He verified that he had had a couple of drinks and that he had on a shirt I had remembered him wearing, and which I described to him.

Remembering the other people in our memories helped us a great deal. We were then able to verify consciously with them what we remembered. It also helped them, for when they had a little piece of a memory, or a very confused memory, we were usually able to help them sort out what had happened. This assistance helped them to move along faster through their awakenings. It has also been a big plus that both Bert and I remember the same things most of the time. However, helping them out has created some challenges for us. We usually recalled more of these memories and in greater detail than our friends did, yet we had to abide by the law of non-interference. In order not to interfere with their conscious development, we had to retain certain information we knew until they learned of it through their own growth process.

The Andromes can move around during the daytime as easily as they can at night as I soon found out. Two days before Valentine's Day, I was taking a nap. I hadn't remembered much from the previous night, and I hoped that Beek and Magna would help return the memory for me. I slept for almost two hours, and when I awoke I remembered, but it was confusing. I relayed to Bert what I had recalled.

I remembered being nearby a large loading door, the type that semi-trucks load and unload from. I could smell someone frying chicken, but I knew that Andromes are vegetarians. I remembered walking or floating through a crowded hallway with Beek and Magna. Bert and our kids were near. I seemed that we were shopping. I was waiting while Bert and the kids found what they wanted. Once they found it, we followed them up to the counter. The clerk had temporarily stepped away and was just coming back to the counter. She didn't seem to notice me as she walked by. She was busy talking with another clerk in the next aisle. I heard part of the conversation. She was talking about pay day, the union and its rules. I thought she shouldn't be so worried about pay day, she ought to be worried about doing her job. This portion of the memory was also confusing, as we know the Andromes use no currency.

As we all stood there waiting, Beek, Magna and I looked over some of the colorful items on the shelves next to the register. Finally we left through the busy hallway.

The next portion of the memory that I was able to recall was watching as Bert and the kids placed their package on a kitchen table and then moved it to the coffee table. I floated over the objects, thinking they were pretty. Then I realized that the objects were for me—they were Valentine's gifts.

That was all I had recalled. I told Bert that I thought it was just a dream, because on top of everything else, I was sure the Andromes didn't celebrate Valentine's day. And I couldn't recall Bert or the kids speaking to me once throughout the whole memory. I only recalled conversation with Beek and Magna. Bert shrugged his shoulders and said he wasn't sure what it all meant either.

Two days later, however, Bert and the kids explained what it meant. They had known all along. While I was taking my nap, Bert had taken the kids shopping to get me a Valentine's gift. They hadn't told me beforehand that they were going anywhere, and of course when I had awakened, they were in the house. I had no idea they had gone anywhere.

Bert retraced their steps for me. They had walked past a loading door as they had gone from the parking lot of the mall to the door. Next to the entrance was a restaurant; they could smell the food as they walked past. The mall was crowded as they made their way through the hallway. Once they found what they were looking for in one of the stores, they moved up to the checkout line. The clerk was just stepping behind the counter; she was talking with another clerk about their union. Bert said that he and the kids also looked over some colorful items next to the register while they waited for the clerk.

Bert also relayed what they had done once they got home. He said he was worried when I got up from my nap and told him what he and the kids had just done, that I would also recall what the gifts were. I didn't, other than that I had liked what I had seen and had thought how pretty they looked.

We decided to experiment. If Beek and Magna had done this for me, perhaps they would repeat it for Bert. Bert went to take a nap while the kids and I left the house. When we returned and Bert woke up he recalled what he had seen. He said that although he knew there was more to it, he seemed to be able to remember only a small portion of it. He recalled that he had followed me next to a restroom in a store. Just outside of the restroom there was a rack of some kind of shiny objects, but he wasn't sure what they had been. He also said that he thought there was a dark-haired lady standing nearby.

Bert was correct—he had recalled what had happened. While the kids and I were out shopping, we stopped to use the restroom. Near the door was a shelf of shiny metal curtain rods and accessories. There was also a dark-haired lady browsing in the aisle next to the door.

We were excited over these new capabilities. Beek and Magna had begun to initiate us into just what it meant to be in their world. We knew what it felt like to float unseen through crowds of conscious people. We felt as if we were a part of what was happening, yet we weren't; we were the observers. We were the ones who could not be seen or heard; yet we could see and hear all that was going on around us.

But we knew when the others were around. As I went with Beek and Magna to follow Bert and the kids, he said that he had felt their presence. He had known that they were with him. He was surprised, however, that they also had me along. And I knew as well, that I felt their presence most strongly when I was near the restroom.

We were learning about them and about us. We were also learning about others, both human and Androme.

When we first discovered that we had been "abducted" by "aliens" we were frightened. Who were they? Why us? How did it happen? The words "abducted" and "aliens" were, in the beginning, very much a part of our vocabulary as we tried to discover what had happened to us. Now we find the word "abducted" almost laughable, and the word alien seems almost as insulting. Alien is, after all, a relative term. Whomever you call alien finds you just as alien. To the general public the word alien, when used for extraterrestrials, usually implies horrible, ugly, green monsters aiming to crush our small planet. The beings we know are hardly alien in this sense, and we do not feel that we have been abducted in any way.

Once we began to understand our own past history with the Andromes and began to understand ourselves, our path through the awakening began to be enlightened.

Our first pre-adult meetings were primarily with Dets, the captain of one of the meeting ships. He was the main factor in those last teen-age years that Bert and I spent together. He prepared us for the decisions we would have to make. He was a father figure to both of us, especially during the early years when Beek, Magna, Bert and I joined and started our combined family.

Dets had a very difficult job as captain of his meeting ship. He had to ensure that all the Andromes on board were able to carry on their relationships with their human counterparts without jeopardizing their on-board responsibilities. He had to oversee all the safety requirements of both humans and Andromes and at the same time contend with his own human relationship. Because of the time we needed for our awakening, and the large size of our combined family, Beek and Magna were required to move from Dets' meeting ship to the mother ship, where the environment is similar to that of Earth. There are hills, vegetation, streams, a lake, sidewalks, some roads, houses and buildings. Unless you look directly into the sky, you don't feel as though you are on a ship. If you do happen to look up, though, you see that the sky is dome-shaped, back-lit and a very pale blue.

The mother ship serves as a residence for many of the families that are involved in human relationships so that couples who have children don't have to spend all of their time on the smaller meeting ships. The children have a home, a school, and a place to run and play. There is enough room for human families to share a domestic life with their Androme families.

Artificial lighting within the ship is used to enhance togetherness. When we have daylight hours, the Andromes have night-time hours. In this way, when subconscious humans are brought up at night, the ship is alive and buzzing with the Andromes and their daily activities. The families can then share at least a partial life together.

We learned much about Beek and Magna through the hypnosis of our early years, but we learned even more after we began to visit the mother ship. This phase of our interaction with the Andromes has included at least partial participation of our conscious minds.

As memories of the mother ship began to make more sense to us, we began to see something very confusing— Beek and Magna had hair on their heads. We were sure that we hadn't seen hair on them before. At first we believed that either our conscious minds were transposing images or that we had been seeing them with hoods over their heads.

Then, one evening, Magna and I went to a store on the mother ship. She took me to a counter and picked up shampoo, not just for my hair, but for her hair as well! Beek and Magna helped us understand what was going on on the meeting ship. Andromes weren't allowed to grow hair for security reasons. Our Earth scientists could gain a lot of information from just one strand of their hair, and the non-interference law prohibits the leaving of evidence that could alter a human's conscious growth path. Neither could the Andromes risk leaving a strand of hair that might cause problems, if it didn't match the spouse's hair. The Andromes we saw on the mother ship, who had no hair, still maintained these security rules.

Our visits with Beek and Magna now involved the new transports they were given. They were slick, black and fast, and they were used primarily by us. It took two of the black vehicles to accommodate all four adults and all of the children, but we also used them to pick up other people. Beek and Magna also had use of the larger white transports that were used mainly for picking up quite a few people all in the same night.

It was the smaller black transports they taught Bert and me to drive. At first it seemed very much like driving a car, except that it was all hand operated and there were no pedals. Any other comparison to a car ends there, however, for these vehicles never touch the ground. They accelerate at an amazing speed, although you don't notice it except for the speed with which you pass outside objects. It didn't take very long to get used to driving these transports, although Bert seemed a lot more comfortable with it than I did. He doesn't have the fear of flying that I do, and I was scared when this fear filtered through to my conscious mind.

During our first few weeks on the mother ship we met one of the top security guards for the Andromes. Now we saw, as Beek and Magna had explained to us before, that they do have other allies who are not human. It was during this visit with them that we truly realized what they had tired to tell us.

The top security man for the Andromes was not an Androme. He looked like a reptile, like an upright alligator, although I don't believe his mouth was as long as an alligator's, and he did speak our language. His smile lit up his whole face. I walked away from that meeting thinking this was too jovial a character to be a head of security! I suppose that is a very earthly attitude, though, and there is no doubt that the Androme security teams are nothing less than professional and effective. Bert and I both remembered this on the same night, and since then we have fondly referred to our new acquaintance as "the alligator man."

Another interesting being we met later on the ship was a very hairy being, six feet or taller, who reminded me of an English sheep dog. No insult is meant, of course. Sometimes the only way we can describe some of the things we have seen is to compare them to something we can understand consciously. We met him only briefly on the mother ship as we were walking to the apartment. We never were quite sure who he was or why he was there. While it may seem preposterous to believe that puppy-dog worms, alligator people or sheep-dog people exist, we must remember that the universe is incredibly immense and diverse.

Once Beek and Magna were moved onto the mother ship, we finally began to have some sort of "normal" family relationship. We enjoyed spending time together in the apartment. Magna and I would go shopping together for the family. Beek and Bert would stay with the kids while Magna and I took one of the transports to what we would know as a grocery store. Since the Andromes use no monetary system, their concerns lie in quality and environmental factors. Their packaging is efficient and either reusable or recyclable. We have also been to their "recycling center," and there were a few times when I thought I had actually seen Earth-made products there. I had to suppose that I was again transposing images to which I could relate. The real reasons, however, we will discuss later.

The grocery carts are also unique. The basket is on a platform. The platform is just large enough to let children sit down along the sides of the basket. The shopper stands behind the basket on the platform and operates it so that it floats down the aisles.

Magna and I chose the vegetables, spices and other items carefully, taking only what we would use, which is how their system works. They use many of the same vegetables and spices that we do, although they have several other vegetables and flavorings with which I am not familiar. It was truly the first time that she and I could bring our households together and share our motherly chores. It's like having a best friend living with you, with lots of giggles and fun while the work gets done.

After we returned to the apartment I recalled one of the older boys calling me "Mom." It was quite a shock for me the first time my conscious mind was awake enough to hear that, just as it shocked Bert the first time he recalled one of the younger boys calling him "Daddy." Even though we knew the children were ours, it was still amazing the first time the conscious mind was actually able to be involved with them.

Bert and Beek spent a lot of time during the visits taking the older children down to the lake or stream to play in the water. Andromes seem to be very fond of water!

We also spent some of the time during the visits helping

to remodel the house. Everyone chipped in with the talents they had for either construction, interior decorating or whatever was needed. Besides us, and Beek's and Magna's relatives, other Andromes also were there to help. Everyone was helpful and willing to give of themselves, their time and their expertise, just for the joy of helping one another.

Before we moved into the remodeled house, we were again subjected to an evaluation. The evaluation was not as detailed as the first time, and it didn't require that we go before the committee members. It was given to us by the medical doctor and a counselor. The doctor reported on how far we had come with the changes in the monitor and how well we had come through the changes.

The counselor examined each of us separately, then as a group. His questions covered the new phases we had gone through and how we felt our conscious mind was reacting to the situation. He asked our children how they felt about having four parents instead of two and how they felt about their Androme brothers and sisters.

Christy remembered replying that she liked having Beek and Magna as parents and that it was fun having so many brothers and sisters. She knew she had understood the questions, that she had felt her own emotions as she answered them and that she had meant what she had said, but now that it was morning and she was here in our Earth home, it all seemed strange to her. She didn't feel confident that she knew Beek and Magna or the other children well enough to make decisions about them, yet she had feelings that were telling her differently.

We explained to her, as we had before, that as the conscious mind begins to experience more of these visits it may become confused. It is seeing and hearing things that only the subconscious was previously aware of. Her confusion was in the division between the conscious and subconscious minds. Her subconscious feelings were strong enough to come through to her conscious mind, yet her conscious mind doesn't fully understand these things as yet.

It is because of this division and lack of conscious

knowledge that the awakening was brought about slowly and carefully. Our conscious minds were allowed to become slowly accustomed to the things our subconscious had known for years. The subconscious and conscious minds were allowed to slowly merge into one.

The evaluation reports were then sent on to the committee members, and they again approved the continuance of our awakening process.

After the evaluation Beek and Magna began to show us other things about their mother ship. They had all sorts of animals on board. Magna loves being around horses and she took us horsebackriding. Their horses are built somewhat differently than earth horses, and they don't get as big. Their size is slightly larger than the Shetland ponies we are used to. But Magna showed us that there is another difference between their animals and ours—they can telepathically communicate with theirs!

The first time her horse tried to communicate with me, I was shocked. I couldn't believe it. I still can't say I am completely used to it yet. Their animals use a very basic telepathy. They can't convey long intelligent conversations, but they can give and receive simple thoughts, as a very small child might express himself. They convey simple ideas such as "I'm hungry," or "I'm cold."

I asked Magna why we haven't been able to sense such telepathy in our own Earth animals. She explained that it required more than our being practiced at using the telepathy; it also required that the animals be taught to use their own telepathy as well. If our mind isn't strong enough to relay accurate thoughts to our animals, they can't learn to relay thoughts back to us.

Magna explained that the Andromes cannot communicate as well with our animals as they can with their own, for that reason. Our animals aren't practiced enough. Our animals are thus more unpredictable to them. The Andromes can't always sense what our animals may be thinking. Therefore, they need to be careful about pets they have never met before.

A drawing of the house owned by Magna's uncle that has been remodeled to accommodate all of us. This house is located on the mother ship near the lake. Magna's uncle is with the security team. He and his wife live in a remodeled room in the basement.

They can also put our pets into their subconscious state, thus easing the initial stress the animal may feel towards their abrupt appearance. Even if the animal knows them, it may still panic when the Andromes instantly become visible.

There were a few times when we were permitted to bring our own animals up to the mother ship. Our dogs really seemed to enjoy these trips, although they weren't allowed to run around as much as the Androme animals are allowed to do.

Magna's uncle has several dogs of his own. They are close to what we know as beagles. We have also seen other dogs on the ship that are like our breeds here. Perhaps they even came from here. The Andromes have cats, too, but they are different than any we had seen before. The hair of the cat was like that of a lamb. Apparently the Andromes like our Earth cats as well, because just recently we were shown a litter of them that are now on the ship as well. In addition to dogs and cats, a wide variety of very colorful and beautiful birds fly free throughout the ship.

The Androme love of land is as strong as their love for animals. They are natural-born farmers, and they farm for themselves and others. In the spring of 1989 we helped Beek and Magna plant their garden in the field by the house. We also planted flowers, since Magna enjoys them as much as I do. The fruits of our labors eventually ended up on our own table, and the extras were put in the store for others to use.

The house was finished in late spring and was ready for us to move into. We helped Beek, Magna and the kids move their things into the house. We spent several visits rearranging and getting things just right. The children loved the added room as well as the lake, which is not far from the house.

The house has a large workshop where we work on projects with the children. The projects vary from toys to furniture. One particular project we worked on with the children was making dolls resembling themselves. All of the kids had a great time with this project, and Beek impressed us all by hand-carving a bed for the master bedroom.

Bert and Beek also spent a lot of time on some of the more sophisticated equipment such as the "skycycles," transports, and computer systems. For a short time we had a transport that seemed continuously to be giving us problems. Neither Bert nor I could understand the system or

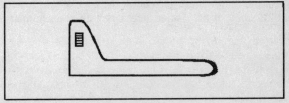

A skycycle, used as a children's toy. It is floated about 15 to 20 feet above ground and is driven about 10 to 15 m.p.h. When the hand controls are released, the skycycle stops and the person slides forward and falls off the vehicle. The anti-gravity belt on the person catches them as they start to fall.

the problem consciously, but it had something to do with its computer system.

Magna and I worked on some sewing projects. She did most of the work, since I was still learning. These projects are all a part of the Andromes' lifestyle. Some of the projects are taken to market to be given away. It's like a very large swap meet, and the Andromes prepare for it as though it were a celebration. It's a wondrous thing to see and to be a part of. These swap meets seem to be held monthly and they include singing, dancing, eating and carnival rides. It is a time of sharing with each other and giving thanks to the Creator for all that they have.

Another part of our daily (nightly) activities with our family was to put the kids in school—Androme school. Here the children learn more skills that can be incorporated into their daily lives. They also learn the arts, because music and creative expression are very much a part of the Androme society. It is common for them to express themselves in a shared song or dance. The children learn the basics of learning, reading, writing, math, etc., but they have begun to learn the Androme way.

Bert and I have also started school, although right now our time is limited because our meetings include so many human responsibilities and contacts, that we simply haven't had enough time for classes. It's just like being on Earth. When the children are in school, the four of us often take care of some of the riskier meetings with other humans.

14

Attacked by Humans

As we began to clearly remember more of the meetings, we learned more about our lives and how we had affected Beek and Magna's lives. We learned that we were picking up other humans for many reasons. These people often fit into our conscious lives, but sometimes they were strangers we had met only with the Andromes.

The people who were already fitted with monitors were, of course, the easiest to pick up for a meeting. With these people it was only necessary to wait until they were asleep and then activate their monitor with the light device. Once their monitors have been activated and they are sleeping, the subconscious is allowed to surface. Then it is simply a matter of waking them up physically by giving them a gentle shake or saying their name. Once awake, it's business as usual through the subconscious mind, while the conscious mind continues to sleep, unaware.

It isn't as easy, however, if the person is conscious, even when they are actively involved with the Andromes. There are a lot of risks involved if it's necessary to pick up a conscious human. The human might remember something that might normally be very frightening to them, and not understand what was happening. Time factors are involved as well. Picking up people during their normal conscious activities creates missing time that they, or others, may become aware of. We have not been allowed to participate in this type of pick up primarily because the majority of the humans we have picked up would recognize us consciously.

There are a few humans who are fitted with monitors but who are not currently involved with the Andromes. Usually their spouses are involved, and it is necessary at times to include the uninvolved spouse in some of the meetings, especially when subconscious decisions may have effects on the conscious life. These people can be difficult to pick up, even though they are normally cooperative. Some may actually turn violent.

Humans not fitted with a monitor can be extremely unpredictable. They too are subjected to a light beam that temporarily brings their subconscious mind to the surface. But the conscious can return at any time during the contact. The monitor provides a mechanical means to control the accidental awakening of the conscious mind as well as to control the storage of memories. The memories of a contact may partially or fully surface (independently or under hypnosis) in a person with no monitor installed. These memories will be shocking simply because the conscious mind has never experienced another species of humanoid extraterrestrials. They may feel that something was done to them medically or that they were offered something special but then refused it. Normally this means that they were offered a place within the Andromes' society and they refused it. When the Andromes refuse them, they have usually based their decision on the humans' personality traits.

There are other reasons why a human may be picked up only once or twice. Usually the reasons are because of human relationships, not Androme.

Because we haven't had enough training, Bert and I have not been allowed to participate in an unmonitored human pick-up. A specially trained Androme security force usually handles such cases. These Andromes are specifically trained to deal with reactions these humans might have. We've been allowed to go along with Beek and Magna, however, to witness these pick-ups.

Once these unmonitored people have been picked up and secured, it is determined whether or not they could pose a security threat. If they do present a threat, the extent of the threat is determined, and then appropriate measures are taken to protect everyone involved. Most of the time this simply means the person is set apart from the general population with guards nearby. The person is made comfortable and is usually sitting at a table. If the person is extremely violent, he or she is usually not taken out of his or her own residence or area of the pick-up. The reason for the meeting is then quickly revealed on the spot and the meeting is ended, usually with no further meetings.

There have been rare cases in which monitored and unmonitored people have suddenly and unexpectedly turned violent. But if such an event does occur, we have been equipped and trained to use hand-held equipment that stuns the physical body. This simple, triangle-shaped machine fits in the hand and has a silver object that pops out at the touch of a button. The silver object is placed flat against the upper chest area and/or the upper back area of a violent person. It emits a strong signal through the body that temporarily brings about paralysis. The person usually remains awake, because the signal doesn't affect the functions of the brain. In this way, the person can be brought under control while maintaining communication, and the violence can usually be resolved.

The majority of the time we never had a problem. The Andromes were usually prepared for the individuals they were to deal with; however, during one meeting, we learned how, in spite of all their technology, and their physic advancement, the Andromes can make a mistake. On one particular night we picked up a female human. She was to be involved in a meeting with other Andromes and humans although, as far as we understood, she herself was not involved in any relationship with the Andromes. Her role of conscious involvement with the other humans there made the meeting a necessity.

We had brought her to Beek and Magna's house while we waited for other people involved in the meeting to arrive. It wasn't expected that she would be a serious security risk, but we did realize she needed to be watched to some degree. Her attitude was somewhat indignant, and it seemed that she wanted nothing to do subconsciously or consciously with the Andromes or the humans we were waiting for.

Bert and Beek took most of the children outside to play while Magna and I watched the smaller children and the other woman indoors. While we were busy with the children, the woman walked into the kitchen and found a knife. In the ensuing scuffle Magna and I managed to get the children out of her way. I recalled that I had something in my hand. I didn't get a chance to use it before the woman lunged at me. I caught her wrists, trying to get her to drop the knife. We both landed on the floor. I was trying to keep her from cutting me with the knife, while Magna burst past me and out the door. She had placed the children in a back room, and she was yelling for Beek and Bert.

I finally managed to pin the woman down, although she still held the knife. I wasn't sure how much longer I could control her, since she was bigger than I. Bert suddenly burst through the door, and he held a dark triangular object in his hand. I started to yell for him to stop her. He placed his leg partially over her chest to hold her down, and then he pushed the object in his hand down on her upper chest. An instant later she went limp, not fully unconscious, but temporarily paralyzed. I slumped back onto the floor to catch my breath. I had been very fearful that she would hurt the children. Bert kept his position a few seconds longer to be sure that she was under control before he too relaxed.

At this point of the memory, neither Bert nor I could recall any further details. The memory we retained was in itself very shocking when we both recalled it for each other in the morning! The next few times this woman was picked up, it was done by the Androme security team.

It was this memory, however, that made us realize that the Andromes aren't always accurate in judging human reactions. It also showed us that this woman, even in her subconscious, was full of hateful, violent tendencies.

We weren't very surprised later to find out that this woman, whom we didn't know personally on a conscious level, was a manic-depressive, had a history of violence, and had been on medication that was supposed to control her emotions.

This frightening memory also showed us that we had been through some type of training with the Andromes, because we both reacted in a way that we didn't realize we could. We both felt that perhaps we needed more of the training.

It wasn't the worst, however. One incident that happened was completely unexpected. I woke up first that morning as I was shaking and gasping for breath. My heart felt as if it was coming out of my chest. I went into the bathroom and stood in front of mirror. I was stunned. I told myself that this had to have been a genuine nightmare or my conscious mind must have really become confused over what it had seen while visiting with Beek and Magna.

Beek awoke sometime later looking pale and upset. He told me that he hadn't recalled anything, but that he did have a terrible nightmare. He began relaying it to me. He had been in a house talking with several humans and Andromes when he heard a woman screaming. He and another man ran out of the house towards a workshop. From the door of the workshop Bert said that he saw a woman standing there, bleeding from her mid-section. He thought she was going to die. He ran to the woman and was attacked by a man holding a type of woodcutting tool. The man swung at him, and that was where his "nightmare" ended. As he finished recalling his "nightmare," as he put it, I was stunned into silence.

Finally I told him what my "nightmare" had been. I had been in a workshop, and I was alone. Suddenly I turned to see a man coming up to me. At first he just tried to grab me. He was talking about being mad at someone else and that by hurting me he could get even with this person. I was frightened and pulled out of his grasp. He then grabbed some type of a tool from a work bench and started towards me. As I started screaming and ran for the door, he cut me off. I stepped back from him, and he just kept coming at me, swinging this tool towards me. I thought he had hit me with it but I felt nothing but fear. I ran for the door again. In front of me another man stepped into the doorway, and the other man attacked him. The ensuing moments were confusing. Then I realized my rescuer was on the floor; he was bleeding from his stomach. Then an Androme was there. He was floating as he spread his arms out and came between the man and myself. In both his hands he held the stunners as he then swooped down on this man. I feared he was going to be hurt too, but his movements were fast and precise. One hand placed the stunner into the man's upper back while the other hand placed the other stunner into the man's chest. The man went limp instantly.

In the next portion of the "nightmare," I could remember coming out of another room where I was being helped by someone. I was in the medical area. Bert, Beek, and Magna were there waiting. Bert had a wrap over his stomach. The man who had attacked us was there too. He sat like a zombie, bandaged on his back and chest. Magna's aunt was also in the room, and she was angry. She was talking severely to Bert and Beek about having let this happen. I remember trying to explain to her that no one could have known this would happen, but I don't think she accepted that.

As I finished relaying my "nightmare" to Bert I lifted my shirt and showed him a red mark across my mid-section. He in turn checked his stomach and found a deep red colored mark; the area around it looked slightly bruised. We realized that this experience hadn't been a nightmare, but a memory. After all the years and all the fears of aliens, we were attacked and hurt, not by extraterrestrials, but by human beings. We remembered Elizabeth and her question about whom to trust.

15

Companions Along the Way

Many of our memories included visits with other humans as well as Andromes. Luckily, the majority of these contacts went well. These relationships became a very important part of our learning process. Being able to verify aspects of these memories consciously helped us further our progress through the awakening.

Reginald and Elizabeth became a confusing part of our memories. At first Elizabeth was not cooperative in these meetings and voiced both consciously and subconsciously her dislike for the Andromes. Yet she consciously continued to go through hypnosis, while Reginald, who seemed at home with the Andromes both consciously and subconsciously, could not get far with hypnosis. He was able to recall one memory while under hypnosis, but his progress seemed to stop there.

Reginald tried to videotape what happened while they slept, because physical phenomena were happening, such as door locks unlocking on their own, clocks changing time, sounds occurring in their apartment, shadowy figures appearing and light shows being displayed. The video camera malfunctioned each time they tried to tape themselves sleeping. Reginald owned the video camera and he was very familiar with it.

He was frustrated because he felt he had no proof of the existence of the Andromes. It was pointed out to him, however, that he did have evidence. Why did the camera malfunction only when he tried to tape the Andromes coming and going?

Meetings with Reginald and Elizabeth continued for a while, although we weren't sure why. Elizabeth seemed to be recalling a lot of the memories each morning. She even recalled some of the problems she could remember having with the Andromes and the humans in these memories, yet Reginald still recalled nothing in the mornings.

One night both Bert and I recalled that we had again picked up Elizabeth, but we couldn't recall Reginald being there. Neither could we remember exactly what the meeting had been about. I could only recall a blouse Elizabeth had been wearing.

Bert spoke with Reginald later that day and discovered that there was a reason why we hadn't remembered him. Reginald had been changed to a graveyard shift at work and hadn't been home. He also said that the blouse I had described was one he had just purchased for Elizabeth. Even though they lived in another state, we were seeing them often enough at night that we felt almost as if they lived next door.

The memories that we recalled of meetings with them helped us because we were able to verify items that we had no access to consciously with them, such as new pets, Elizabeth's new hair color, and their locations on certain nights. The subconscious verifications were the memories that we, as well as Elizabeth, remembered.

For a time all memory of Reginald and Elizabeth stopped completely, and we no longer remembered meeting with them. They verified that during the same period they felt as if the Andromes were no longer around them. The physical occurrences had stopped, as had the restless nights, and Elizabeth could not recall any memories.

We learned later, once our own awakening had progressed further, that their awakening had been put on hold because neither one was ready for the awakening and its changes. When an awakening can't be achieved it is simply

stopped and the relationship between the human and Androme is taken back to the original subconscious level until
the awakening can be continued.

We also discovered that we had seen Reginald and
Elizabeth during this time, but our subconscious minds had
agreed to not allow our conscious to remember it at that
time. If we had known consciously exactly what the reasons
were, we might have attempted to interfere and help. This
wasn't our responsibility, however. Again we were subjected to the non-interference law that the Andromes abide
by. Reginald and Elizabeth began to awaken again several
months later, but at a slower pace.

Dave and Ellen were other humans we recalled meeting
on board the mother ship. We consciously verified these
meetings with Ellen, who began to recall portions of the
memories very early in her awakening. Consciously, they
experienced blinking lights, nose bleeds, marks on the head,
restless nights, children sleepwalking, the stereo changing
stations by itself, feeling a presence, hearing noises at night
and seeing light shows. They had also begun to become
more spiritual, editing out a lot of the media because of its
violence and sex. They had begun to change their diet and
were considering becoming vegetarians for health reasons.

One of the memories that I was able to verify with Ellen
was a new purse that I had recalled seeing at one meeting.
This purse had a sort of striped pattern on it, but I wasn't
sure exactly what the pattern was. Ellen told me in a phone
conversation just shortly after the meeting that she had
bought a new purse that week and that the striped pattern
was the face of a tiger.

In another memory I recalled that she had changed her
hair back to a style that seemed similar to the way she had
worn it once before. Her current style was long with a
permed look whereas previously she had had shorter and
softer curls. I called her to ask about it. She confirmed that
she had changed it back to the way she used to wear it.

Ellen had many subconscious memories that matched
what we recalled, but normally we didn't call anyone to

verify what we remembered. Knowing that others were not as advanced through the awakening as we were, we could not interfere with their growth process, so we waited until they told us what they had recalled.

Ellen called several times, usually after each time we had recalled seeing her. She was often able to remember other humans who had been present and describe something of the situation, such as the vehicles being used. Much later she was able to describe most of the surrounding area near Beek and Magna's home. From the point of her first shock, Ellen's awakening had gone fairly quickly, although now she needs to remember the years prior to the shock. Without fully knowing her relationship with the Androme community, she can only come so far. Dave has not completely accepted his first shock as yet.

Paul, of whom we have talked earlier, has also been coming through the awakening process at a fairly fast pace. As with Ellen, Bert and me, Paul has benefited from being able to verify his subconscious memories with other people. After Paul's first shock of realizing that the Andromes exist and that he was involved with them, he quickly was able to recall some of the meetings he had had with them. He recalled the evaluation committee, the apartments and area surrounding Beek and Magna's home, and some details of the rooms inside the house. Paul, however, was different from anyone else we knew who was awakening. All others were able to recall only the visits with other humans and Andromes. Paul, however, began to recall also the private life he shared with his Androme family.

Even though he was able to recall small portions of this life, his memories were not clear, and he did not progress further. Until he completes further changes in his life and goes through the phase of remembering the prior years, we are sure that he will stall at a certain level.

We do not yet completely understand some of the larger meetings that include a lot of humans. They take place in a large auditorium and usually have guest speakers or teachers. These meetings have been very difficult to recall, and the only reason we can imagine is that we are not yet allowed to consciously understand much of this information. Perhaps it would put us or them in danger. Perhaps we would violate non-interference by recalling too much about the other humans who must remain anonymous to our conscious minds?

We and other humans were educated by the Andromes about a certain government that may have captured some Andromes. Some of them may still be living and are being held where the Andromes cannot as yet get to them. Others of them were apparently experimented upon. This situation has been shown to us several times now, but we don't know why. Perhaps at another time they will clarify who has captured their people and why it is important for us to know this? Perhaps there is a way we can help.

In the spring of 1990 Bert and I began to remember bits of memory relating to the publishing of this book. Beek and Magna told us when and where we were to go to meet the publishers consciously. They also explained that it wasn't imperative that we both go, but Bert had to.

I have to admit that I was doubtful over the recall of this information. Bert also recalled that Beek and Magna would see to it that the publishers would come to us, and that we would personally deliver the book into their hands in our home. Knowing a little about the workings of what it takes to get a book published, I had severe doubts.

At that point I was having trouble believing that there would indeed be a book publisher present when and where they had said, or that this publisher would come to our home and accept our book from us. My conscious mind just couldn't accept this much. In the meantime Bert was full of confidence.

One Sunday Bert went to a meeting. It was the first time he had ever gone to a meeting of this group. His purpose in going, of course, was to meet the publishers. It was a meeting of the Portland UFO Group, (PUFOG, now called NUFOG, the Northwest UFO Group). Bert did meet the publishers there, and within two weeks they came to our

home, where we personally handed them the first draft of
our book. They accepted it for publication shortly after that,
and the evidence is in your hands at this moment.

It was also during that time period that we were taken
during a meeting to a little girl who was very sick. She had
to have some procedure like dialysis to clean her blood. This
procedure was apparently done about once a month. We
didn't know why we were shown this little girl and it wasn't
clear to whom she belonged. It was upsetting to us to see her
like that and we realized that even with the Andromes'
sophisticated technology, they could not cure everything.

We had another evaluation in the spring of 1990. This
time, however, the evaluation was in front of the full
committee in a court room of some type. Quite a few of the
Androme residents were present as well. Magna and I went
in together. She vouched for me, as Beek did later for Bert.
I stood before the committee and answered their questions,
most of which dealt with how I felt about the Androme
people and their society. I answered as clearly as I could,
expressing my deep regard for them and their way of life.
Bert took his turn later, as he too expressed his thoughts and
views of the Androme people.

We were allowed to continue through the awakening. We
hoped that this evaluation was to be our last, but as it turned
out we had much more growth to contend with.

The next level we went through seemed to go somewhat
faster. We were remembering better, especially the meetings
with the Androme doctors. One of our doctors on the mother
ship was a female who had a female doctor in training with
her. While this trainee was a full doctor, we were to be her
first humans. She worked alongside our doctor learning how
to work with humans. Another of our doctors was a male
who seemed to work quite often with the monitor adjustments.

The Androme doctors helped us when we decided that
Beek and Magna would have another child, even though
baby Einga was only a few months old. One of the relevant
memories were extremely confusing. One morning I re-

called that we had been shown, through the use of their medical equipment, two fetuses. I thought we were being shown that Magna was carrying twins. Then after thinking about it further, I decided that perhaps we had been shown how earth women carry one human baby and one Androme baby. After all I couldn't believe that Magna would be carrying twin girls.

Magna was due sometime between the months of December and January, as far as we could judge from the time of the memories. This would make the twelfth child among the four of us, counting both Zeema, who passed away in 1985, and Teaka, whose birth we learned of only later.

The house on the mother ship was considered to be just as much ours as theirs. In the master bedroom we discovered drawers and closets full of clothing that had been sewn for us. I had shoes in the closet, and I knew them also to be mine. Magna and I together arranged the rooms for the children, and it included our Earth children.

As we reviewed our nightly meetings we were sure that part of the conversations were about our living with them on a permanent basis. Yet at times this possibly seemed so far away that we wondered if we hadn't confused what we were remembering. Perhaps the conversation was actually about our living with them as we were now, at night. Would we be allowed to stay with them, consciously? We just didn't know. We do know that if it is offered to us we will go.

During the times we have spent with Beek and Magna on board the ship we have gradually developed our personal relationships as well as the family relationship. The personal side of the relationship between the four of us is difficult for me to write about, but it is important, and it too must be shared so that others will understand.

The relationship between the four of us is as complete as any other married union. We share ourselves with each other by making love. It is a beautiful and loving relationship. They are not much different than we are, although they are built smaller. They make love the same way we do, and they desire it as often. We share our private time in the privacy of our bedrooms in our home and on the ship.

We share all that makes up a marriage and a family—the work as well as the fun. We all take turns taking care of baby Einga, and the other children. We share the responsibilities of washing the laundry, cooking and cleaning up. For entertainment we and the children hike, skycycle, swim or play ball in the park. Sometimes we just stay in the house or workshop and work on hobbies. The Andromes have an active interest in the arts and theater. We have gone to several "plays" that have been put on by the children as part of their classroom learning activities. We have even watched Androme television with them. Its content is different from ours in that they show more theatrical productions and documentaries, and their community standards are reflected in this entertainment. We saw all sizes of TV screens, from small portable ones to very large screens.

All that we have come through these past three years has been confusing and hard for the conscious side of our lives. During the level changes and monitor adjustments we have had a lot of physical problems as well. Many times these changes can cause spotty-to-severe nose bleeds in more sensitive individuals. They are not harmful, but it is hard on the conscious mind seeing blood of any type. Some of the later changes are painful at times. Pain on the skull or inside the brain is hard to ignore. It never gets severe, but it is noticeable.

The agitation and frustration after each new level of change can be hard to deal with. These changes temporarily confuse and disorient the conscious mind and the recall of the meetings. It usually smoothes out within a few days, with Beek's and Magna's help. But going through these changes time after time can be trying.

Consciously living with subconscious nightly excursions is challenging. It seems like we are forever watching what we say when we were around other people. We can't say anything to people who have no knowledge of our situation, and we have to be careful of what we say around people who have been with us at some of the meetings.

We began to react to the changes. Each level would assault more of what the conscious mind had learned as reality, and the conscious mind would have to reshape itself. We were overwhelmed at times to learn that there was so much more to creation than we had been taught on Earth.

Beek and Magna too had times when they became frustrated with us. Much of their time and effort was expended helping us awaken. They acted out of love, which at times was the only thing that held the four of us to our goal. During the hardest times Beek and Magna lifted our spirits and helped pull us through the agitation and frustration.

At times we just didn't want to believe that it was really happening. I was especially guilty, even though many times we verified the Earthly aspects of the meetings, such as knowing things about other people and their homes that I just couldn't have known otherwise. Sometimes we would get angry and brush Beek and Magna away when we could feel them touching us. We would deny that they could really exist even though we could sense their presence, see their light shows and feel their invisible touches. We knew full well that there was no other explanation for all that had happened and for all that we had recalled, yet we still tried to deny it.

One time Bert was upset with me because I wanted to give up, and deny their existence. I had felt that I couldn't continue through the changes any further. Bert said that if I didn't straighten out my attitude I'd find myself floating upside down by my ankles. Sure enough during the meeting that night Beek and Magna had me float upside down for the benefit of my conscious mind! It helped, though. Upon awakening in the morning and recalling that portion of the meeting, I did cheer up and gained some of the strength I needed to go on. We have come through the awakening because of their extra little efforts for our benefit, their fun and humor, and their deep love.

The Androme people have hopes and dreams, as we do. They have families and live in communities together. Their housing isn't much different from our own. They even have problems with their plumbing. Bert and Beek have worked together in the house on a stubborn utility sink and its plumbing.

They work, go to school and shop much as we do. They celebrate a lot of the same events we do, such as births, marriages, birthdays, etc. They plan and dress for these occasions. The Androme uniform is not the only clothing style they have. They have seamstresses who create beautiful clothing, and they have the wonderful clothes they sew at home for their families.

They wear scented oils and worry whether their hair looks just right. Magna, who was not allowed to grow hair for many years, lets hers grow just past her shoulders. One night she said that it was time for her to get it cut. She explained that she normally didn't wear it so long, but since it had been a long time since she was allowed to grow it at all, she preferred it longer for a while. Their technology is different from ours. Many of their products are different in content and packaging, mostly due to the environmental ethics that they live by and cherish.

Their goals in life are somewhat different from humans' in the sense that none of their life's dreams are oriented towards money or power. Their goal is for each individual to achieve fullness and richness of mind and soul. They want to create a society that obtains its wealth from the gifts of life that our Creator has given us.

They are not gods, angels, demons, evil scientists, or monsters. Neither are they humans, but like humans, they are a natural part of creation, from the "one Creator."

16

ETs on My Couch

We hadn't seen the last of the evaluation committee, and as the months went by, we discovered that we were to see a lot of them. As part of the testing, drawings were used to evaluate how advanced we were in the awakening process. We were shown a large wall mural depicting how the conscious mind recalls what the Androme people look like. The drawings showed several variations of how they have been recalled by humans.

The drawings ranged from very short beings with huge heads and huge black eyes, extremely tall and thin beings, seemingly floating like feathers. Some drawings resembled dwarfs or trolls, and some resembled small fairies. Some of the drawings depicted bald, large-eyed, noseless beings whose looks seemed cold and scientific, while others showed beautiful beings with translucent hair. Some resembled ugly wrinkle-covered monsters; others showed smooth, creamy, white skin. Some appeared to be dark skinned, while some drawings showed extremely pale skin. Some were dressed in one-piece jumpsuits, while some had "astronaut" suits on. Others were dressed in long gowns, and some seemed to be covered from head to toe in a hooded bulky cape.

The mural paralleled what we had gone through, from our earliest memories to our current level. We had come to realize that how we saw them depended not only on the level of our awakening but also on the circumstances of the visit. Like humans, their appearance is strongly affected by how they dress and how they are illuminated. For instance, when I dress in certain clothes I tend to look shorter, rounder, thinner or taller. The colors I wear and the lighting I am in will tend to give my skin a milky white, pale, yellow, or even a dark appearance. My hair color can vary from extremely light to a dark shade in different lights. The Andromes are subject to these same effects of style, color and lighting.

We also discovered that our perception of them depended on another source—the media. We were much more likely to remember them as scary monsters if we had just viewed a scary alien film on TV or video. We found the media and its violence less tolerable and we learned that the violence depicted was doing subtle damage to us. During the test we chose the drawing that we felt resembled what our conscious mind was viewing.

We were also tested psychically. With the joining of the conscious and subconscious mind comes an increase in psychic ability. It is necessary to teach the conscious mind to control these abilities and to protect the knowledge that the monitor has released. Prior to awakening, the subconscious mind and the monitor controls these memories, preventing the conscious mind from accessing them. After awakening, it is possible for other humans with advanced psychic abilities to "read" these memories and the information in them. The conscious mind then has to not only recognize when someone is psychically contacting it but also deny them access to this information.

Further testing monitored how well we were accepting the Androme way of life, how our conscious thinking was being affected and how much we were changing. The evaluations seemed tougher each time because the conscious mind felt more stress as it became ever more consciously aware. Our goal of a full awakening seemed to be within reach.

Several times Beek and Magna stressed that they would

Denise's first drawing of how she thought Beek looked.

Bert's first drawing of how he thought Magna looked.

Denise's later perception of Beek around the end of 1990.

Bert and Denise's later perception of Magna around the beginning of 1991.

not contact us during the night while we were fully conscious. They understood that too many years of being in American society had filled us with too many fears of ghosts and goblins stalking the star-filled nights of bogey-men waiting under our beds or in our closets. The stress and shock of fully conscious contact would be unduly aggravated if it were to take place during the night. True to their words, they did not begin the conscious contact phase until the sun was up and the day had begun.

When we imagined what a fully conscious contact would be like, we expected a complete, one-time shock with no return to subconscious meetings. But that wasn't how it was handled. As with all of the other phases, the conscious contact phase was a slow, steady progression so that the conscious mind did not overload.

The first conscious contact was verbal, on July 30, 1990 at almost 5:00 A.M. The sun was up and shining lightly through the curtains of the window. I could feel Bert lightly leaning on my shoulder, his fingers touching my ear as he quietly said my name. I started to turn over to face him, but he pressed harder for just a second and then let go of me. I turned my head and saw that Bert was lying with his back towards me, sound asleep.

I realized then that I had heard Beek in the room, and not just telephatically. When he had finally gotten me awake, he didn't initially let me turn over until he had time to activate his invisibility. It wasn't much of a conscious contact, but it was a beginning, a physical voice in the room. There was no telepathy and no recall of a meeting.

The next morning Bert was awakened by a voice next to him that whispered, "Good morning, Love." Thinking it was me, he turned over to answer, but found that I was just waking up myself. He then realized that the term "Love" was one that Magna used often, not me. The female voice he had heard was Magna's. This contact too had been in the light of day.

The next couple of weeks were difficult as the balance between our subconscious and conscious minds began to change rapidly. The monitor adjustments became physically tiring and were therefore made over the weekends.

Along with the physical changes came emotional ones. We would go suddenly from a state of agitation to near tears. By the first part of each week, however, the confusion would clear a bit and the meetings would again be easier to recall.

Each weekend became tougher for all of us. Bert and I were getting sore in different areas of the skull, and I began to get bloody noses each day. The children began to sleep restlessly, and to experience bloody noses as well. New marks began to appear on all of our heads.

Then on August 11, 1990, a new conscious shock hit us. I wakened early at 6:30 A.M., and the sun was up. I rose and came into the kitchen. Then I decided that since it was a Saturday I could treat myself to some more sleep. Not wanting to wake Bert up by getting back into bed, I lay down on the couch instead. A few months earlier we had adopted an orphaned kitten. This kitten decided that he wanted to cuddle up with me on the couch and purr in my ear as I tried to drift off to sleep.

Suddenly the kitten stopped purring and jumped out of my arms, landing on my rib cage. He was looking at something just behind me over the arm of the couch. Slowly he backed up and over my side towards the back of the couch. I didn't need to turn to know what he was staring at. At that time on a Saturday morning with everyone but me sleeping, there was only one possibility.

My next thought was, "Not now, I haven't got my glasses on and I haven't even showered and dressed yet. I'm not ready yet." Slowly I turned and sat up, and there was Beek, standing near the end of the couch, watching me and my reaction. I stood up and, walking past him, I went to the table where I had placed my glasses. If I was going to meet him I needed to consciously see him clearly!

When I turned and walked back to the couch, both Beek and Magna were there. They sat down together on the couch, leaving me enough room to sit down next to Magna.

At first my heart pounded in my ears, but now it seemed to be under control. The flow of adrenaline had quieted, too. My mind was conscious and my body felt calm. Too calm—it had received help from Beek, Magna and the monitor.

I leaned over close to Beek, comparing his reality to what I had been able to recall from the subconscious meetings. Although he was similar to my recollection of him, no hazy memory compares to a physical present person. He smiled a huge smile at me, and he spoke to me, but my ears didn't seem to be listening. I continued to stare first at him and then at Magna.

She sniffed slightly, and I heard Beek explain that they both had colds. I looked at Magna's hands and thought that her index fingers looked much longer than I had been recalling. I know I heard them talking to me, but I didn't seem to be able to find my ears or my voice—I only seemed to be able to stare. Then everything was black. When I opened my eyes two hours later, I was lying on the couch again.

Later, after reviewing my conscious contact, I could have slapped myself. Finally I was able to meet extraterrestrials in my living room consciously, and I stupidly froze. Out of the ten thousand questions Bert and I wanted to ask them consciously, I couldn't voice even one!

Bert and I hoped that soon he too would have a conscious contact with them, but it wasn't to occur just yet, however.

The weeks following were marked by weekly changes again, and the effects were very tiring physically. Emotionally they almost seemed to whirlwind us through the confusion and on into clearer memories.

As the weeks continued to flow, our memories and lives began to change even further. The memories were clearer, yet they began to contain so much detail that its very mass caused confusion. It seemed all wrong to recall Beek, Magna, the children and we having meals together and sharing our days. A part of our conscious minds still reached out and said this can't be happening, that these visitors from another planet wouldn't waste time or resources on us. Why would they make such an effort to pick us up at night just to share a meal, a conversation or a hobby? Wasn't there a world crisis that they should be solving?

The answer though has been there all along—they do it for love and for family. They are not here to solve the problems of our world that we have created. They are here because they need help, and for those of us who have chosen to help them in one form or another, they have imparted to us a greater understanding of all life.

Our understanding continued to grow as we shared our nights with Beek, Magna and all of the children in their two-story home. By our standards, their houses resemble a generation gone by, the 1920s through the early 1940s in architectural design. Some even seem to belong to our late 1960s and early 1970s. As our daughter Christy described one visit with them, it is as if they live in an old mansion that has been turned into a museum. Everything is antique and beautiful.

The contrast of the technological vehicles and equipment compared to their humble lifestyle is quite stunning. It is a shock to the senses to arrive on the mother ship in a transport and park it beside a house that we consider "old-fashioned."

The adjustments to the monitors disturbed us severely towards the end of October, 1990. Bloody noses happened more frequently to all of us. Bert and I both recalled that further work to the monitor was being done through our mouths. This process included removing a tooth, using the opening to perform the surgery, then replacing it. The only symptoms left in the morning were a slight soreness to the mouth and occasionally some light bleeding.

Another disturbing procedure was done to our eyes. I woke up one morning recalling the doctor placing an object into my left eye that was similar to a soft contact. The memory was so vivid that I went straight to the mirror to look at my eye. I was shocked to see a red mark on the white of my eye!

One morning not long afterwards Bert also woke up recalling that the doctor had placed something in his right eye. He too discovered a red mark on the white of the eye. As the marks faded over the next few days, I noticed that they left a very faint discolored area. Checking my right eye, I could see that this eye had a similar area located in the exact same area of the eye. We could not find a similar mark on Bert's left eye. Our children did not have such marks at all.

Bert recalled the Androme doctor explaining that the implant was like a video camera and would make it possible for them to see what we see rather than depending upon telepathy alone. The implants were installed for our security. Later we recalled seeing a split-screen television in Beek and Magna's home that displayed what we were seeing.

Changes to the monitors, however, did make the memories easier for us and the memories led us to believe that soon we would not only visit with them consciously but that we might possibly be allowed to go with them. Our hopes were raised one morning when both Christy and Stacey also began to recall memories from the previous night.

We also recalled Beek and Magna bringing Reginald and Elizabeth to us to say goodbye. We were told that if they accomplished the phases then one or both of them might also go through full awakening. It was a decision that was up to them as individuals.

It was this memory and others like it that seemed to all point to the possibility that we would make the full awakening, until one night, when everything seemed to change. This memory was rushed and confused. All that either of us seemed to remember was that something important occurred, something of an emergency. The next night I recalled being taken to the medical building where we visited Magna and a new baby. The baby was in a respirator. The memory was confusing—I was so shocked by this tiny baby and the equipment it was hooked up to that I couldn't retain the other portions of what had happened.

Together Bert and I came to the conclusion that Magna had delivered the baby prematurely and consequently it needed medical attention.

This theory didn't hold up, however, as in the next few nights we recalled Magna being still very pregnant. She was in bed and there was talk of how she wasn't feeling well, as well as talk of a baby and a birth. Our memories held nothing that we could recall to clear up the confusion. We decided there was nothing to do but have patience and wait until they were able to help us through our memories. We knew there was something wrong because the touches from Beek and Magna had suddenly just about stopped during the daytime.

The evaluation committee made the next few nights very busy. Both Bert and I woke up with very powerful but slightly confused memories of them because of our high level of consciousness. Their position of high authority and their habit of floating caused them to appear to be very tall and imposing. Of course once they put their feet on the floor their height was less than ours, and although they were in a position of authority, they were gentle and courteous.

It was concluded that we had not yet fulfilled the changes we needed to go through. One reason was that this book was incomplete. We were going to continue working both towards full awakening and towards publishing this book.

I continued to see a newborn baby, at first in the medical building, then at the house. Yet both Bert and I recalled that Magna was still pregnant. One morning, however, Bert woke remembering having watched Magna deliver the baby she was carrying. I woke up with a faint memory of this but a vivid recall of a particular sentence I had heard: "We have twin girls!"

I'm not sure who even said it, but this recalled phrase brought everything into place! Almost nine months ago I had recalled a memory of being shown that Magna was carrying two female fetuses. We didn't believe that it was possible that she could carry twins, and we had forgotten that memory. We had originally calculated that she had been due in December or January. The first twin was born in the last part of October and the second in the second week of November. They were both premature, and they were named Mary and Marion.

In November of 1990 Magna answered questions about the use of telepathy for me. She explained to me that although they can use the telepathy just as we can use speech, they will not use it under certain circumstances. For instance, as I stood there I could feel that she was indeed reading my thoughts, yet unless I was to directly question her with these thoughts, she would not react in any way.

Although the Andromes can freely speak with our subconscious, they will not interfere with our conscious thoughts out of respect for our way of life. It can be very disturbing to have another person comment on our private thoughts, so they will not react to our thoughts unless we specifically ask them to. This behavior can make them seem emotionless, since they will not react with facial expressions either.

We were shown to a room that I recognized immediately from my own memories. This room is a veterinary clinic. Animals that they have "collected" from earth are taken to this room before being brought into their society. If they locate an animal that has been injured to the point that it will not live and there are no humans in the area, they may take the animal with them and try to save it. If the animal lives it will be taught and then introduced into its new home.

Equal to their love for animals is their love for nature. The vegetation on the mother ship for the most part seems much like the forests of evergreens here on Earth, specifically reminding us of the Black Hills of South Dakota, although the trees are not as tall. Yet they do have other plants that are not familiar to us, like their fire bush, a three-foot-tall bush in which a red liquid courses through the almost clear branches. From a distance its luminescent qualities and movement make it appear to have a fire dancing across it. There is also a tree in the shape of a giant banana, whose bark resembles something like the surface of a pineapple.

There seemed to be so many facets to their life that we at times wondered if we would ever learn all that they were trying to teach us.

One day we got an odd, unplanned verification of a previous night's memory. It was basically a slip-up on all of our parts. During the visit with Beek and Magna, Bert had left to visit someone on his own! He was allowed to take a transport and visit a human. Neither of us could recall who it was that he had gone to see. I had stayed with Beek and Magna and kept an appointment with them to talk with one of the commanders of the mother ship. Apparently Beek needed authorization on something regarding his position on the ship. I didn't understand consciously what he had been asking. It was denied.

The three of us returned and we waited for Bert. When he pulled up he was eating from a box of earth cereal! Neither Bert or I could accept this portion of the memory in the morning. Why would the Andromes have Earth cereal?

Later that day as I was cleaning the house I lifted the cushion of the couch to vacuum under it. And there was a single, uncrushed piece of this same type of cereal!

We traced every possible means by which this cereal could have ended up in our couch. It wasn't ours—we hadn't even had that particular brand of cereal in the house. I had also steam cleaned the couch twice that year and had recently been vacuuming it every day for cat hair. It also couldn't have been under the cushion long since it was uncrushed. We

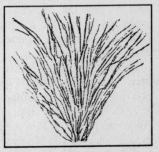

The fire bush that is located near Beek and Magna's house.

also had no other cereal that resembled it. So it hadn't been from our house. Next we checked with the people who had visited with us the past few days and found that only one had that brand, but they hadn't eaten any of it yet. Then Bert checked with Paul and found that he did have that cereal but could not verify whether any was missing from the box.

A plant that Magna has inside the house.

Bert and I laughed over this single piece of cereal. We even considered not mentioning it in the book. What were we supposed to do, tell the world we have a piece of cereal left over from one of our visits? It seemed ridiculous, yet the fact was that the memory of that cereal being eaten was odd in itself and it was even stranger to find the physical verification in our home the next morning.

The only question left was, whose was it? Was it Beek and Magna's, or was it Paul's? It was then that other memories fell into place. The stores on the mother ship also carried some earth items. Why? Again because of the non-interference law, everything must be put back after a visit so that the conscious mind has no leftover clues, especially before the awakening process. These items include a wide range of personal items—makeup, colognes, deodorants and so on.

Other items carried in their stores and homes are personal items that humans use. Even a subconscious person has needs. If you need an earth product, then you are allowed to have that item on the ship, and you also have items that are Androme products. It is a full life. The earth products are brought on board by involved people from their own homes, but it is done in such a fashion that the conscious mind does not notice anything missing or out of place.

We mentioned earlier the clothes we had acquired since moving onto the mother ship. For quite some time we had been remembering outfits that were ours subconsciously, yet not known to us consciously. There were shoes that were ours, but not ours consciously. On the mother ship a full life requires more than just the pajamas you wore to bed, your earth clothes, and the jumpsuits that are worn by the Andromes on the meeting ships. Casual and formal clothing is required for different visits and functions.

Although the Andromes allow humans to bring with them what they want or need, we did not think this meant such things that were against their way of life. The Andromes are vegetarians, yet we and other humans have recalled meat served at some of the meals. A large number of humans were gathered at one meal that was particularly disturbing for me. Only a small portion of these people are currently going through awakening while some are not involved at all with the Andromes except through us. These people brought and served their own meat. Those who wanted it took some, and those who didn't want any or who no longer eat meat passed it by.

At first we couldn't see why the Andromes would allow meat on their ship. To us it seemed offensive. But the Androme way is not to interfere with a person's right to choose. They do not force their wants, needs or way of life on any one. They will sit and talk with you as a friend about what you are doing, but they do not force change.

It was sinking in that we had another full life with a home, spouses, children, chores, hobbies, vehicles, schools, Androme relatives and work responsibilities. As the memories became clearer, we also realized that even with the hypnosis we had gone through we had missed recalling the January, 1982, birth of Teaka, Bert's child with Magna. Beek and Magna tried to show us our error, but we had been confused consciously. Considering the phases we had gone through and are still going through, it is understandable that not everything has come through to our conscious minds clearly and accurately. It also shows why they have to show us some things over and over again for them to be remembered accurately by the conscious mind.

Although I had begun to suspect that we had another

child, it wasn't clear until one night when I recalled a memory with enough conscious mind present that I could not deny the emotions I was feeling. We and some other humans were visiting at Beek's and Magna's house. I went into one of the bedrooms to check on the smaller children who were playing together. Besides Stacey, Kehalma, Christopher, Beek, Jr., and Bert, Jr., there was another little girl there. She was upset and sitting quietly by herself. I knew what was wrong with her as any mother would know what was wrong with her child—she had been feeling left out. Between the activities and the limited time, neither Bert nor I had been able to spend as much time with her as she needed.

I bent down and hugged her, and I told her that I loved her. Consciously I was flooded with feelings for all of the children, and I felt how limited our time with them always was. This memory of a dark-haired, eight-or-nine-year-old girl suddenly brought through the many times we had remembered her previously. This little girl was Teaka, the one with the medical condition that requires blood cleansing once a month. Now our collected children numbered thirteen by our count, and we consciously remembered each of them.

Even though we had tried to remain open-minded towards all that was happening to us, we realized that we still had reached some incorrect conclusions and that we had closed the door on re-evaluating them. We had felt that we had remembered through hypnosis all the most important events, and that having accomplished this task, there was nothing more to look for. In so doing we overlooked the birth of one of our blended children and made her existence hard for Beek and Magna to prove to us.

Having missed one child, we had to admit that we might have missed others, too. Now we try to make fewer snap conclusions, and we accept the fact that we do still have much to learn.

In December, 1990, further adjustments were made to us and the children. Bert and Christy both related that their memories were beginning to become clearer and that their consciousness was becoming fuller. Stacey complained that upon waking most mornings it felt to her as if she had just lain down. She also asked if the memories we had of the ETs were like very real dreams.

Now that the children were beginning to awaken again, they were at a lower level. Christopher was still having a hard time remembering, but the Androme doctor explained that both the breakthrough of the memories and the adjustments to the monitor would help him. He too began waking up with a bloody nose.

Other things began to change as we connected again with Madaline. She wasn't surprised to hear from us, and she said that slowly over the past year other people had come to her under odd circumstances, and that even she had undergone changes.

She explained that she had changed as a person; through her work she was now helping many people on their path. She felt that her life's work had changed and that it was about touching the soul and teaching people the importance of fulfilling the journey of the soul. She had begun teaching what she had learned to her clients.

Now she was teaching people to trust and believe in God, the universe and higher powers. She was teaching about vibratory levels and the importance of eating properly and of being a vegetarian. She was teaching the importance of universal oneness, of our connection to all living things, and of each of us being a part of the other. She had also become a speaker about extraterrestrials.

We were happy to hear her speak of these things, and we relayed to her the changes we had gone through since we had last seen her. She was now convinced that the extraterrestrials wanted her to do further work and to each people about them.

One morning Paul recalled clear memories of being with what could only be described as the evaluation committee. He explained that after the evaluation he went to a two-story home, that he recognized yet didn't know consciously. He recalled going into the kitchen/dining room area and discovering that he was late for the meal. He said that there were four women in the kitchen and that they had fixed him a sandwich.

Paul drew a sketch of the kitchen/dining room area as well as he could remember it, and we compared it to one that I had drawn weeks earlier. Paul had neither seen the drawing nor heard any detailed description of these rooms prior to his own memory of them. The sketches were amazingly similar. Later he was also able to describe the area around the house and the lake.

During the first part of January, 1991, Ellen telephoned to relate a memory she had recalled. She accurately described in detail the area near the house and lake. She also recalled floating over the side of a mountain in an Androme vehicle, a situation that was scary to her conscious mind.

Reginald and Elizabeth also shared with us their new level of awakening, in which Reginald was able to recall meeting with the Andromes on the mother ship. He remembered the transports, as well as the area near the lake and house.

Elizabeth relayed that for a time her "dreams" were spiritual in content. Then she had gone through a period of no recalled dreams. During this same period she and Reginald felt that the Andromes were no longer around them. Then one morning she had awakened with a new outlook on life. She said that the following three days she was very enthusiastic over changes she had planned to make within herself, but she soon realized that the changes wouldn't happen easily or quickly. She went on to say that since then she had been "dreaming," but that she was sure they were just that, "dreams."

After having her relay her "dreams," we were able to tell her that these had not been just "dreams," but memories. She had been able to describe certain areas of the mother ship that only Bert and I had recalled up until then.

As for the changes she wanted to make within herself, we explained that they were the same ones we had been working on for almost two years; they wouldn't happen overnight. Reginald and Elizabeth also relayed that they again no longer felt alone. They were fairly confident the Andromes were present again.

Hearing this news from Reginald and Elizabeth lifted our spirits considerably. What they told us verified our own memories of what was happening to them and confirmed that they had worked out what they needed to continue the awakening.

January, 1991, seemed to be another turning point in all of our awakenings. Christy began to recall more details of the meetings, including driving the transports. Now twelve years old, she woke up overly excited one morning and told us how Magna had instructed her to operate the transport. She had earlier vague memories of this, but this time she had no doubt. She had been learning how to drive the transports on the mother ship. She also recalled that they were hand operated.

Several other memories both recalled by us and by some of the other people going through an awakening dealt with group meetings. The discussion revolved around the Persian Gulf War. The memories for all of us were somewhat confusing, and we didn't understand if we were getting relevant information or simply discussing conscious fears.

In February, 1991, Christopher began to remember each morning the meetings from the previous night, but Stacey still couldn't quite recall her dreams, although she felt they had been realistic. Bert and I felt excitement over the children's progress.

One night Beek and Magna showed us more about the tests the Andromes use to select human spouses. Because they need to breed out certain genetic problems, they cannot have an Androme and a human with similar genetic deficiencies conceive children. If the two are in love, as has occurred sometimes, they can wed without having children.

The genetic testing the Andromes use shows that the gene structure of humans has been going through changes that are not beneficial for either the Andromes or for humans.

Although the period of time over which these changes have been occurring wasn't made clear to us, the reasons for the changes were: We and those who will be born in the future are being poisoned by chemicals, pesticides, fossil fuels, nuclear radiation, food additives, meat and its preservatives, harmful medications and many other man-made substances. Our technology has improved our lives but has created a slow death for our world. Even if we were to change our ways immediately, the biological damage and changes that are already in progress probably can't be reversed. The Andromes told us of genetic changes that our society knows about, but which it lets pass because our "risk assessment" of them was low. They spoke also of changes that we do not yet have the capability or technology to detect. There may even come a day when the residents of Earth find that they need "outside" help to continue their own civilization. I wonder how our society would handle such a problem.

Environmental damage is not the reason for the genetic problems the Andromes face, however. Their technology does not pollute. We found out later on that their genetic damage was due to an excessive burst of radiation from their sun.

Later in February, 1991, the last chapter of this book was yet to be completed when we let a few people who have become a part of this book read what we had finished. We weren't too surprised to hear from each of them that they had experienced increased Androme activity from the moment the book was in their hands. The Andromes were helping them to consciously confirm the reality of their awakening.

Elizabeth and Reginald not only experienced an increase in the presences and light shows, but they also experienced physical phenomena. Reginald was working late one night and left for home at about midnight. The drive normally takes him 15 to 20 minutes, but he didn't arrive at home until about 2:00 A.M. He couldn't recall what had happened to him during the missing time.

Elizabeth called us one morning to say that she couldn't

remember anything from the previous night, although she knew that something had occurred. Her reason for calling, however, was to ask if we could explain to her why she had found her shoes wet that morning when she went to put them on.

I laughed and explained to her that I was glad she had called. Our memories from that night had been odd. Bert had recalled that we had all been playing down by the lake and stream on the mother ship. I had recalled being near water, but what had been most pronounced in my memory was that I could recall being worried about clothes and shoes getting wet. My shoes were not wet in the morning, so I can only presume that it was Elizabeth's that I was worried about.

While Paul had possession of the book, he too felt the presence of the Andromes more strongly. He even felt some of their feathery touches. One night he was awakened in the early hours of the morning by sounds coming from his kitchen. In his relaxed but not fully conscious state he listened to the sounds of the Andromes as they left the house. He thought to himself, "I really don't want to bother with this right now." Then he went back to sleep.

In the morning he was surprised by his reaction from the night before. Had he been fully awake, he knew that he would have rushed into the room to see exactly what was going on but by not being fully conscious, he had a slight merging of the subconscious into the levels of consciousness. He knew at that point that the sounds were caused by the Andromes and that they were leaving after having brought him back home.

Another couple, previously unmentioned, also had odd occurrences happen to them from the moment they received the book. Exactly what took place they wouldn't say. We were asked by them to "prove the existence" of the Andromes by having Beek and Magna tell us what happened to them. If we could give this couple the correct information, then they would fully believe that the Andromes did exist.

On several occasions other people had "dared" us to prove the existence of our unseen friends. In the beginning we wanted to take up these challenges and shock these people into belief, but through our awakening we had come to realize that such grand-standing would be potentially dangerous and a breach of the non-interference law.

It's not up to us to decide when others should awaken. That is strictly between their subconscious selves, the Androme leaders and the specific Andromes they have a relationship with, whatever the relationship may be. It is not a game of truth or dare but a highly spiritual and psychologically precise journey into understanding and discovery.

When the awakening process of some of these people has reached a certain level, correlating memories can be shared with them, as Reginald, Elizabeth, Paul, Ellen, Bert, I and some others have done. Sometimes these memories have even been used as a portion of a person's "first shock," but only because it has already been planned by the Andromes and the humans subconsciously involved.

The same law of non-interference holds true when we are asked, "Am I involved with the Andromes?" or "Do I have another family?"

The questioners will have to discover the answers to these questions on their own. We listen to our inner promptings, and we can no more answer these questions for them than Beek and Magna could answer ours in the beginning. There are no simple yes and no answers—all the answers require a depth of growth and understanding into one's own memories, emotions and spiritual growth, which only the individual can discover.

Among the people who were given the book to read in advance was Madaline. She too knew that the Andromes were with her as she read through the book. She could feel their presence, and she concluded through her psychic abilities that the Andromes were proud of the job we had done on the book.

During February we went to a psychic fair. Not having been to one before, we weren't sure what to expect, but since we had met with Madaline, many of our stereotyped views of psychics had changed, and our own psychic abilities had grown. Since Beek and Magna had helped us develop our psychic gifts, we had become able not only to perceive when other people were "reading" us but we were also able to "read" other people, even when we didn't want to. Their thoughts, emotions and energies seemed to just be there for us to know.

The psychic fair was interesting and it featured a variety of psychics. One gave short readings from a photograph of your aura. The photographs were made by a camera that was devised specifically to record the energies of a person's aura. It uses a process similar to the Kirlian method.

Bert convinced me to have my picture taken and have a reading of it. As I sat next to the woman who was to interpret this photograph, both Bert and I realized that she wasn't looking just at the picture. She was reading me. I didn't mind, because I knew that she would not be able to get any important information concerning the Andromes.

What she did "see" about me was quite accurate, though. She began by stating that I was an environmentalist, which is true. She also added that my environmental concerns and views didn't come just from the issues in the media, they had begun in another lifetime and were carried on into this one. She went on to explain that I was an "old" soul who had been reincarnated several times on Earth.

Bert and I recalled meetings with Beek and Magna in which we had gone to a spiritual center to learn more about our inner selves, including reincarnation. Through prayer and meditation there, we learned about our own past lives and how the soul develops through its reincarnations on its path back to God. The Andromes have souls as we do, and they too must, through reincarnations, take the path back to the Creator.

The psychic went on to tell me accurately about my personality, but when she looked down at the photograph in her hand, she announced that I was not alone in the picture! She went on to explain that above my aura were three spots of light that were spirits. She said that there was a holiness about them and that I could look at them as a type of "guardian angel."

Before I could ask her more about these three "guardian angels," she continued to "read" the photograph. Pointing first to the right side of the picture then to the left side she said that there was something else here. She said that they were not spirits in the way that we would think of "ghosts" but that there was more to them than this. She thought they were some type of entity.

While she was trying to find the right words to explain what she was seeing for us, Bert asked her if she felt that these other spirits could be extraterrestrials. She said they could be, and she explained that she had come upon such images from time to time during private readings with people.

She explained that the colors in the photograph indicated that I had been through major changes recently and also that I was completing a healing process in the shoulder, neck and head area.

Before we left she looked at us both and commented that she could feel the changes we had gone through and that whatever it was we had been working towards was near at hand. We were about to reach our goal.

What had been especially nice about meeting this psychic was that she had absolutely no knowledge of Bert or myself prior to the "reading" or the picture. What had been exciting was that Beck and Magna posed with me for a photograph!

Of course this photo wasn't a full physical rendition of them. It only photographed them as they appear while they are giving a "light show." A comparable picture would be like those seen of "ghosts," a sparkly white, almost transparent, floating cloud.

We had gone through a lot of changes in February. No longer were the monitor changes just followed by pressure headaches or soreness—now they were followed by pain and exhaustion. The last levels before full consciousness were marked with extreme agitation and anger. It seemed that our conscious mind wanted to put up the hardest fight to save the last portion of the old reality. It hadn't been clear until then, although we had suspected, that we held the key to fully conscious contact. It had been ourselves all along. We understood completely.

We began to fully understand when Bert began to have problems dealing with the relationship among the four of us. Until this relationship came up into a higher level of consciousness, he had accepted what we had discovered, but it was his full consciousness that held the most years of the Earth's standards, dictations and habits.

Bert's conscious mind began to block off memories that dealt with the personal aspects of the relationship. The monitor had released all locks on the memories, and Beek and Magna induced their recall, yet Bert's conscious mind stopped them.

One day, when his frustration had peaked, he heard Magna's voice. She said that it was OK for him to recall these memories. After hearing her voice he began to recall the relationship and the final problems they raised with his emotions at the new level of awareness. He knew that until he could work these out within himself he would not be able to complete the awakening.

I had the same problem. Once the relationship was raised to a higher level of consciousness I didn't know whether I could accept it. I wanted to meet them consciously and never return to the subconscious meetings again, yet I couldn't accept the relationship. Neither Bert nor I knew whether we had grown enough to open our marriage and family to the full extent of our newfound family.

Then while trying to nap, but not being able to sleep, I lay with my eyes shut. Images of the relationship ran through my mind, and their emotional impact. Suddenly I wasn't alone in the room any longer—Magna also was there. From the sound of her voice I knew that she was near the window, and she asked me to look at her. I wouldn't. I told her I was sorry, but I wasn't ready.

Magna cried. She asked again for me to open my eyes and look at her; I refused again.

I then realized what had been happening all this time. Until we could completely accept them on every level of our mind, *we*, not they, controlled when the complete contact would be made.

We had come through all of the phases, the shock, the remembering, and partially through the growth and learning. We had accepted who they are, where they come from and why they were in our life. What we hadn't truly accepted was who *we* were. We weren't just Bert and Denise with three children, some pets, and a middle-class life style; we were Bert, Denise, Beek and Magna, with a house full of children on an extraterrestrial mother ship.

Could we open the final reserves of our hearts and consciousness to them? We could, but it was going to take time to prepare for the full conscious reality of this higher level of consciousness.

17

Cast Out with the Demons

Once we realized that we held the key, we worked harder at trying to understand this subconscious relationship we were in. The remaining layers of rules set forth by our society seemed to be formidable. We could not seem to accept this other marriage. The concept, reasons and fulfillment of the decisions didn't seem enough to justify the result—polygamy.

As we struggled to understand our relationship, we gained further insight into Androme society. Beek and Magna knew, that through a deeper understanding of them and us, we would eventually accept the marriage without reservations. We didn't realize just how naive we still were, towards not only Androme society, but also our own society. We had come such a long way with our new reality of them and us, yet we still had far to go.

It seemed that our "tunnel vision" was still a problem. The conscious mind has an uncanny knack for accepting only what it wants to accept as reality. Breaking down these boundaries seems to be a never-ending internal struggle. The subconscious self is always trying to get new ideas and realities through the closed door of the conscious mind, while the conscious mind finds excuses to ignore them and yet claims to be open-minded.

Although our religious beliefs were not carved in stone, our faith was. We had the deepest belief that no matter what was happening to us, God would keep us safe. Our trust was with Him as we went through our awakening. We even believed we were open-minded, but our beliefs were put to the ultimate test when we recalled being taken to the Community Religious Center with Beek and Magna to be introduced to "Jesus." Our conscious minds rebelled, believing that Jesus died about two thousand years ago. We refused to believe that Jesus would be on a mother ship, or anywhere else besides "heaven," for that matter. Was the memory wrong? Was it confused with a dream? Were we transposing an image of a verbal conversation onto some being on board the ship? Was Jesus really on the mother ship waiting for His second coming? The theological implications could be staggering, and we didn't know what to believe.

More than once on the ship we recalled seeing this entity known as Jesus as well as being surrounded by light. At first we told no one of our encounters with this Jesus and His "angels," fearing that other humans would react the same way we did, but then we began hearing of other humans who also recalled seeing Jesus and beings of light. We do not yet fully understand his appearance there, nor do we know its true implications.

Although we had never before felt a real need to be active in the church, we suddenly found ourselves wanting to share our faith with others, as we were doing periodically at night at the Community Religious Center. We felt that even though religions are often prejudiced, overly controlling and closed-minded towards each other, they seemed to have a place here on earth.

So we decided to share our earthbound community spirit and be counted as church regulars. We didn't go to church to build our faith, we went simply to share it. Our personal faith was still expressed at home within our family, through regular prayers, conversations, Bible readings and a respectful lifestyle.

We chose our church by accepting an open invitation given to us on several occasions by our neighbors, Bill and

Janice whom we had known for almost two years. Their children and ours played together and even went to Bible school together. They knew nothing about our ET experiences. During October of 1991, when we became dissatisfied with the public school system, they had introduced us to other families from their church who home-schooled their children.

We attended their church for several months and enjoyed sharing our faith with others, but we knew that the time would come when we would have to tell our friends and the church about the other half of our life. We weren't looking forward to it!

We didn't always come away from a Sunday sermon feeling good. Our views on reincarnation, other worlds, other species and the things we'd learned about the Creator from the Andromes didn't always mesh with the interpretations the pastor and his congregation expressed, but we expected this. When we first became friends with Bill and Janice, we didn't know whether they were involved with Andromes, although through ordinary conversations we thought that they might have some of the symptoms. However, they were unaware of these as "symptoms."

At times we thought we recalled meeting with them while we were with Beek and Magna. We wondered whether we were just transposing them with some other people that our conscious mind found easier to accept. But we had memories that included touring their new house with them prior to our seeing it consciously, and we recalled personal information that also proved accurate later. These and other memories confirmed that whatever their relationship with the Andromes was, they were being picked up.

One night Beek and Magna informed us that the time had come to tell the church and our unsuspecting friends of our secret life. Difficult subconscious meetings began to prepare Bill, Janice, the pastor and a handful of other new friends from the church. It was clear that their subconscious minds were already definite that their conscious minds would force them to turn their backs on us, and the church would ask us to leave their congregation.

I cried after one subconscious meeting, and I was still crying when I woke up later at home. Bert was depressed as he weighed the odds. He wanted to oppose what had been agreed upon by our subconscious minds and the others at the meetings and not tell anyone anything, but we knew we had to. Beek and Magna were so much a part of our lives that we knew we would have to be open to our friends or we would feel that we were being dishonest with them. Being honest about this subject was going to be very hard not only for Bert and me, but for our children as well. By being honest we would both lose our relationship with the church and our neighbors' friendship.

We managed to put it off for over two weeks, but one evening Bert decided that it was time. I took the younger children to a Bible school meeting that evening. Bert went to speak to the pastor in private, which was arranged with Beek and Magna the night before.

The pastor was to be told on that Wednesday evening, prior to our telling Bill and Janice on the following Friday evening. We decided on this arrangement so that the pastor would be aware of what was happening in our life prior to Bill and Janice finding out and seeking his advice. It was done this way out of respect for the church, since the pastor is in charge of his church family, and he feels his responsibility deeply.

Bert said the meeting with the pastor went well, even though there was some shock, of course. The pastor had never dealt with this type of situation before, and he wanted time to think about it before making any type of comment on it. He did ask, "Am I involved?" Bert didn't give a direct answer to this question.

Friday night came too soon for both of us. We were already well aware of what was going to happen—they would turn their backs on us.

After the children were busy playing, we sat down, and Bert began to tell Bill and Janice of our involvement. There were times during that evening when we thought Bill would get up and walk out, but he is a polite person, and he listened. At times they both seemed to be handling it well, but for the most part Bill seemed angry. Janice recollected that when she and Bill were dating they had watched a light in the sky one evening while they were parked in her parents' driveway. At times the symptoms, strange events and memories seemed to mean something to them. When they left that evening we thought that perhaps, for a change, the memories were wrong. Maybe this would all work out, and they would not reject us. We had plans to tell another church couple the following weekend, but our hopes were dashed. The pastor called at the beginning of the week and requested that we meet with him and a church elder. What we recalled from the memories was about to be fulfilled.

The "meeting," which was how the pastor initially referred to it, was termed a "hearing" by the pastor and the elder by the time we arrived. During this "hearing" they asked us many questions regarding our relationship with Beek and Magna. We answered with what we knew. The pastor said that he didn't for one minute doubt the recounting of the events nor any of the things we were expressing. He was satisfied that we were expressing honestly what we believed had happened to us. What he questioned was the true source of our experiences. The elder, on the other hand, scoffed at life elsewhere in the universe.

They told us that "if" we were involved in this relationship then we were committing adultery. We explained that we were not committing adultery. We were in a sanctioned, four-way marriage, and there was no adultery. They told us we were committing a sin by marrying more than one other person, and they cited scripture to back themselves up. Not being as well versed as they are in the scriptures, we were at a loss to respond.

They told us that they believed that we were not involved with aliens but that we were involved instead with demons. They told us that we were in bondage to demons, as our families probably had been for generations.

We told them we were not in bondage to demons, and that we also explored many possible explanations such as possession and demons during our awakening. It was our faith in our Creator and the "signs" we were shown that led us into this other society and made us feel free of any type of demonic possession. We knew full well who demons were, and the Andromes weren't demons.

I told them that I had counted on God all my life, and that I fully trusted God to show me who Beek and Magna were. God had never and would never let me down.

They told me, with scripture for back-up, that God was purposefully deceiving me and giving me His signs to lead me in the wrong direction, just to see if I would go the wrong way. In essence, God was lying!

I told them that a loving God would never do that. I did not believe that if I handed over my heart, soul and trust to God, that he would never deceive me while knowing the unrest in my soul. I could not believe that I could ask for truth and be deceived in return.

They cited scripture that said that all had been revealed to man, and in that scripture nothing was said about aliens. Therefore aliens cannot exist. They cited more scriptures, although they disagreed with each other about their correct interpretation. Yet they told us it was a black-and-white situation and that we were in bondage to demons.

Our insufficient knowledge of scripture left us unable to challenge them in return, which we discovered later was actually to our own benefit, as it prevented us from "debating" with them in a no-win situation for either side.

They asked us why we were going to their church. We explained that we felt a need to share our faith within the community and that we did not need to find God. We said we already knew God in our heart, which was probably not the right thing to say.

The pastor then told us that if we were to come to the church, admit that we were in bondage to demons and ask to be set free, then we could remain as part of their church family. If, on the other hand, we were to insist that these events were occurring because of aliens, then we were not welcome at the church. Further, we were not to associate with anyone belonging to their church family, including our neighbors Bill and Janice and another couple we had invited over for the following weekend. They left the impression that this other couple had already been told of what we were planning to tell them and that they agreed with the pastor and the elder. We found out later through an accidental meeting that they had not been told about us.

We ended the meeting politely and left. We didn't talk to our children about it until the next morning. We explained the conversation to them and told them that we could continue going to the church and being friends with people we know from chruch if we met the following conditions: we must admit our ETs are demons and that we are in bondage to them. Then we must ask the church for help to free ourselves from them. All three of them stared at us in disbelief and cried, "We can't do that! They aren't demons!" and "We would be lying if we said that."

We talked with them and cried with them over the loss of friends, but we were in agreement—we could not do what the church wanted us to do. We would be lying to them and to ourselves. Bert and I explained to the children that we shouldn't feel angry toward the church, because, after all, we did put them in a very awkward position. The children easily understood, because we have lived with the "awkward" position placed on us since we consciously became aware of our extended family. It hasn't been an easy position, and possibly this incident was the hardest on the children. As hard as it was, though, we were awed to see their strength at their young ages as they refused to buckle to society's pressure, even knowing the consequences. This kind of strength has been hard at times for Bert and me to maintain. We did have one small ray of hope, however—we knew from the memories that these reactions were initial ones and not necessarily the final ones.

A few days later Janice called me on the phone. I explained that we were not supposed to be in contact with her, and I explained to her what had happened at the "hearing." I also told her that since then both Bert and I had done further studies of scripture and had contacted other religious leaders. What we discovered was that several of the passages used against us during the "hearing" had other interpretations, and we found passages that would have directly opposed the scriptures they were using against us. There is an answer for everyone in the Bible.

Janice gave me further passages that would have been of benefit to us. She said that she wanted to find out more information about the subject of aliens, but that she couldn't find anything at the Christian supply store. I was not surprised. She also said she and Bill still wanted to be friends with us. She didn't appreciate the church deciding who her friends could be.

I promised to gather up a list of books for her to look for that would help her with her search, but I explained that out of respect for the pastor, we could not contact her. She promised to call back, but as of this writing she has not.

We continued our search into the world of the Bible. We discovered that each scripture is subject to the reader's interpretation and can be taken in many ways. We discovered how the Bible was made, how it was decided what would and wouldn't go into it and the many changes since then.

We decided that we would consider ourselves belonging to the Androme faith and that we would continue our private conscious life with prayers, Bible readings, and talk of our Creator. What it taught us was that the guilt we still held inside ourselves for not actually belonging to a church and for insisting that our church was in our heart and home first and foremost, was unfounded. Even though we felt comfortable with our views, we still let society's rules fill us with a sense of guilt. We still feel that churches are important, but like other organizations, people and governments, they still have much to learn.

Our further exploration of the Bible taught us that some marriages were polygamous. Some of these seemed blessed, others not. The God of the Bible seems to be a personal God. It seems that He takes each person's circumstances and judges by the heart. Behaviors that are true and from the heart and have logical influences can sometimes change the rules, even man's rules. Whereas displayed behaviors that covet greed, lust and such things are subject to penalties.

As for Bill and Janice, we settled on a subconscious, nocturnal friendship. We talked about the questions and problems they were having with the information we gave them and of the times their conscious minds almost broke down and called us. These occasional visits with them were very hard for us consciously because we knew we could not interfere and take the initiative to call them.

As we mentioned earlier, one of the reasons we became involved with our church friends was our growing dissatisfaction with the public school system. Many months before, Beek and Magna showed us their school system, which is very different from ours, because much of the basic learning is done at home. Knowing that there were better options in other worlds, we felt that it was time to find better options here in our world.

Our children's school was using techniques that were opposite to what we taught at home. An incident occurred at the elementary school, in which the children were being rewarded with candy, movies and parties in order to encourage appropriate behavior and scholastic goals. We saw it as bribery.

At home we teach responsibility for the goal of improving oneself and gaining an awareness of others. We were trying to teach the children that learning and growth are wondrous and never-ending parts of life.

We also restricted the TV and movies that we allowed our children to see. We were amazed at how much more time we found for activities we enjoyed doing as a family. Yet the school seemed to be teaching bribery and showing movies that we didn't want the whole family to watch.

I called the principal of the school to discuss these concerns. She said that the use of candy, movies, parties, etc., is acceptable at school in order to achieve the desired behavioral goals. I told her it was bribery, and she said, "Yes, it is. But it works!" She also revealed that she limits her own children's intake of sweets at home!

Christopher, who was in fourth grade, was having frequent stomachaches that seemed to start just minutes before getting on the school bus in the morning. It got to the point where we sent him anyway, only to have the school nurse call us an hour or so later.

The school counselor called me in for a conference. She steered the conversation towards the fact that perhaps Christopher's problems were due to my going back to work. It was true that I went back to work during the summer of 1991, but his stomach problems didn't start until school began. Also, I stopped working two months before we left public school, but he continued having the stomach problems until he was no longer in public school.

Two other factors convinced us to try home school. We really began to worry about the increase in violence, drugs and gangs in both the elementary and middle schools. Also, the children were spending the first term of school reviewing the previous year's work. They were bored with this review, and as a result their lack of interest was beginning to show in their grades.

We researched home schooling, met other families who home-schooled and made our decision. We were surprised at the growing number of people who home-schooled their children. Even more of a surprise was the number of public school teachers who either had a spouse home-schooling their children or had enrolled them in private schools. Their reasons were even more numerous than ours.

At the time, I wasn't getting enough rest between our nightly visits, working full time and taking care of the household. We decided it was best that I quit work, stay home and home-school the children. We debated about my retaining a part-time position but decided that home schooling would take up the majority of my time, and it has.

We took the children out of the public school over

Christmas vacation, 1991, and began to home-school after that. They loved it! They completed their assignments in less time than it took them at public school, and they were learning more. Now we knew what they were learning and how they were progressing. For the most part they received one-on-one instruction in the comfort of our own home.

And the extra time allowed us all to begin learning piano and to volunteer at the nursing home and public library once a week. There are still some bugs to iron out, but it's becoming a nice part of our family. Christopher only had one other nervous stomach problem the whole year, which happened when we took Stacey to the emergency room, and we were all worried. Things turned out fine, however.

Another of society's institutions—the importance of our schools—was swept from our conscious imprint. Home-schooling is not a sin or something only fanatics do.

18

Compassionate ETs

One interesting part of the mother ship is the animal reserve. It is a veritable Noah's Ark. Lions, bears, wolves, birds and elephants are to be found there. The majority of these animals are from Earth, although the Andromes have also brought animals from their own and other planets.

The animals that they have taken from Earth are animals that were injured to the point of near death. If they find a dying animal, and there are no humans nearby, the Andromes take the animal and try to save it. If the animal lives, it is worked with and taught to communicate, and if it is a natural animal of the wild, it is put in the reserve, free to roam. Andromes and visiting humans walk freely among these animals. The domestic animals are given to families.

The Andromes have shown great compassion, not only for animals but for every living creature, no matter what its origin. They are especially compassionate about their disabled, aged and ill. The Andromes do not use mental institutions as we do here on Earth. When possible, the Androme who is mentally or physically afflicted lives at home. If the condition is too severe, they live in a facility more like a large home than an institution. The caretakers are everyone from their society, including visiting earth people. Like everything else, this responsibility is shared by young and old alike. Even the most severely disabled being is given an opportunity to experience family and growth.

This compassion prompted us to doubt certain aspects of their actions that we still didn't understand. Why would they interfere and offer medical help to people in some instances, but not in others? We began to understand that there was a complex array of reasons for their behavior. First, always, was the non-interference law. They could only help medically if they did not interfere with the conscious mind.

Second, the Andromes considered the physical problem's role in the person's growth. Was the problem a requirement of the reincarnated self? The Andromes cannot correct a physical ailment that is part of a growth process whose origins stretch back to previous lives. Third, the Andromes determined whether the problem was due to an environmental cause. If the only cure was to remove the cause, then the Androme doctor might assist but he cannot change our environment in order to cure the person's illness. It seems that the non-interference law stretches into "laws" we weren't as familiar with. Each medical problem a person has is treated or not treated according to that individual's holistic needs. If the Andromes and your inner self took care of every bothersome situation, the conscious mind might fail to find challenges in life and might become dependent upon this help. Without challenges, one's growth is stunted, so helping the individual too much can be harmful. The conscious mind might even become angry at the lack of control of self; this is a very sensitive area to a person aware of their subconscious involvement.

We have related occasions when Beek, Magna and other Andromes have taken care of needs such as Bert's pneumonia and heart problem. They also removed cancer from one of his lungs, as Elizabeth also recalled. At one point they removed a section of my intestine, which had been ulcerated by colitis. They treated Christopher's sty, and they've treated, but not cured, Stacey's environmentally-induced asthma.

Recently Stacey accidentally choked on a quarter. We dislodged it but it went down into her esophagus instead of out of her mouth. We took her to the emergency room and

X-rays showed that the quarter had not gone into the stomach. They gave her some medicine to relax the esophagus, allowing the quarter to pass into the stomach and on through the digestive system. It didn't work, and we were transferred to a children's hospital where a pediatric specialist could do surgery on her to remove the coin. We arrived at the hospital around midnight, and the doctor suggested that the surgery be done in the morning. I stayed the night with Stacey in the hospital while Bert went home to stay with Christy and Christopher. There were no other patients in the room. I slept fitfully, my longest period of sleep being one and a half hours. During that time Beek and Magna did come to the room, but because of my tensions and worry over Stacey I couldn't recall many details. Bert reported the same thing when he arrived in the morning.

That morning Stacey would not wake up. We could rouse her just enough to get her into the wheel chair, or to move this way or that, but then she would immediately fall asleep. I was puzzled! Because of Stacey's asthma she has had plenty of adrenaline shots and is therefore very leery of needles. When it came time for them to hook up the IV, I felt very anxious, knowing that Stacey would start crying and yelling and then physically try to get away from the needle. But instead she lay there with a dazed look on her face, and just watched the nurse. When the needle was poked into her skin she remarked, "Ouch," in a quiet and almost emotionless voice. It was unreal. I commented to the nurses and doctor about it. They said that perhaps she was just tired from all the excitement of the hospital. After hearing that response several times I finally said, "Maybe." But I know Stacey. Having asthma, she is used to hospitals, and never before has she become sleepy, not even during the most severe attack! She always reacted with a lot of high energy, even prior to the adrenaline shots, and she always wanted to know everything the doctor or nurse was about to do. Her half-conscious behavior was totally out of character. I asked about the medicine they had given her the night before to relax the esophagus. I was told that it wasn't a sedative and that it couldn't be responsible for her behavior.

Bert and I decided then that perhaps the Andromes had done something to ease Stacey through the trauma of the surgery. We can't say for sure.

They didn't have their doctor remove the quarter because that would be conscious interference with the hospital. If that quarter had suddenly disappeared, we'd hate to imagine what type of tests they would have put Stacey through trying to locate it.

Why not push the quarter into her stomach? Perhaps in Stacey's case that would have been a mistake. Perhaps that coin wouldn't have gone through the digestive system as it normally should. The next best thing for them to have done was to relieve Stacey of the turmoil and stress of what was happening, and if they did do something, it worked well! Stacey had the quarter removed successfully that morning.

While we were writing the first part of this book, Magna gave birth to Danny, who was born prematurely in October, 1991. Danny was biologically parented by Beek and myself, but Magna was the surrogate mother. I was unable to carry a child because of a hysterectomy in 1987.

An Androme doctor took sperm from Beek and an egg from me. The fertilized egg was then implanted in Magna, who carried the baby for just over seven months without a problem. Then one night she was upset—something was wrong. She told me that she could not get through to the baby, that he wasn't responding. She was speaking of the "bonding" that occurs between mother and child while the mother is pregnant. Because of the Androme's great psychic abilities, they telephatically convey to the baby their thoughts and emotions. This bonding or communication is also conducted by others in the family and by those close to the mother.

Magna was taken to the Androme doctor, and baby Danny was delivered. He was put into a clear circular incubator and remained there until he had developed enough to survive without it. Even now he still has medical problems that don't seem to be severe but do require regular medical attention.

Andromes, as we have explained earlier, cannot have children within their own society because of severe genetic disturbances that have occurred to their race in recent generations. The few surviving children had severe mental or physical disorders. Not all of these conditions have been "bred" out yet, and some new genetic defects have appeared as well. Their use of Earth DNA to supplement their own gene pool has not been without complications. Earth genes carry genetic disorders, too, and even with testing, not all of the possible problems can be foreseen.

Our little girl Teaka was born with a genetic defect and she still requires dialysis. The twin girls Mary and Marion were also not right. Mary was born prematurely with a birth defect—her legs had not developed correctly.

She was placed in an incubator where her growth could be stimulated. We were told that by the time she was five years old her legs would be a normal length. She will be in a mobile version of this incubator for most of the time until then. She has been lucky—this is one genetic problem the Andromes can repair over time. Others haven't been so lucky.

Because of the high incidence of premature births, the Andromes are quite adept at using the techniques needed to help these babies survive. They can raise a fetus from conception to birth, strictly with the use of their "incubator," but this is not preferred. Even with the complications associated with mothers carrying two fetuses, the experience of the fetus and the bonding family takes precedence over the sterile laboratory methods. These methods are for survival, not convenience.

Because of the Androme/Earth effort a second generation is now being born. The first children of this union are now having children of their own as well. They marry into either society or into the new mixed generation.

A human awakening to the Andromes is often confused by their varied appearance. The different physical characteristics of the two peoples and the combinations thereof creates such a wide variance of descriptions that confusion about who is whom is an understandable occurrence.

One reason for apparent variance in height comes from the astonishing fact that the Andromes can manipulate size! They can shrink themselves and others as well. It took several meetings and the recollections of other contactees for this twist in their technology to get through to us.

Beek and Magna set up several meetings to prove this capability to us, but it was a meeting in which they had Elizabeth participate that finally proved their point. I knew from a conscious point of view how my height compared to Elizabeth's. Elizabeth and I began our meeting in a shrunken condition, but she was returned to her original height in front of me. That showed me what was happening. Elizabeth also retained a part of that particular memory.

Extraterrestrial spouses, Jesus on the mother ship, and now shrinkable people! What next in this incredible universe?

19

Balancing on the Edge

Retaining a balance during the awakening is a matter of enormous concern to the Andromes and both the conscious and subconscious selves. During the awakening the conscious mind is faced with integrating a vast expanse of information. Sensitivities of emotions develop, as do faith, psychic abilities and concerns about world and universal affairs. How do you balance and harmonize the subconscious self's involvement with people from another world with the conscious self and its strict, unbending Earth rules? How do you get up in the morning and get ready for work or household chores when you remember flying in an extraterrestrial transport? How do you concentrate on the customer at the other end of the phone line, or shop for groceries when your mind is recalling the recent birth of your blended baby? How can you coexist with a monetary, prejudiced, self-destructive type of society, knowing that you also live in a society that by comparison seems almost perfect, even with its shortcomings?

Balance is walking the tightrope, precariously perched on a fine line between the conscious and subconscious minds. We've learned to listen to the inner self, but to not be hasty. Perhaps someday we will live with the Andromes on a permanent basis, but until then we aren't going to quit work, sell off all of our worldly goods or sit in an empty house, waiting.

The meetings in which we've recalled discussing living with the Andromes have caused us to want to pack a suitcase and stand by for the ship to pick us up. Part of the reality shock to the conscious mind is an overly exuberant excitement, which must be contained. We feel that we know what is coming, but until that time we must live our conscious day-to-day lives. We can't plunge off either side of that tightrope. Rather, we must retain a balance between the two sides, continuing straight ahead until we accomplish our goal.

We wanted acknowledgment without prejudice from both worlds, but the majority of people here on Earth don't react well to stories of extraterrestrials and eyewitness accounts of sightings and encounters. That, of course, has been very hard on us, as this book reveals. Yet we are also stressed by wanting acceptance from the Androme counsel members and their community. They can, with good reason, be leery of Earthlings and their ability to change. So again we walk that fine line, stressed by both worlds.

Yet a new understanding of that stressful wish for acceptance from either side has begun taking shape. We cannot hope to please both planets, and we can't bow down to our society's pressure and say that extraterrestrials do not exist. Neither can we tell the Andromes that we are as advanced in body and soul as they are.

Bert, Beek, Magna and I have all made advancements, improvements and changes. We have all learned much from each other. But we are all individuals, and we can only change the things that can become a natural part of ourselves. For instance, we could never have become vegetarians and stuck with it unless it was truly a part of who we have become. Regardless of the source of the "promptings," none of the changes we made during this awakening process would have remained with us, unless they were growth that we were ready for and wanted.

We accepted our children on the ship more easily than we accepted the four-way marriage. Beek, Magna and we talked of how all the children, our three as well, were the children of all four of us. We recalled Beek and Magna referring to our three kids as *their* kids, yet it wasn't until recently that the impact of that actually hit us. They have always referred to our three kids as a part of the whole group, yet our conscious mind ignored the implications of other adults asserting parentage over our Earth children. At first we felt a mixture of emotions towards this awareness. It seemed natural that the four of us were the parents of the children on the ship, yet it seemed that Bert and I held a double standard for our three.

So many of the adjustments we have gone through were part of a series. After each reality shock we'd feel that we'd put something to rest, only to discover that it still hadn't been settled. One still unsettled shock concerning the children emerged during a short conscious meeting when Bert asked Beek how many children we had. Laughing, he told Bert that we had more than fourteen, in fact, we had twenty-five children! Apparently this was a surprise to Bert, and he couldn't recall much after that point. We still aren't sure if Beek was joking or not, and even other subconscious and conscious meetings with them haven't cleared that up.

During the period of our awakening, our meetings had included many aspects of psychic phenomena—awareness of it, awakening of it, practicing with it, and testing our progress with it. Yet, when we suddenly began having meetings that contained a significant amount of confusion and conscious transposition, we were stumped. Our only clue was that we were suddenly having a lot of déjà vu. What did it mean?

One day I recalled the image of an older woman in a wheelchair. She had long gray hair with some odd strands of the original black. Attending her was a young man who was dark haired and dressed in a white shirt and black slacks. I had the impression that he was her son or a very near relative. He left her alone for a minute, and suddenly the woman fell from her wheelchair. The young man rushed to her aid, lifting her in his arms.

These images made no sense to me until the next day. As the children and I got into the car after grocery shopping, I noticed a man and a woman coming out of the store. I turned back to start the car, then it hit me. I looked back, and the woman was as I had recalled. She was the elderly woman in the image, and the young man with her was dressed and looked as I recalled. As he was pushing the wheelchair to their car, he left her while he put the sack in the car. The woman leaned forward slightly, and the incline of the pavement caused the chair to tilt, spilling her out of the chair. The young man rushed to her aid, lifting her into his arms.

I was staring out the window, dumbfounded, and the kids asked me what was wrong. Both Bert and I had been experiencing precognition, but this experience had been very exact and quite detailed. It was as if I were watching the event a second time, but this event had just happened!

A new fear arose in us. Now that we understood a fuller sense of the psychic ability Beek and Magna were trying to teach us, we weren't sure that we wanted it. Do we really want to know in that type of detail what is about to happen?

We were used to experiencing a sense of something about to happen and to getting fuzzy images, but a detailed account is hard to get accustomed to. What has helped us, however, is knowing that if we see what is about to happen we can sometimes change it. And we have done just that when we were able!

What we can't change is the fact that we are involved with the Andromes. What we don't understand is *why*?

Initially, we thought the Androme's reasons for involving us were one-sided. They needed our help to strengthen their genetic line. As we later discovered they weren't the only ones who needed help. The key was a series of meetings that included many Earthlings. These meetings were unclear in the beginning, mostly because we were not ready consciously to accept what they were about. Many of these meetings took place in large gatherings, others were on a smaller scale, but they all included discussions, video viewing, computer simulations and extensive disaster training.

These skills might be needed here on Earth in the not-too-distant future. Is it Armegeddon? Revelations? The "Second Coming?" An economic crash? Another axis shift? It doesn't matter what name it is given. Drastic changes seem to be about to happen.

Are the extraterrestrials here to help us through these changes? Maybe. We believe that they are here to help those of us who will accept the help, and they are also here to be helped by us. The Earth does not stand alone in the universe. We are all one together, and our actions affect each other.

We can't tell you exactly what will happen, or when or how it will happen. We don't know how many will be taken from this planet, nor even whether we will ever be taken. We believe that this decision is not ours, nor the Androme's.

We still have much to understand and much to help others understand. Yet what we do know places us further into their consciousness and way of life as each day goes by, making it harder for us to stay here. We started our awakening in May of 1989, and at this writing it is now December of 1992. Three and a half years of our conscious existence has been taken up with the knowledge of extraterrestrials in our lives, the knowledge that we have been involved possibly since birth or before. We have learned many things about the Andromes and about ourselves. Some things we have been able to share in this book, and other things we have not been able to share. We have come through many changes, and we have met many new people, on their side as well as on ours. We have lost friends over this, and we have made new ones.

We've asked ourselves if it's all been worth it, considering what we've come through and what is to come. It is worth it. As hard as it is to shrug off the Earth-learned consciousness and suffer the losses involved in order to awaken to a higher consciousness, it's worth the struggle. Let's join together and awaken.

"It's time."

Appendix

THE CHILDREN

By Parentage	By Date

Beek & Denise
Ankra (male), b. November 2, 1978
Unnamed (male), miscarried May, 1981
Beek, Jr. (male), b. October 12, 1984
Danny (male), b. October 16, 1991

Bert & Denise
Christy (female), b. November 3, 1978
Christopher (male), b. November 24, 1981
Stacey (female), b. October 15, 1984

Bert & Magna
Zeema (female), b. autumn 1980 -d. autumn -1985
Teaka (female), b. January 21, 1982

By Date
Ankra (male), b. November 2, 1978
Christy (female), b. November 3, 1978
Unnamed (male), miscarried May, 1981
Zeema (female), b. autumn 1980 -d. autumn -1985
Christopher (male), b. November 24, 1981
Teaka (female), b. January 21, 1982
Anthro (male), b. January 1, 1983
Beek, Jr. (male), b. October 12, 1984
Stacey (female), b. October 15, 1984
Kehalma (female), b. October 21, 1985
Bert, Jr. (male), b. December 8, 1988

Anthro (male), b. January 1,
1983

Kehalma (female), b. October
21, 1985

Bert, Jr. (male), b. December
8, 1988

Einga (female), b. November
14, 1989

Mary (female twin), b. October 21, 1990

Marion (female twin), b. November 8, 1990

Einga (female), b. November
14, 1989

Mary (female twin), b. October 21, 1990

Marion (female twin), b. November 8, 1990

Danny (male), b. October 16,
1991

SUMMARY OF "THE AWAKENING"

The following is a brief summary of the various phases through which the Andromes lead us. The "awakening" is a very individualized process and does not necessarily follow the steps in sequential order. Depending on the person going through the awakening, some of the phases can be combined. But it has been our understanding that no one who has been involved with the Andromes for a lengthy period can complete the phases to the goal of a full, permanent conscious contact until all of the phases have been fulfilled. The phases, although broken down here into a very brief summary, are neither simple nor quick. Our awakening has taken over three years and we understand that we have progressed fairly quickly. The process of the awakening encompasses every portion of one's personality, beliefs, faith, and emotions. It is a complex adjustment to body, mind and soul.

Phase One:

The beginning of the awakening is also known as the first shock. It is the time when the subconscious mind decides that the conscious mind is capable of safely handling the knowledge that it is involved with people from another planet. This phase will typically last until the person either moves into phase two or the subconscious mind decides that the conscious mind cannot be awakened and slows the process down or stops it altogether. Starting a daily diary of the events and keeping a firm faith in God will ease the shock of this phase.

Phase Two:

The second phase of the awakening is known as remembering your involvement. Prayer, meditation and hypnosis can be used in this phase to allow the conscious mind to understand further the involvement of the subconscious with the ETs. It is very important that this memory process begin with the earliest memory and work sequentially into the adult years.

Phase Three:

This phase of the awakening is marked by changes in personality, life style and learning of the Andromes. Recollection of meetings with the Andromes or possibly other ETs usually begins in this phase. These meetings begin as very vivid dreams until the levels of the subconscious have merged with the conscious and the meetings are at a fully conscious level.

Phase Four:

Full, permanent conscious contact.

SYMPTOMS

These are some of the more common symptoms or occurrences we experienced. It is by no means a complete list.

- Blinking lights
- Stereo switching itself off and on
- Alarm clocks ringing at times not set at, or turned off
- Locks breaking or unlocking themselves
- The feeling of not being alone, feeling another presence
- Unexplainable sounds
- Shadowy movement
- Nose bleeds

- Pressure headaches
- Red patchy marks on the back of the head
- Restless nights
- Sleepwalking
- Vivid dreams
- Missing time
- High frequency sounds that come and go
- Pets suddenly becoming jittery and restless
- Belief in UFOs
- Unexplained scars, marks, bruises.

Other symptoms that may appear as you progress through the awakening process:

- Light shows
- Touches
- Recall of ET memories
- Areas of soreness in the head and neck
- Fluttering sensations
- Body temperature changes

CHANGES

During the awakening there will be changes in every aspect of the person's life, such as changes in

- Personality
- Emotions
- Morals
- Faith
- Psychic abilities
- Habits
- Lifestyle
- Viewpoints

LETTERS

The following letters are from other friends and acquaintances who have also begun this journey with us. Where applicable, pseudonyms have been used to protect their privacy.

Letter from Reginald

March 9, 1991

I have known Bert and Denise well for around seven years and only the last two have involved the awakening. Interestingly enough the first five years seemed to be a very normal and happy lifestyle, with what I considered the normal bumps and bruises; like maybe an occasional flat tire, common cold or low cash that we are all familiar with. But then to have your close friends tell you that for at least the last seven years, you have been picked up by UFOs, probed, prodded, and visited with time and time again makes one think they walked right into the middle of a bad movie without a clue, hence my concerns for them. It didn't make sense, Bert and Denise have a very stable family life and realistic and logical points of view. It wouldn't be like them to make up something like this, so I believe them, which is the best that anyone from an outsider's point of view could do . . . until one evening while visiting them.

That evening I went under hypnosis and remembered an event that happened with Bert and me. I recalled visions and events which happened while I was out on an errand with him in October, 1984. After the sessions they showed me a transcript of Bert's memories of that trip. Until the night I had my hypnosis, I had not seen or heard any of the details that Bert had recalled through his own hypnosis, yet the two separate accounts were identical. Since then I have called them after having strange dreams of encounters and before

I could get halfway through, Bert or Denise were able to finish the last half of my dream for me. I think this is a little more than coincidence. Something is happening to them and to us and I only wish that I could remember more on a more conscious level.

Reginald

Letter from Elizabeth

February 11, 1991

I have seen the "light shows," as Bert and Denise have named them, for years. I have asked doctors about them and have received strange and blank looks as a result of my inquiries.

With me the "light shows" vary in intensity from a vague illusion to an almost blinding fog. I've seen them at all times of the day and night and in most locations that I have been in. Although they can be quite an annoyance, they can also be breathtakingly beautiful.

Since I was four or five years old, I have been followed by a ghost. I gave this ghost a name and used him as a scapegoat. My family seemed to accept my ghost, however now I find myself wondering whether this was a ghost? Could this have been an alien? Or was this the imagination of a child?

I have also had severe nose bleeds which occurred between the ages of five and ten. These nose bleeds were sudden and severe, but they seemed to clear up when my aunt placed some medicine in my nostrils during an episode of the bleeding. Could there have been a cause other than some type of childhood disorder?

I've also been plagued by vivid realistic dreams most of my life. My son, now three years old, has also begun having these dreams. I have also felt the "presence," heard strange sounds and had other odd occurrences happen.

Of the shared dreams or memories, of course, those involved have different minds and so a part that is important to one may be less so to another, but the similarities cannot be ignored. I found it easy to explain them with some form of ESP, or even coincidences; but when my son, my mother, Bert, Denise and Paul, who I have never even met and none of us live in the same state, tell me of dreams that they had that are the same as mine, I have to rethink what is happening.

I must admit when I saw Bert and Denise changing their religious views to include reincarnation, I became very frightened for them. Among other religious views I had always believed in reincarnation and was told that I was a non-believer and put down for my beliefs. So I assumed that I was wrong. Perhaps this assumption led me away from God, but I have always felt him in my life and needed him there.

I cannot picture my subconscious self as closed-minded or rigid as Bert and Denise seem to remember me from their memories, but few of us see ourselves as others do.

I would like to see an alien for all the reasons one could think of. I would like to be involved and awakened, but I, my conscious self, would wish to do so before my kids were involved to ensure myself of their safety and to ease their way.

I have always dreamed of living a life such as Bert and Denise say the Androme's lead. Am I involved? Will I be awakened? I hope so.

Elizabeth

Letter from Paul

March 6, 1991

I am writing a brief note about my involvements with these "beings" and the other people in the book. I have never given much thought about aliens or ETs until recently. In the fall of 1989, Bert told me of some of his experiences. I was fascinated by his story. I quickly forgot about his story, however, until about three months later. I was in a lounge when something strange happened. I couldn't call Bert as fast as I would have wanted to, to ask him questions about this strange topic. Ever since this point in my life strange things have happened to me. I started remembering dreams and they seemed realistic. Prior to that I hadn't been able to remember any dreams except a dream when I was about five years old.

I have read a draft of the book, *Secret Vows*, and everything written about me has happened. The book talks about various things such as touches, meeting people I have never met consciously, and the light shows, etc. These things happened to me and only recently I have experienced the light show. One night while I was relaxing in my recliner, I experienced the light show. All of a sudden a circular pattern of about 500 sparkles didn't move with my head movement. I then sensed that one being was in front of me. I thought during these two minutes that this being would appear in the flesh, but it never happened. I knew this was an ET; I was getting used to them.

Paul

PHONE INTERVIEW WITH ELLEN

March 9, 1991

Denise: How do you feel about the strange occurrences you and your family have experienced? You know, like the restless nights?

Ellen: Kind of eerie. Kind of different.

Denise: Have you woken up thinking someone else was in your house?

Ellen: Yes. Things occur that are out of the ordinary.

Denise: Do you think it is all imagination?

Ellen: Well at first we did and then after a while when you really look at it, you know it isn't.

Denise: Do you see the light shows?

Ellen: I've seen the shadows, and we've had the heavy fog or thickness in the room.

Denise: Blinking lights?

Ellen: Yes, we've had the blinking lights, and we have had the light bulbs burn out. And we had Dave's car radio switching stations on its own.

Denise: How do you feel knowing that you and your family may be involved with extraterrestrials?

Ellen: I don't know how I feel. At first I got an uneasy feeling, like it was a violation. Because it's like all of a sudden they are there and you don't know what to do with them. How to deal with them—are they good? Are they bad? Where do they come from? I didn't understand them and I didn't know anything about them until I talked with you two and found out a little more about them, that they aren't physically going to harm anyone.

Denise: How does that make you feel?

Ellen: It doesn't seem to bother us as much now and it makes us want to know about them. It brings out our curiosity.

Denise: How do you feel about the dreams (memories) that we have all shared?

Ellen: They are different. It is odd to have someone call you and tell you things that have gone on in your life and knowing that they live that far away. You can't figure out how else they could have known those things. There was also that one time right after Dave had his surgery and Bert recalled visiting him at the hospital with the extra-terrestrials. I feel that they could have been there and that they may have had a part in Dave's recovery because he had a miraculous healing, even the doctors were amazed at how quickly he healed.

Denise: What about the dreams that you have had?

Ellen: A lot of mine have coincided with yours. The things that I was able to remember were things that you had remembered and they happened at the same time.

Denise: How does that make you feel?

Ellen: Like I still need to know more. Our society doesn't acknowledge them being there. We've been told there is a possibility, but to actually think that they are there has never been accepted as normal. It makes me curious. I want to know more and learn more.

Denise: Do you feel that you have gone through any changes since you first realized you were being visited?

Ellen: Our spiritual background has gotten a lot stronger. A priority. Our family has experienced a lot more togetherness and closeness. We do more things as a family.

Denise: At first you two thought we were crazy, right?

Ellen: Well, yes, to be honest.

Denise: Then it got to the point with the things that began happening that Dave made the comment about Bert needing to come and get his "friends."

Ellen: Yes. One night when the lights went out and two of the bulbs blew out, Dave said, "You call Bert and tell him to come and get his friends." I told him I talked to Bert about it and Bert said, "Those were our friends," that I have my "friends" and you have your "friends." And Dave replied back that "No, these are Bert's friends, tell him to come get them." (Chuckling)

During the remainder of our conversation we discovered that on Saturday, March 2, 1991, we had a similar odd occurrence. Both of our families went out for the day, neither of us knowing what the other's plans were going to be for that day. Ellen and her family arrived back home at nearly 5:00 P.M. while Bert, the children and I arrived home at a little past 4:00 P.M. Both of us found that the clocks on our microwaves had been reset. Of course, our first thought was that the electricity had been off, but on checking we found that no other electric clocks in our homes had been reset. Coincidence? No. We are neither on the same electric company, nor even in the same state!